BIRTHRIGHT

Book 5 of:
The Stone Legacy Series

Theresa Dalayne

BIRTHRIGHT

Limitless Publishing, LLC
Kailua, HI 96734
www.limitlesspublishing.com

Formatting: Limitless Publishing

ISBN-13: 978-1-68058-603-9
ISBN-10: 1-68058-603-3

DEDICATION

This final Stone Legacy book is dedicated to my mother, Winnie Donat, who bore more responsibility than her share, all to see me fulfill my dream of completing this series. You pushed me forward, challenged me to write better, and cooked more dinners than I can count so I could hide in my office and meet deadlines. I know that without your ongoing support and encouragement, I wouldn't be celebrating this success. I love you so much, Mom.

And I promise if I make a boatload of money from this series, I'm totally buying you that cabin in the woods. Now it's in writing, like a contract signed in blood. But that's creepy, so not really.

CHAPTER ONE

Zanya

The road was deserted just outside the city of Tikal. The car was quiet, and the air was thick with tension, making it harder and harder to breathe.

Zanya slouched in the passenger seat and pulled her knees to her chest. "I can't believe that just happened." She combed her fingers through her hair, pulling strands away from her heated cheeks. "I don't understand. I mean..." Her bottom lip trembled through her effort to hide it. "My mom wanted me to choose between you and her. How could she?"

Arwan trained his gaze on the long, straight highway, gripping the steering wheel so tightly his knuckles turned dusky, and the tendons that wound up his forearm bulged with every movement. "She should understand." He flexed his jaw. "She fell in love with a human once, even though nobody approved of their love."

"But they never bonded." Humans and Riyata

1

couldn't bond, but then again… She dragged her gaze to Arwan's angled jaw and dark, piercing eyes. "What happened back there? We shouldn't have been able to bond."

For the first time, he tore his attention away from the road and examined her. "I don't know."

The lights of aurora never should have chosen her and Arwan to be soul mates. He as partial underworlder, and she as the Stone Guardian. They were incompatible—or so they were told.

A flutter rolled in Zanya's belly as she looked into Arwan's smoky eyes. It was just hours ago, while standing on the grassy hill that overlooked the solstice celebration, she was sure any hope of them being together was lost forever. Now her world had been turned upside-down, and their bond had been sealed. The heaven spirits—the gods of Tamoanchan—must have seen something in him. Something that made him worthy.

She exhaled and placed her feet back on the floorboard. "Where are we going?"

"Into the city. We'll at least have a place to spend the night."

Heat wound around her muscles and crawled down the backs of her legs. Spend the night? As in—together? After their bonding, it never occurred to her what came next. She flushed just from being near him, let alone staying the night with him.

Her first solstice was over and the effect it had on her carnal instincts was supposed to have worn off. Apparently that wasn't the case. It didn't help she sensed the anchor of their bond deep in her bones. Her skin flushed with another rush of heat.

"Are you okay?"

Zanya tucked hair behind her ear. "Yeah, I think so. Why?"

"I can hear your heart racing."

"Right. I forgot about that whole instinct thing."

He grinned, ever so slightly. "At least you're not crying anymore."

Her soft smile vanished as her mind flashed back to her mother's death-glare. She really hated Arwan, with every fiber of her being. The way she seethed to see them standing together was chilling. Her mother had never seemed so cold.

"We'll stop at an ATM, and then find a hotel. I'll call Renato. He'll know what we should do."

"An ATM? Did Renato give you a bank card or something?"

"No." He stole another glance at her. "I have some savings stored away."

"Savings?" As far as she knew, he'd spent his entire life at Renato's house. "How did you save anything? I thought you'd never lived outside of Toledo."

His features grew sober. "I inherited enough to keep us comfortable. It was the one tangible thing my mother left behind."

From his mother who abandoned him? That didn't sound like something a careless woman would do. But it was too sore of a topic to bring up now, and in all honesty, it wasn't important. As long as they had enough money to eat and keep a roof over their heads until they figured out what to do next, everything else was secondary.

As long as they were together, it didn't matter.

Zanya leaned her head against the leather seat. They'd taken the car from the solstice celebration—another issue they'd have to deal with later. The hum of the engine and the muffled roar of wind flowing through the cracked windows blended into white noise and relaxed her rigid muscles.

Her stone vibrated from its pouch on the bracelet her mother had given her. She sucked in a tiny breath. Her stone. It must have been terrified after everything that'd happened, even though it hadn't translated it to her. In fact, it seemed calm.

She opened the pouch and slipped her stone into the palm of her hand. "Hey." She held it between her fingers and rolled it around. It glowed with warm hues of orange. "I know it's a lot to take in." It glowed brighter, blanketing her with tranquility. "Hm. Not so tough, then, huh?" She glanced at Arwan. "Yeah, he's not so bad."

"I suppose I'll have to get used to you talking to your rock?" He snickered.

"Shh." She hugged it against her chest. "It'll hear you call it a rock."

"And?" Arwan's eyes lit up. "What's it going to do?"

"You shouldn't be afraid of what *it'll* do." She pressed her index finger on his biceps and summoned a pulse of electricity to course over her hand. The shock kissed his skin with a thwack of light.

He swerved and shouted. "Are you trying to kill us both?" He rubbed his arm, still half-grinning.

Zanya couldn't tear her attention away from his caramel skin, dark lashes, and teasing smirk.

4

His grin spread. "Your heart is racing again."

She blew out a puff of air and slouched back in her chair. "You've got to stop using your heightened senses for your personal advantage."

He placed his hand on her thigh. "Why?"

She suppressed the quiver crawling up her leg.

She hadn't been with anyone before. Jayden was her first real boyfriend—if there were such a thing in a mental institution—but they'd never gotten past second base.

It was all too much to wrap her mind around at once.

Arwan slid his hand down to her knee and squeezed it, just once, before returning his hand to the wheel, as if he knew what she was thinking.

The coil that gripped her lungs slowly relaxed, but not before she realized the light in her chest had flickered on—a dead giveaway to her anxiety.

She drew in a slow, deep breath and turned on the radio. Some music would help pass the time, at least until they got to the city. Then they'd call Renato and find out when it was safe to go home.

Something told her it would be a while, if ever, before her mother would welcome them back.

***

Arwan

He'd driven through the night, watching the secluded desert terrain morph into wide highways and twinkling lights from towering buildings in the distance.

5

Zanya had been asleep for almost an hour. Her rhythmic breathing and steady heartbeat kept him calm while he searched for an explanation.

She was right. They never should have been allowed to bond.

He grabbed his cellphone from the cup holder and flipped it open. He'd hoped to talk to Renato in private. This would have to do. Once Zanya woke, he didn't want to shut her out, though he didn't want to alarm her with his conversation with Renato, in case anything unexpected came up.

He tapped his thumb over the buttons and pressed the phone to his ear. It rang just once before Renato picked up.

"Arwan. Are you two all right?"

"Yeah. We're okay."

"Where are you?"

"Driving." They'd spend a few nights in random hotels, but he still didn't know where they'd go after that. "We're both confused, and Zanya is still trying to wrap her mind around her mother's ultimatum."

"I know. I'm sure you are both very shaken up. Ellie hasn't given Marzena a moment's rest since you two left, begging her to somehow connect with Zanya using her ability. She's terribly worried for Zanya's safety. She still believes you're going to hurt her."

The mention of anyone hurting Zanya drove a spike of adrenaline through his blood. He'd protect her from anyone or anything, no matter what, and with his life. "Tell Marzena we appreciate her giving us our privacy."

6

"Marzena has insisted nothing less. I've spent every waking moment researching, trying to understand exactly what happened. The gods of Tamoanchan must have somehow blessed your union with—" There was a brief pause. "Your bond. How could I have neglected to congratulate you? I'm terribly sorry. It's just that under the circumstances—"

"Don't worry about that, Renato." The corners of his mouth turned up while he admired Zanya for a fleeting moment—curled into a ball, still deeply asleep. "Thank you. It's…" His chest tightened as the link between them deepened, boring into his soul. "It's nothing like I ever thought possible. I don't…" To say it aloud felt somehow wrong, but it was the absolute truth. "I don't hate myself anymore. It's like I'm finally at peace."

"That's truly outstanding. I couldn't be happier for you both, even if the union is somewhat unconventional. How is Zanya coping with the bond? Neither of you expected it, and I'm sure the sudden link has had a jarring impact on you."

"So far we're both handing the bond fairly well." In fact, not a lot had changed for him. He had always been connected to Zanya. Even before Drina interpreted the passage from the book of Popul Vuh, revealing they were truly destined for each other, he somehow knew.

"Very good. Please keep a close watch over her, as I know you will. I'll work to get Ellie under control and find a way to bring both of you back."

Arwan nodded. "Okay. Meanwhile, Zanya and I are going to stay in the city."

7

"Why would you choose to stay there?"

"What choice do we have?"

Renato was silent for a long moment. "There is a second option. Perhaps it's time to tell you."

"Tell me..." He paused. "Tell me what?"

"About your home."

Arwan's throat tightened, and he pulled the car to a stop in the emergency lane. "Home?" He gripped the wheel tighter with one hand. "What are you talking about?"

Renato breathed into the phone—the kind of breath you let out when you dreaded what you were about to say. "Do you remember the home you grew up in, before you came to Toledo? Before you lived with me?"

He could barely remember what his mother looked like, let alone his childhood home. If it weren't for the sketches hung on his bedroom wall in Renato's house, Drina's brief link outside her hut in Belize, and the fleeting moment he watched her through Contessa's magical haze in Moscow, he probably would have forgotten her entirely.

"I'll take your silence as a no." Renato's voice snapped him out of his thoughts. "Spend as long as you'd like in the city, but when you're ready, travel to Mexico."

"Mexico?" His breaths quickened. "Is that where I'm from?"

"That is where you were born, and where you spent your childhood—in your mother's home."

"It's still there? You're sure?" It had been nearly fifteen years since he left when he was six.

"I received a piece of mail many years ago with

nothing but the deed to the home in your mother's name, postmarked. I could only assume it was your mother who sent it. It wasn't signed, and there was no note to accompany it."

"Why didn't you tell me this before? You gave me my money inheritance, but not this? I should have known—" He clamped his teeth and gripped his chest tighter. His darker half whipped and burrowed into him. Arwan groaned and leaned into the steering wheel.

"Are you all right, Arwan?" Renato's voice was muffled in his ears. He drew in a shaky breath, concentrating on putting his darker half at rest. Soon, it settled down and became dormant again.

"Text me the address," he whispered, not wanting to wake Zanya and worry her. "I have to go."

Arwan hung up the phone and tossed it in the back seat, then mounted both hands on the wheel and stared ahead. His palms were clammy and his head throbbed from the rush of darkness slithering through him.

There would be no staying at a hotel. He'd push through this and keep driving—all the way to the airport.

Chapter Two

Zanya

A rhythmic pinging sound woke Zanya out of her sleep. She blinked at the morning sun beaming through the windshield and covered her eyes long enough to adjust.

The car was parked and the driver side door hung open, allowing the pungent scent of gas to assault her senses. She crinkled her nose. "Where are we?"

Arwan crouched and looked at her through the doorway, one hand placed on the hood of the stolen car. "We're getting gas, and then..." He checked the clock on the dash. "I have something to tell you."

Her muscles immediately tensed.

Very few good things started with those words.

When Arwan was done fueling, he sat in the car, shut the door, and cranked the engine.

"What's going on?" Patience this early, before a cup of coffee, was too much to ask.

He shifted the car into drive and pulled onto the

road, speeding deeper into Guatemala City. It was the only place close enough to reach in a night's drive.

"I called Renato while you were asleep."

"Okay?" She sat up straighter and gathered her hair to the side, then combed her fingers through it until her waves were tamed. The urge to ask about her mother was tempting, but she didn't give in. It was too soon, and it'd be a good long while before Zanya forgave her for exiling them both.

"He told me about a place in Mexico we could stay."

"As in a different country? Who's in Mexico?"

"Not who. What."

She groaned. "Are we going to play twenty questions, or are you going to tell me what you're thinking?"

He pulled into a vacant spot beside the curb and turned in his seat to face her. He brushed his fingers together nervously while searching her eyes.

She hesitated, and then asked again, with a softer, more cautious tone. "What's in Mexico?"

"My home."

"What? I thought…" She waved her hand in the air. "You know what? Let's talk about this over coffee. Please." A little caffeine and something to eat would clear the cobwebs in no time.

He skated his fingers through the tips of her hair. "You're tired, I know. I am too."

She examined him again, more carefully this time. The thin lines in his forehead were creased, and dark circles shadowed the skin above his cheekbones. She tilted her head, suddenly hyperaware of what a grouch she was being. "You're the one who should be tired. You haven't slept all night." She laced her fingers between his. "You need to get some rest."

"I can't. Not until I see it."

"See…your home." It came out very matter-of-factly.

"Yes. The home I grew up in."

Whoa. That changed things. She bit the inside of her cheek. Sleep and a hot shower could wait, but breakfast couldn't. "We grab something to eat, and then we leave."

He frowned. "No. You need to rest. We can find a hotel and—"

"No good." She pulled her hand back and brought them both back to her lap. "We leave now." His eyes lit up. "On the next flight." She waited a moment, and then waved him forward. "What are you waiting for? Drive."

He grinned and pressed his foot harder on the gas, thrusting them toward the signs pointing to the airport.

After grabbing a bite at a drive-through, Zanya was coherent enough to travel. They used Arwan's bank card—which was apparently tied to a hefty inheritance—to book their tickets, and they'd left the "borrowed" car in short term parking. It'd be towed when nobody came back for it, solving *that* issue.

She was getting used to hopping around from one city to the next, and had even learned to ignore the sensation of her stomach lurching into her throat through takeoff and landing.

The two connecting flights to Mexico went smoothly enough with little sleep and nothing but the clothes on her back. When they made it, they flagged a cab, and soon were on their way...home.

Zanya watched Arwan in the back seat of the taxi. He tilted his phone side to side with a compass app open. The digital dial bobbed side to side before settling in one direction.

"Didn't Renato send you the address?"

"There is no address. Just a latitude and longitude. We'll have to hike there once the cab drops us off."

"More camping. Perfect." The last time they slept in the jungle, they were going to the caves of Naj Tunich, and Balam nearly scared them to death by stalking them the entire way. Not to mention the bugs. The hairs on Zanya's arms stood on end.

Arwan pulled her against him, pressing a kiss on her temple. "Thank you for doing this for me." His hot breath rolled down her neck, making her skin flicker with electricity. The cabby glanced in the rear view mirror, but didn't seem to be paying attention to much more than the Latin music carrying through the speakers. Thankfully, she'd learned how to control her abilities and could smother the occasional outburst of her powers when they popped up.

She rested her head on his shoulder and drew in a deep breath, inhaling his warm, musky scent. They were bonded now. His history was her history. His future was hers too. They were in this together, no matter what.

"We'll stop by a sporting goods store before we

head out there. We'll gather some supplies and a tent."

Zanya nodded, though her nodding gradually stopped. "A tent? As in...one?"

"We don't need two. It would be more to carry, and the terrain won't be easy."

"We didn't have tents last time we camped."

"It was the dry season. This time we should expect rain. A lot of it."

Her body rushed with a sick heat. It's not like they'd never slept beside each other before. They had in the coffin house in Victorian London, and again when they traveled together to the entrance of the underworld to retrieve Jayden's soul. But it was different. In both cases, someone was around. In the coffin house, the English security guard made his rounds every few minutes, and while camping, Balam and Cualli were always close by.

Now they would be alone, and there would be...expectations.

She slouched in her seat. Her stone buzzed, blanketing her with a sense of comfort. She ran her fingers over the leather pouch on her wrist where her stone was tucked away.

As the Stone Guardian, she was strong, fast, could conjure fire and wind, heal, and even use telepathic manipulation like Marzena. She could do it all...if she only knew how. Training had only gotten her so far. If she'd learned one thing, it was that having the *capability* to do something and actually being *able* to do it were two different things. She needed to be instructed by someone who had mastered the skill, and then she would have to practice.

Until then, she'd have to agree to the one-tent thing. Otherwise the pack would be too heavy, until she learned how to utilize Renato's strength ability, at least. Hopefully it wouldn't be as exhausting as the wind conjuring ability. Some powers took more of a toll on her than others.

Zanya pursed her lips, making a mental note to put training on the top of her to-do list.

A few hours later, the cab pulled to a stop in the parking lot of a store. Arwan leaned forward into the midday sun beaming through the windows, and said something in Spanish before pushing open the door and stepping out of the cab. She followed him onto the paved ground and into the store, where everything they needed for a hike into the Mexican jungle sat on shelves and hung on shiny silver hooks with bright yellow price tags.

Zanya grabbed some clothes, travel size toiletries, a portable water filter, hiking boots, and a handful of other necessities.

After checking out, she crouched in the corner, filing everything into her pack as quickly as possible. Arwan dropped his pack beside her and did the same. While he worked, strands of dark hair hung in his face and his muscles bulged under the tightly fitted black tee.

"This reminds me of when we hiked to the caves."

His smoky eyes met her gaze. "Minus the dressing room."

Heat spread over her cheeks. "Right. Minus that."

15

"Right." The corner of his lip turned into a grin.

Her flush deepened, and she forced her focus away from his sharp cheekbones and olive skin to the cool, smooth flint stone in her hand.

Arwan zipped up his pack and threw it over his shoulder with little effort, even though the thing must have weighed a hundred pounds. "Ready?"

She stood, slipped the pack onto her back, and nodded. "I'm ready." Before he turned toward the front door, she took his hand. "Hey." She bit her bottom lip. "Are you sure you're ready for this?"

He lifted her hand and pressed a kiss on her knuckles. "Don't worry."

"I just know it's a lot for you to wrap your mind around, that's all."

"No, I meant about the tent—about us. Don't worry, I won't push."

CHAPTER THREE

Arwan

Once the cab dropped them off at the edge of the jungle, Arwan pointed his phone left while analyzing the map. Northeast was the quickest route as long as they didn't run into any obstacles that would force them to detour.

From what he could tell by the coordinates of the home, it was hidden deep in the jungle, away from most villages and far from any big cities. It stood out there, all alone, just how his mother intended it to be.

Zanya lifted her backpack off the ground and fitted the straps around her. Once she'd adjusted the sternum strap and hip belt, she gathered her hair on top of her head and tied it into a messy bun. "Okay." She slipped an aerosol can out of the side pocket and sprayed her arms. Mist floated through the air. The pungent scent burned his nostrils. He turned his head.

Since the bonding ceremony, his senses had been

even more heightened. He always had the ability to hear the change in Zanya's heartbeat or smell the light odor of her sweat when she hiked beside him. But now, everything was sharper and more focused. It had to be the effect of the bonding. That, or the fact the beast had been awakened inside of him.

"Are you ready?" She secured her raincoat in a knot around her waist. "You lead the way." She held out her hand, encouraging him forward.

He laid his hand on the hilt of the machete strapped to his side and pivoted toward the game trail leading into the thick, winding foliage. Dozens of shades of green shimmered in the afternoon sun that speckled the jungle ground with light. Colorful flowers and delicate baby ferns reached up from the mossy earth, surrounded by glistening rocks slick from the morning dew.

The jungle was a mysterious place. He hadn't spent much time in Mexico, which made these jungles even more unpredictable. It meant keeping a close eye out for anything out of the ordinary and never letting his guard down. He withdrew the machete and took his first swing at the overgrowth.

Hours later, they'd kept a steady pace, sometimes being forced to veer off one game trail only to fight through thick overgrowth. The wet season had brought with it thick, goopy mud, making every step laborious.

Zanya's quickened breaths caught his ear. He braced his hand on a half-dead tree branch beside him. "Do you need to stop?"

She wiped sweat off of her forehead and fanned her flushed face. "This is way different than the other times we were in the jungle."

"This area is more like marshland."

"And it stinks." She covered her nose with her forearm, stealing several deep breaths through her mouth. "What is that?"

He analyzed the mixture of strange smells. The back of his throat closed, and he couldn't help but cough. "Decaying plant matter, I think. Rotting fruit." The branches above them rattled, and the distant scream of monkeys echoed through the trees. "Monkey scat."

"Yeah, that's gross. Let's get out of here as quickly as possible. I'd prefer not to be sliding around in monkey poo if I can help it."

He poised the machete in front of him. "I couldn't agree more." With a few more swings, they were out of the thick patch with endless wetlands ahead. Arwan paused and looked back at Zanya. "Let me go ahead. I'll clear the next few yards and you can follow me."

Zanya propped her pack against a tree, her chest heaving with every breath. "You know, it's not the weight of the pack or the mud that's bothering me as much as the humidity and the disgusting stench." She swatted at the air in front of her. "And the flies."

A streak of guilt ran through him. He should have made this journey alone.

Her eyes narrowed and she pointed at him. "Don't even think that. I'm glad I'm here. Ignore my complaining. I'm just being a big baby."

He cocked his head. "How do you know what I'm thinking?"

"You give the same pitiful stare every time you feel bad about something. So knock it off and go clear some creepy jungle vines so we can keep going." She winked.

***

Zanya

The last few feet of mucky, gross, sloppy, stinky jungle wetlands were enough to suck every ounce of strength from her legs and land her on her ass on the jungle floor.

But at least it was dry jungle floor.

She could deal with that.

"Can we stop soon?" she panted.

He pointed up a steep hill where a cluster of trees grew out of the sloped, grassy angles. "As soon as we make it up there."

She perched her hands on her hips, scaling the near forty-five-degree angle straight up, leading to a stone structure buried in thick foliage. "Is that a ruin?"

"A small one, but it'll give us some cover."

First the marshland, and then a small mountain. Fantastic.

"Don't worry. It's just so we are away from the wetland." He peered up at the sky. "Trust me, you'll be happy for the shelter."

She pushed flyaway hairs away from her face and nodded. "Okay, then. Let's do this."

After a vigorous hike up the rocky terrain, Zanya clawed her way the last few steps—victorious. She groaned and slipped off her backpack, then collapsed to the ground by the ruin and let her hands splay to the sides. "Oh. My. God." She turned her head to look at Arwan, and lost her breath at the sight of him stripping off his t-shirt and slinging it over his shoulder. His muscles bulged with every movement, his skin shimmering with a thin layer of sweat.

He took a few gulps of water from his camel pack and slicked his hair back with his fingers. "This trip has already been more difficult than I anticipated. It's as if my mother wanted to stay hidden."

Zanya watched him for a moment before pushing onto her forearms. "Even if your mother was trying to hide, that doesn't mean she was trying to hide *you*."

He held her gaze for a moment longer, and then gave a soft smile. "Maybe." He went back to digging through his bag.

She lay back on the grass and rolled onto her side, resting her cheek in the palm of her hand. "Besides, look at the bright side. I could have used my transporting ability like Hawa and left you in the dust if I really wanted to."

He smiled—a brilliant white smile this time— and let out a low, quiet laugh. "I know you could. Thanks for waiting around for me."

"You can show me your gratitude by setting up camp." No more hiking for the day would be a fine reward.

"Is that all?" He yanked a tightly rolled tarp from his pack, followed by a bundle of poles. "Consider

21

it done." He leaned against the aged stone structure and pulled out more supplies, stacking them on the lowest step of the Mayan ruin.

Surprisingly, the sight of the tent didn't grip her chest.

She tilted her face, staring at the canopy of green and wavering leaves with streaks of blue peeking through the branches. Now that they were out of the swampland, it was all uphill from there. Literally. Tomorrow was going to be a death march. They were headed up the worst side of a mountain, studded with rocks and riddled with possible dangers. She dragged her fingers along the dry ground, finding a tiny green vine reaching out from the thick plants.

She coiled the vine around her finger before tugging on it gently, then letting it spring back.

The small gesture reminded her of the times Peter, their healer, would play with her best friend's curls. Zanya frowned. She'd left Tara behind a second time. What kind of friend was she?

A gentle pull on her finger brought her back to the moment. She turned her head to see the tiny, beautiful vine reach out to the mid-afternoon sun. Its velvety texture hugged tighter, as if it were acknowledging her presence.

The coil tightened, and the tip pricked her skin, drawing a single plump drop of scarlet blood.

"Ouch." She pulled back her hand and sucked on her fingertip.

"I'm almost finished with the tent." Arwan's voice stole her attention away from the vicious plant. "Do you want to collect some firewood?

Almost everything will be wet, but if you stay under the trees, there should be some dry kindling."

"Um…sure." She looked at her finger, now with just a tiny red blemish. She'd better be careful while searching for firewood. The plants around here were carnivorous.

Against the protest of every aching muscle, she pushed to her feet. A cool wind wove through the trees, rattling the branches and showering her in leaves.

"Change of plans." She glanced back at Arwan, whose face was tilted to the sky. "It looks like the rain will be here sooner than I thought. The ruin will shield us from the wind on one side, but the trees will only give us so much cover from the rain."

"I thought the whole point of being up here was so we had cover."

"Yes." He drew in a deep breath and closed his eyes. "But this storm isn't going to be just rain."

"How do you know?" She searched the blue sky and grayish clouds overhead. Sure, it was overcast, but it didn't exactly scream torrential downpour.

He opened his eyes. "I can smell the rain in the air and feel the electrical charge building in the atmosphere." He ran his hand down the length of his arm. If she didn't pay attention, she wouldn't have noticed his hairs standing on end. He returned to assembling the tent. "We should get camp set up and prepare to ride it out."

Chapter Four

Zanya

In Ohio, when Zanya lived in the orphanage, rain meant the gentle tapping of water on the metal roof and a deep drink for the plants outside. However, here, in the jungles of Mexico, rain meant something entirely different.

Inside the tent, Zanya pulled her knees to her chest, hoping the fiberglass frame and water-resistant fabric walls would stand up against the assault. As leaves smacked against the sides of their shelter—and even though she lay on top of a thick sleeping bag—she could feel the ground beneath her turning soggy while it soaked up the endless supply of water.

Another gust of wind hit the left wall of the tent. She tucked into a tighter ball and ground her teeth. At this rate, it was possible they'd get tossed off the hillside.

A flash of lightning and a clap of thunder made her suck in a sharp breath. She cringed at the rolling rumble as it echoed around them and then morphed into the familiar sound of the downpour. With another strike of lightning, the earth trembled as if the bolt of electricity had just missed them.

The only perk to this whole tropical storm was it took focus off of them sharing a tent for the night.

"Try to get some rest." Arwan lay down, laced his fingers behind his head, and closed his eyes, as if Mother Nature's assault had exactly zero effect on him.

"How can you sleep through this? The marsh could rise overnight, right? I mean, what if we wake up to a flooded tent?"

"We're at least twenty-five feet above the marshes. Flash floods are heard of, but I doubt the water will come up that high."

"Oh." She relaxed her muscles. "That's good." Another gust of wind battered the tent, sending a shiver up the backs of her legs. "I didn't know it got this cold in the jungle."

He drew in a sleepy breath. "It's the wet season."

She nodded, thankful for his exhaustion. She was tired to the bone too, and even if it was hard to sleep, she had to try. She slipped into her sleeping bag and curled into a ball. Arwan's eyes fluttered closed as he drifted off to sleep. It seemed like he was already dreaming, though it was impossible to determine whether it was good or bad. Maybe it was about what he'd find at his mother's home, but maybe…maybe it was about her.

She blinked sleepily, fatigue coiling around her muscles.

He seemed so peaceful, lying there beside her as

rain poured over their tent. But one thing she'd learned was even if things seemed peaceful—even for a stretched moment allowing you to forget—that didn't mean it would stay that way.

She let her eyes close and drew in several deep, cleansing breaths. Tomorrow they'd reach his mother's home and deal with whatever they found.

As her mind drifted between asleep and awake, a soft, beautiful voice broke through a brief pause in the violent storm. Zanya opened her eyes and listened to what sounded like a lullaby. When the tune drifted into the distance and vanished, she closed her eyes again. It was probably just fatigue mixed with wind from the storm, or maybe the beginning of a dream.

She reached out and lingered her chilled fingertips over his hand. Knowing he was there made the night a little less scary, and her a little less consumed by the grief still clutching her chest from her mother's betrayal. His grip coiled around hers in his sleep.

With her eyes closed, the gentle voice returned, humming a sweet, lulling tune. Her stone hadn't buzzed or shown any sign of alarm.

She quietly sat up, careful not to wake Arwan, and unzipped the entrance to the tent just enough to peek into the endless darkness.

The wind had died to little more than a breeze, but the rain was still falling in sheets. She peered outside, scanning the hillside and the area near the rock wall of the long-abandoned ruin.

A low growl caught her attention. Zanya's gaze snapped to the right, where a pair of bright yellow eyes spied on her from a distance. She swallowed, her muscles frozen as she stared at the creature in silence. It could have been anything in the jungle, but from the looks of its reflective irises in the flashes of light, it was definitely feline.

It could have been Balam. It could have been something else entirely.

In a split second, the figure vanished into the jungle, and Zanya finally let out the breath she'd been holding. She zipped the tent back up and slipped into her sleeping bag, resolved to never look outside the tent at night—ever again.

***

Arwan

The next morning, Arwan opened his eyes to various jungle sounds. He turned his head to Zanya, who was still asleep beside him. Strands of dark, wavy hair splayed around her in every direction.

He sat up and unzipped the tent, squinting at the morning light. Though the storm had passed, the air was now chilled, leaving the jungle floor blanketed with a thick mist of fog. Perhaps it would lift as the day progressed, but with the canopy of trees and high levels of humidity, it would take at least a few hours.

He turned to Zanya and brushed hair away from her face, letting his fingers slide down the curve of her neck. She was like a sleeping angel—the closest to heaven his damned soul would ever come.

"Zanya." He spoke softly at first, careful not to

27

startle her awake. "We have to get moving."

She groaned and pulled the flap of her sleeping bag over her head.

He smirked and tugged the fabric below her nose. She squinted at him, her eyes covered in a glassy sheen. "We have to wake up if we want to get to my mother's home today."

She pushed onto her forearms and inspected outside through the open tent door. "You mean your home?"

He paused, and then nodded.

"Is the storm over?"

"Yes." He slipped on his socks and shoved his feet into tan hiking boots. "The ground will be wet and slippery. We have to be careful."

She gathered her hair into a bun and secured it on top of her head. "I know." She rubbed her eyes. "For more than one reason."

He paused. "What do you mean?"

"I heard this weird voice last night. Like singing. And then I looked outside and saw eyes, I think from a big cat."

"Singing?" It had to have been the wind, or perhaps her imagination playing tricks on her. But a big cat? The threats in Mexico were similar to what they'd be up against in Belize, which wasn't good. Predators were plentiful now that they were isolated in the wild, and the reality was, they weren't on the top of the food chain anymore. "We'll keep an eye out while we're hiking today." Thankfully, he hadn't smelled any large animals around, or noticed anyone nearby. Now that his senses were on high alert and in tune more than ever before, at least they'd have an indication if something were closing in.

Zanya nodded through a yawn. "Okay. Do we have any breakfast?"

He dug in his pack, pulled out a Powerbar and a bottle of water, and then offered it to her. "This will hold us over for a few hours."

She sighed. "A breakfast for champions." As she reached out to take the rations, her fingers drifted over his hand, leaving hot streaks across his skin. Her breath hitched and she stilled, watching him. He held her gaze, searching for any indication of what she was thinking in that moment. What she wanted, and more importantly, what she wanted from him.

Though their bonding was unexpected, now that they were united as one soul, he wanted more of her. But she had been through enough. He wouldn't push. He wouldn't move in until she was ready. That was how it had to be to earn her trust, and he'd be patient until that time came, no matter how difficult it was.

Arwan cleared his throat, pushing away the urge to cup her cheek and press his lips to hers. "You eat, and I'll start to pack." Zanya tore open the energy bar and bit off a chunk before offering him the other half. He shook his head. "You need it—"

"What? More than you?" She chewed a few more times before swallowing. "I'm the Stone Guardian, remember? If anyone needs the strength, it's you."

He chuckled. "Point taken." Deep down, she was more advanced than he was in almost every way.

She was faster, stronger, with every Riyata ability at her command and an enchanted stone to fuel her abilities. She was incredible, and she was his. He still couldn't believe it. Not completely.

He took a bite of the energy bar. "Thank you."

"Well…" She pushed her bag aside. "What's mine is yours, right?"

He winked. "Absolutely."

She paused, her smile widening. She blinked quickly, and the blush in her cheeks made his chest tighten. She let out a soft laugh, averting her gaze. "This is…" She ran her hand down the length of her arm and shrugged. "Strange."

His smile disappeared and he lowered his head. Maybe it was too good to be true. "I'm sure you're wondering how you ended up with me. I mean, how you ended up with someone like me." He clenched his jaw. "Some*thing* like me." His darker half clawed at his belly, consuming him from the inside out.

"Hey." She touched his face and ran her thumb over his eyebrow, her fingertips lingering on his temple. The warmth of her skin cast his darker half back into submission. "I don't know why the gods of Tamoanchan chose us to be bonded, but regardless of what you believe about yourself, they know you're special. And so do I."

He closed his eyes, memorizing the way her palm felt against his cheek. He'd go back to this memory when he was desperate for relief from being what he was—half underworlder, half Riyata. She was all he had now. His everything.

The scent of a familiar animal wove through the

air, alarming his senses. He opened his eyes and looked toward the opening of the tent.

"What is it?" The light in Zanya's chest winked on, and she sat back in silence, waiting for him to respond.

He drew in a breath through his nose, analyzing the scent. He cocked his head, tuning in to every sound, but locking in on just one—padded paw steps over the leaf-littered jungle floor and a low, passive chuff.

"We're not alone."

CHAPTER FIVE

Zanya

The cool rush of light in Zanya's chest spread, saturating every cell of her body. Her light—the stamp of power marking her as the guardian—had illuminated on cue. If something was nearby, she had to be ready to fight. The light gave her more strength when using her abilities—if it came down to that.

"Is your stone telling you anything?" Arwan asked.

She blinked and looked down at her wrist, where her stone was kept in the leather bracelet her mother had given her. If there was danger nearby, her stone would usually be the first to alert her, but it hadn't made a peep. "No, actually. It hasn't." She looked at him. "Why?"

He pulled open the flap to the tent and peered outside. "Because. I'm fairly sure it's Balam."

"Balam?" Zanya's muscles relaxed and her light faded until it was gone. "Is Cualli here too?" The middleworld goddess had to be the source of the singing from the night before. It was a relief to know she hadn't contracted some kind of weird jungle disease or hallucinated after an unintentional encounter with another dangerous plant.

"Come on. Let's see why they are here." Arwan combed his fingers through his hair and then stepped out of the tent, leaving her alone.

Zanya fitted on her socks and shoes, then flattened down her flyaways. If she were going to see Cualli and Balam, the least she could do was look halfway decent.

She followed Arwan out of the tent and walked to his side. He scanned the thick, green jungle. It was like a wall of leaves and vines—impossible to see into more than a few feet.

A loud flapping of wings made Zanya flinch. She spun to spot a great white owl with caramel feathers around its face perched on a branch over their camp. The majestic bird swiveled its head from side to side, examining them with large, round eyes.

Zanya took Arwan's hand. "It's good to see you again, Cualli."

The owl spread its wings and launched from the branch, its feathers morphing into the figure of a tall, elegant woman with fair skin and blonde hair that draped down her bare back. Her feather-covered gown hid very little, though it was just enough to keep her from being nude.

Cualli walked toward them. New, supple grass sprouted from the jungle floor to cushion her every step. "It is very good to see you as well, guardian."

"Zanya, please." Sarian called her guardian. The term was never endearing after that.

Cualli gave a slight, regal bow of her head. "Of course."

Arwan stepped forward. "Can you tell us how this happened?"

Cualli pouted her lips, as if she were puzzled. "What, exactly, half-breed?"

Though Cualli's comment didn't carry any hint of dislike, Arwan visibly cringed.

Zanya cleared her throat and took back control over the conversation. "I think what he means is…" She squeezed his hand. "How did we bond? Why?"

Cualli's pouted lips spread into a soft smile. "It was fate."

Zanya recalled the passage from the Mayan holy book, the Popul Vuh, and what it said about her and Arwan being destined for each other, though the reason was still unclear. If the gods of Tamoanchan wanted their souls intertwined, there had to be a reason. Underworlders and Riyata weren't compatible…until now.

Balam sauntered out of the jungle in jaguar form, his tail flickering from side to side and his ears rotating to every sound. The cat's spotted coat glistened under the rays of sun touching the jungle floor. He rubbed his muscular body along Cualli's bare legs and chuffed, then hooked his tail around her calf as he passed, circling the group.

"Balam and I have come to congratulate you on your bonding."

"Oh." Zanya glanced at Arwan, who didn't seem nearly as appreciative of their gesture. "Thank you."

Cualli peered at Arwan. "Are you traveling to your mother's home?" He nodded sharply, still unwilling to make eye contact. "Good," she continued. "Balam and I can show you the way if you like. It is almost a day's walk for a mortal."

Zanya stayed quiet. She'd let Arwan answer this once, considering this was his mother's house.

It took him a moment, but he finally responded. "Yes, thank you."

Zanya let out a breath, the tension in her muscles following close behind. Now, with Cualli and Balam traveling with them, there were sure to be fewer dangers. Cualli would fly ahead, and Balam would silently stalk through the jungle on all fours. With eyes in the sky and on land, the rest of the journey would be a cakewalk.

…Or not.

She'd forgotten her own first rule.

When things seem too good to be true, they usually are.

After an hour of hiking, the clouds opened yet again and let out sheets of rain, filling the river they'd been following for several miles. The rush of the white water against drowning river rocks mixed with the patter of rain against jungle foliage blended and morphed into white noise.

It didn't stop coming all afternoon, making each step twice as hard, the rain soaking their clothes, filling their boots with muddy water, and putting poor Balam into a very grumpy feline mood.

The jaguar deity walked beside them, his head poised low and his shoulder blades rolling with every step. His spotted fur was matted, making his spots look more like blurry drops of a watercolor painting.

Arwan hadn't spoken for over an hour. His features were still like stone and his brow furrowed, as if he had spent the duration of his silence in deep thought. Maybe it was the anticipation. That alone had put a knot in even her gut, let alone his.

Zanya sniffled and wiped rainwater away from her eyes. "How ya doin' over there, Balam?"

The big cat gave a long, low growl and flicked his tail, spraying a rainy mist into the air.

She cracked a smile. "That good, huh?"

Arwan nudged her softly. "You may not want to irritate him."

"Why? Worried he's hungry?" Balam chuffed and shook his head, baring his teeth. Zanya laughed. "I'm pretty sure that's jaguar language for, *you're not my type.*"

Arwan glanced at her from the corner of his eye. "Or, *you're exactly my type.*"

Zanya suppressed the urge to roll her eyes. "Don't worry so much. I'm here to protect you." She slowed her pace, peering down at the river with a watermill spinning under the current. "What is that?" She pointed upriver. It looked like the circular paddles on a large ferry, the blades slapping against the waves with every rotation.

Arwan pointed to the far left.

Zanya followed his gesture. Her lips parted. "Oh my god." She stepped forward, examining a home built of solid stone, barely visible behind overgrown bushes and trees. The two-story structure stood on stone stilts, perfectly camouflaged from prying eyes. "We made it."

***

Arwan

Arwan's chest weighed heavier with every passing breath. He stood in a bit of shade, squinting at the stone pillars guarding either side of the entrance. The bottom level was open like some sort of carport, as if the home were built to stand high above floodwaters, or hide behind overgrowth of towering trees. Holding up the carport were some kind of stone totem poles, all covered in Mayan hieroglyphics, as if the home itself told a story.

What seemed like a Roman bath was built into the ground floor, beautiful and sparkling as if it had been cared for every day.

How was it possible the home was in such good condition after all this time?

The windows weren't cracked.

The home was not overgrown.

His gaze drifted down to an unnatural arrangement of stones making a circle around the home.

Perhaps someone had been there…

"Arwan?"

He blinked and looked at Zanya. Her presence was the little familiarity he had. Though this was his childhood home, his memories of it were vague, and it was more of a foreign place than anywhere he'd ever been.

"Do you want to go in?"

He pressed his lips into a tight line. "I don't know." He'd spent so many years fighting not to forget the smell of his mother's cooking and the gentle sound of her voice pouring into every room, and now he couldn't uproot his feet from the ground to take a single step toward that goal. "Can I have a minute to go alone?"

Zanya's smile vanished. "Oh." She blinked. "I mean, sure. Yeah. Of course."

He nodded and took a step forward. "I'll just be a few minutes. Then I'll call you." The truth was, anything could be waiting for them inside. If anyone would step into a possible landmine of dark magic, it would be him.

Each pace brought him closer to his years spent there—his mother's smile, the soft pattering of rain on the terracotta shingles, and the comforting jungle sounds that lulled him to sleep. The memories had been a blur for so many years. Now, with each pace, they flooded back, as if he hadn't lost his home overnight, when his mother abandoned him at Renato's house with hope for a brighter future.

When he reached the stone circle, he stopped, the toes of his boots at its edge. Mayan magic was powerful, and whatever the spell was, it would likely be broken as soon as he crossed the barrier. Good or bad, it was necessary to explore further.

He kicked a few of the stones out of arrangement, and the wind picked up in an unexpected gust, bringing the scent of wildflowers and honey. A ripple of magic carried through the air, washing over the house, and wiping away the faint shimmer that once blanketed the home.

"Hm." He stepped over the barrier, sensing nothing else unusual. "A preservation spell." Likely set by his mother before she left.

He walked to the edge of the textured stone floor of the open bottom level. He used to play there, in the shade, protected from the blistering heat of midday.

A Mayan hieroglyphic was etched into a darker colored stone in the center of the floor. Bright green moss had filled the lines of the carving, making it a focal point.

His mother had always told him not to play on that stone, though he never knew why.

He walked on, carefully swatting away cobwebs, as he grew closer to the arched doorway leading to the upper level of the home. Even in the remote location, his mother would keep this door shut and locked when they were inside. As a young boy he had wondered why they needed a locked door when nothing but the jungle surrounded them, but as a man, it had become clear. She was afraid of who— or what—might try to enter.

Clenching his teeth, he turned the knob and pushed open the door.

He'd expected to find something horrific on the other side. Instead he found wooden steps leading him into an open space flooded with natural light. Stone floors, dusty throw rugs rolled up in corners, colorful walls, and furniture covered in sheets.

He was finally home.

Chapter Six

Zanya

Zanya leaned against a tree, enjoying the cool shade as she waited for a signal to follow him inside.

It'd be a lie if she said it didn't hurt when he left her to wait in the jungle. It was like he'd shut her out of a place in his heart—a place she thought she had full access to. Maybe she overestimated this whole bonding thing. Maybe what she felt wasn't what he felt at all.

Balam circled her once, twice, three times, and then stopped beside her. The cat raised his stout snout toward the treetops, scanning the branches with round, orange eyes.

Cualli, in her owl form, landed above them and hopped along a textured branch.

"Thanks for getting us here," Zanya said. "I know it meant a lot to Arwan." Cualli silently watched her, as if expecting her to say something else. "I, uh…" She glanced at Balam, who was now

40

licking his paw and rubbing it over his face as if no one were around. She couldn't help but chuckle. "I know you guys are happy for us and all," she continued, her attention turned back to Cualli. "In fact, if it weren't for you, I bet we wouldn't have bonded at all." She studied the house and lowered her voice. "But if you don't mind, can you keep the whole 'half-breed' thing down to a minimum? My mom did that to him enough already, and it hurts him. He has a good heart."

Cualli blinked her big, round owl eyes, gave a soft coo, and then launched off the branch, climbing higher into the sky with each flap of her massive wings.

Balam's ears perked and he followed close behind his companion, vanishing into the jungle without so much as a goodbye wave of his tail.

A moment later, Arwan walked out of the house and leaned the inside of his forearm on a pillar. His broad chest pushed against the stretchy cotton of his t-shirt, his torso flexed in his stance. He quickly scanned the jungle before speaking. "Where are Balam and Cualli?"

"They took off. I'm sure Balam wanted to dry off."

He nodded. "You can come in now."

She huffed and walked toward him. "You sure I'm allowed?" she mumbled under her breath.

"I checked. It's all clear."

She sighed, watching him as she grew closer. Those damn super senses of his were going to be hard to get around. He could hear her heartbeat, her whispers, even sense her pheromones rise and fall.

41

It was almost impossible to mask the smallest change in her mood without him focusing on her from across the room. And now that they were bonded, keeping her thoughts private would be even more difficult. If only he were as transparent…

Zanya walked to his side, savoring the cool surface of the stone as she placed her hand on it. "So…" She examined his soft features and relaxed muscles. "How is it?"

"Good, I think."

She bit the inside of her cheek. If anyone understood being torn about returning home, it was her. When she arrived at Renato's, she was less than optimistic, to say the least.

"Come on." He held out his hand. "Let's go home."

She froze. Home?

He skimmed his fingers down the length of her arm and hooked them around her wrist. Amusement played across his lips, making his eyes smile. "You don't have to be nervous."

She stared down at his fingers over her wrist. "That's not fair." She pulled her hand away and crossed her arms over her chest. "You can't take my pulse—like you need to, anyway."

He paused, his smile fading. "What's wrong?"

She swallowed against a dry throat. "I don't know."

"You can tell me."

"It's just, when you went inside…" She frowned. "I just—" Her stone buzzed against her wrist, sending a spike of energy up her arm, and *her* into high alert. She sucked in a breath as light radiated from inside the leather band.

"What is it?"

Zanya unhooked the pouch and slipped her stone into the palm of her hand. Its cool energy saturated every cell of her body, filling her with a burst of power. "Something's wrong."

He squared his stance. "What?"

"I don't know, exactly." She clenched her stone in her hand and scanned the jungle and cued the light in her chest to flicker to life. Better safe than sorry. "Something's out here."

"Balam or Cualli, maybe?"

The jungle could have been hiding anything, and in her world, that could mean just about anything from any realm. "No. Not them." She secured her stone back in its pouch and narrowed her eyes, still peering into the thick foliage. "It's something else."

Arwan took her hand, breaking her focus. "Then we should go." Any trace of the sweet guy she'd been standing beside had vanished, leaving a cautious worrier in his place. He guided her toward the open door leading up several wooden stairs, into an open living room and kitchen.

A musty scent tickled her nose as she scanned the piles of furniture covered in white sheets. She flipped a light switch on the wall, cuing the ceiling fan to start spinning. "I can't believe this place has electricity."

"Hm." He leaned against the window and squinted down at the river. "Watermill. And…" He shaded his eyes with his hand. "A solar panel. Maybe for a water pump, if it's not clogged. But the panels don't look too dirty and the river seems clear."

"Maybe Cualli had something to do with that."

Arwan nodded. "I wouldn't be surprised."

"We'll have to thank her for that later. Running water is always good." She walked through the room, examining the vaulted ceilings with dingy skylights and colorfully painted stucco walls bare of any art or decor. "How long has it been since anyone has lived here?"

Arwan peeked under one of the sheets covering some furniture, then dropped it, sending a cloud of dust into the air. "I'm guessing after she left me at Renato's when I was a boy, she never made it back."

Zanya frowned. "I'm sorry. I didn't…" She bit her lip. "I wasn't thinking."

"You can't change the past. What happened—happened. That's all there is to it." He continued through the space, stopping beside the fireplace. He placed his hand on the thick wooden mantel, vacant of any family photos or cute little trinkets normally found on display. "She obviously prepared to not come back."

Zanya walked behind him, lightly skimming her fingers along his back as she passed. If her touch was as comforting to him as his was to her, she'd offer it.

She walked toward the kitchen, which was open to the living space. The black stone countertops looked like slabs of slate, unfinished and uneven around the edges. But they were beautiful, in a rustic sort of way. The wooden cabinets surrounded sleek, black appliances—a few modern amenities in a house built in the middle of the jungle.

Several area rugs were rolled up and leaned against the wall, cobwebs hanging in every corner. She turned to face Arwan, who still stood by the mantel, his gaze set nowhere in particular. She cleared her throat, causing Arwan to blink, as if he'd returned from some distant place in his mind.

"What do you think?" he asked, leaving the fireplace behind him as he walked across the living room, toward a broad hallway.

"It needs some work, but it's..." She nodded. "It's beautiful." She followed him through the house and down the hall, past two closed doors, to the last door that hung wide open.

Another arrangement of floor to ceiling windows made the far wall, displaying a view of the jungle. A large bed sat in the center of the room with a mahogany frame, matching a large dresser and two night stands.

Zanya leaned against the doorframe as he walked inside. "Was this your mom's room?"

He nodded, his features somber and his eyes a little sad. "She never slept here. It was almost unused. She always slept..." He dropped his gaze, and then glanced up at her. "She slept on the floor in my room beside my bed. Every single night."

He believed his mother hated him. Abandoned him, and then chose to die over watching her son grow into something she hated. Even though he believed those things, it didn't make sense. Why would she take him to live with Renato—to a safe place—if she detested him? Why would she sleep beside his bed, as if she were there to protect him?

"That's nice." She forced a faint smile. "Maybe she wanted to be sure you were okay."

"I highly doubt that." He tightened his jaw. "But I guess I'll never know." He walked past her into the hall, where he paused beside a closed door.

Zanya followed and lingered beside him. She noticed his narrowed eyes. "Was that your room?"

The absence of a response was enough.

She took his hand. "Listen to me." She brushed strands of hair away from his eyes and then rested her palm against his chest. "I'm sure it's all a little scary, but this was—*is* your home." She gripped the aged brass handle. "Whatever we find, we'll face it together."

CHAPTER SEVEN

Arwan

Arwan squeezed her hand a little tighter as the door to his childhood room swung open, revealing a space he'd nearly forgotten.

A twin bed was pushed against the far wall, stripped of any linens or pillows. Above the headboard hung a wooden mask. His mother had hung it there. She said it would chase away evil. Just like the facade of safety she'd held up so well, that, too, was a lie.

It was all so strange, standing in the threshold of the room he'd spent thousands of nights in, believing he was loved, and having no idea of what his future would hold.

His gaze fell to the floor beside his bed. That was where she had slept, every night, as long as he could remember. On top of a round throw rug that was no longer there.

"It's almost empty," Zanya said, bringing him back to the moment. "I guess she packed up this room too."

He grabbed the handle and pulled it shut. "It doesn't matter anymore."

She was quiet, which somehow comforted him. Nothing more needed to be said.

"Hey. I have an idea." Zanya bobbed up and down on the balls of her feet with a beaming smile. "Let's check out what's in the kitchen. We need food, and maybe there's something left in the cabinets."

"Nothing not expired," he said, staring down the hall toward the slate countertops. "But you're right, we do need food."

"Okay. So you go look for food, and I'll uncover the furniture and see what we have to work with. Sound good?"

She was obviously trying to take his mind off of things—keep him busy, for the moment. The gesture was appreciated. He nodded. "It does sound good, but I don't have any tools to hunt."

She shrugged. "So we'll eat clean." She quoted the words with her fingers. "It's the new trend, anyway."

"Right." He wrapped his arm around her waist and pulled her closer. She tilted up her chin, searching his eyes, saying everything words couldn't.

No matter what happened in the past, they were bonded. Nothing would ever come between that, and neither of them would ever be alone again.

He leaned down and kissed her, savoring the taste of her lips and the heat radiating from her skin. Her heartbeat spiked, and then slowed until the familiar drumming in her chest was back to normal.

When he pulled back, Zanya's eyes fluttered open, studying him from behind a thick curtain of lashes. Her wolf gray eyes were entrancing, like looking into a sea of opals.

Her cheeks flushed with color, and she set her hand on his chest, sending a wave of heat through his veins. "Better get going if you don't want to be caught picking fruit in the dark."

"I'm not scared of the dark." He arched a brow. "Especially with you here to protect me."

She snorted. "Like you need me."

He slid his hand around the back of her neck and skimmed his thumb over the curve of her jaw. "That's where you're wrong." The blush in her cheeks intensified, satisfying him—for the moment. He placed a kiss on her forehead and stepped back. "Okay. I'll be right back."

She nodded. "I'll be waiting."

He walked through the living room, out the front door, and outside, where the humid air immediately clung to his skin. The sun was low in the sky, making the heat index more bearable than earlier that day. There was just enough sunlight for him to explore the area around the home and search for fruit-bearing bushes and trees.

He moved around the perimeter of the home, walking the tree line while peering into the foliage. A few small squirrels scurried through the branches overhead. The birds fell silent. The forest grew still.

He frowned. Even in the solitude of the jungle he couldn't escape his inner identity. The dark beast inside him lay in wait for the moment he would unleash it again. First Cualli reminded him of his heritage, and now the animals that sensed the darker half.

He pushed aside branches, winding deeper into the jungle. He scanned the sea of green for splashes of color, and caught a flash of orange overhead. As he walked toward the citrus tree, leaves crunched beneath his feet. He paused and looked down at brown, withered leaves.

It was the wet season. In the tropical rainforest, that meant an abundance of water for green, lush plants, blooming flowers, and animals to welcome their young.

He rammed the toe of his boot into a rotted lump of root, splintering it into dozens of pieces. He followed the trail of flaky bark, the tree dusky and bare of leaves.

Thick, green vines wound around the trunk, strangling the life out of it.

He disregarded the scene and continued to the ripe orange hanging on a nearby branch. He jumped and yanked the fruit from where it hung. The sweet, citrus scent teased his senses, making his stomach rumble. Besides some water and a few protein bars, he and Zanya hadn't had much to eat that day. These fruits would be the perfect supplement for calories and sugar. Though Zanya was capable of taking care of herself, it was his responsibility now to provide for her. It was his job to keep her happy and safe, and nothing would stop him from doing just that.

***

Zanya

Zanya paced the living room, examining the mounds of furniture she'd uncovered. There were two royal blue sofas with raspberry red foot rests, an oval coffee table made of some kind of cherry wood, two side tables, a reading lamp that stood on brass feet with an adjustable neck, and a small dining table with four chairs.

She walked to the kitchen sink and turned on the faucet. The pipes groaned, and a moment later brown water sputtered from the faucet. She crinkled her nose and waited for the water to run clear, then found an old rag in one of the kitchen drawers and wet it just enough to wipe layers of dust from the furniture.

Over the next hour she slid each chair, table, and sofa into position, rearranging them sometimes two or three times before she was satisfied. The reading lamp she set on the opposite side of the fireplace near the double sofa, and tucked the four chairs under the dining table near the kitchen.

She moved into the master bedroom and scoured the room for linens, finding a sheet and pillowcase set neatly folded, hidden in the bottom drawer of the dresser. A thin blanket filled the drawer beside it. She pulled it out, shaking off what smelled like some kind of herbs—maybe to keep bugs and rodents at bay. But the scent was pleasant, and after dusting them clean, she used them to make the king sized bed in the master bedroom.

She cringed at the screeching hinges as the front door swung open. "Did you find anything?" She'd finished tucking the sheet, just like she did at the orphanage. Not the most pleasant memory, but at least the skill came in handy. "I'm guessing that's a no." She grinned.

A gentle humming carried from the family room. Zanya froze.

The sweet melody filled the space, like an ancient Celtic lullaby.

Zanya turned and walked into the hall, heading toward the living space. As the voice grew louder, a metallic scent tickled the back of her throat. She knew that smell. It coated her tongue more times than she cared to recall.

"Cualli?"

Zanya stepped into the room to see the goddess sitting in a rocking chair by the fireplace, her bare feet pressed onto the floor, rocking as she hummed the sweet tune. Her presence filled the home with a bright, clean energy.

Cualli stopped rocking and looked at Zanya. The goddess's gaze drifted down to her neck. "I noticed you do not wear the necklace I gave you any longer. You used to reach for it for comfort."

"Oh." She placed her fingers over the place the wicker emblem would have sat. "I...I don't mean to be offensive. It's just that I didn't want it to break or—"

"No need to apologize, young guardian." Cualli began to rock again with a pleasant smile. She scanned the room and drew in a deep breath, as if drawing the atmosphere into her lungs. "I have always loved this room. It seems different now."

Zanya parted her lips. "You've been here

before?"

"Many times." She skimmed her hands over the polished wooden armrests. "I watched her sit in this very spot when she carried the half-breed."

Zanya drew her eyebrows together, both out of anger and confusion. "Her?"

"Yes. Arwan's birth mother. It's likely the half-breed cannot remember—"

"*Please*..." Zanya balled her fists, working hard to reel back the urge to scold the goddess for her cruel wording.

The goddess glanced at her clenched hands and stopped rocking again. "I apologize."

Zanya mustered the decency to nod, though she didn't deserve it.

"However, that is what he is. How should I call him otherwise?"

Zanya hardened her features, her self-control folding. "You could have the decency to respect him enough not to throw it in his face." The light in her chest flickered on, but her stone hummed soothingly against the delicate skin on her wrist, cooling the heat raging in her veins. "It's not as if he has a choice," she said in a softer tone. The same metallic scent of blood flooded her senses, scraping her nerves. "And *what* is that smell?"

Cualli gestured to the kitchen. "A gift from Balam, from his afternoon hunt."

Zanya walked to the kitchen, looked down in the sink, and jumped at the sight of a small, dead tapir lying, half gutted, with its eyes wide open and its tongue hanging out from under its strange, elongated nose. "Oh...wow. That's..." She searched for her next word, but could only blurt out what popped into her head. "Gross."

Cualli's laugh was like wind chimes in the breeze. "An acquired taste, perhaps."

"Right." Zanya grabbed the rag she'd used to dust the furniture and draped it over the dead animal. "But thoughtful." She looked back at the goddess, who now stood beside the windows, gazing out at the distant view. "Tell Balam I said thank you for the gift. I guess it's the kind of bonding gift I should expect from a big cat."

Cualli pivoted, her long, golden hair flowing around the feathered garment draped over her ivory skin. Her smile blossomed. "May your life here be happy, young guardian."

"Thanks." Zanya tried her best to give a genuine smile, though it was anything but. She still hadn't wrapped her mind around the idea of living in this home—in this unfamiliar place—for the rest of her life. She found herself missing the grand staircase and large library in Renato's home. The music room in the wing, and the strip of glittering white sand making way to aqua waves outside. She missed her uncle's warm smile, his combed hair, fitted suit, and the scent of earthy tobacco that followed him wherever he went.

And Tara. Her best friend, with red curly hair and inquisitive hazel eyes. How long would it be before they were together again?

Tears stung her eyes, and she quickly blinked them away. "Thank you," she managed to choke out.

Cualli paced toward her and gave a gentle smile.

"Being a half-breed is nothing to be ashamed of, young guardian. In fact, in this very rare instance, it may very well save the middleworld from drowning in smoke and fire."

CHAPTER EIGHT

Arwan

Arwan approached the front door, holding a collection of oranges, a few ripe mangos, and some blackberries he'd found on his way back. It wasn't a lot, but it would have to be enough until he could figure out how to hunt without his darker half scaring off the local wildlife.

When he pushed open the door and walked inside, the mixed scent of blood and wet fur flooded his nostrils.

"Zanya?"

"Yeah. I'm here." Her voice was distant from the back of the house.

He went into the kitchen and spilled the fruits on the countertop. The pungent smell intensified, pulling his attention to the sink, where four stiff, speckled legs with three toes protruded from under a rag.

"I see you found our dinner." Zanya crossed the room, wearing a tank top and a pair of stretchy pants that clung to her every curve, her hair in a braid. "The dead critter in the sink was a gift from Balam."

"He was here?" Arwan lifted the rag and peeked at the baby spotted tapir.

"No, but Cualli was."

"What did she want?"

"Besides giving us dinner..." Zanya crinkled her nose at the animal, "...she just wanted to congratulate us on our bonding, and then she left."

"Did she give any advice on how to cook tapir?" He grinned.

Zanya crossed her arms. "Let's get one thing straight. I'm not the best cook. I've had a little experience from when I was in the orphanage working in the kitchen, and I'm generally a pretty adventurous person. Hell, over the last year I've bonded with an enchanted stone, traveled back in time, fought demons, and even voluntarily drowned in a freezing lake leading to the underworld. But I have my limits. There is *no* way I'll gut and skin a dead animal. Ever. So that," she pointed at the animal, "is yours to take care of."

Arwan chuckled. "It's really not that hard."

"Fantastic." She gave two thumbs up. "Then you won't have any problems."

He raised an eyebrow and examined the stiff legs one last time. He'd have to string it up and cut it open before nightfall if they wanted it for tonight. Though he'd never eaten tapir before, if it was a gift from the jaguar god, it would be an insult to not at least try it. "No. It shouldn't be a problem."

She exhaled. "Thank you."

He looked around the space. "I see you've been busy."

Her eyes lit up. "Let me show you around." She took his hand and pulled him into the living room. "There was a lot of furniture under those sheets. I cleaned them up and moved things around where I liked them. There's a dining table over there with four chairs—not that we'll have much company out here, but you never know—and there were a few paintings I found that I hung in the hall. Come on." She led him toward the back of the house, where several landscape paintings were mounted on the walls. "The nails were already here, so it was just a matter of figuring out what should go where." Zanya paused, studying them with a faint smile. "Look at the bold strokes and vivid colors. Beautiful, aren't they?" A moment of silence lingered before Zanya softly gripped his arm. "Come on. There's more to see."

He followed her to the last room on the right. Rather than an empty, cold master bedroom, it had been made into a sanctuary. The king sized bed was made with sage green linens and a white blanket. The windows hung open, allowing warm jungle air to pour inside. Several clay ornaments were arranged on the dresser, and oversized palm leaves reached out from a large brass vase standing in the corner.

"You did this?"

"Yeah." Zanya wiped her forehead with the back of her hand. "I mean, I figured if we are going to stay here awhile, we should make it comfortable."

Even as a young boy, this room had been an

empty shell. His mother only used it to store a few pieces of clothing, and occasionally one of them may have used the shower, but no more. Now the space had been transformed.

Zanya hung her head. "You don't like it."

"No. That's not it." He walked to the bed and lowered himself onto the mattress. Nothing he could say would repay her for giving him his home back. She was the reason this house *was* a home again. She, and nothing else. "Come here." He held out his hand.

She studied him for a moment, then did as he asked. He spread his legs and pulled her close, resting his forehead against her belly and his hands on her hips. The warmth of her standing so close spiked his blood with adrenaline. "Thank you." He slipped his fingers beneath the hem of her shirt and skimmed his fingers over her curves.

"I didn't really do anything."

He tightened his grip on her hips. She had no idea what her mere existence had given him. For the first time, he didn't feel alone. For the first time, he didn't just want to survive. He wanted to live.

***

Zanya

Before long, the howling of monkeys and chatter of insects took over, prompted by the onset of darkness.

Arwan had taken care of the tapir, and even though she was kind of grossed out to admit it, tapir didn't taste half bad.

The fruit Arwan had collected would be breakfast tomorrow. Their bellies were full tonight, but they'd have to figure out a more sustainable way of providing for themselves in this jungle paradise. Sure, Balam would hunt for them as long as they needed, but it didn't seem right not to at least try to be independent. Thankfully, after exploring the house, there were still plentiful amounts of some other basic necessities, like toilet paper, toothpaste, and 2-in-1 shampoo and conditioner. She even found boxes of tampons and some hot water bags to soothe bellyaches. It struck her as odd to find the well-stocked stash if Arwan's mother never planned to return—or planned for *no one* to return. Perhaps it was coincidence, but there was a good chance it was something more…

Zanya gazed out her bedroom window at the sea of stars. The cool night air caressed her skin, rolling a shiver down the backs of her arms.

The door to the master bath clicked open. Arwan walked into the room with wet hair and a towel wrapped around his waist, the corner tucked in at his hip. His hair was a mess, but somehow he pulled off the whole rugged outlander look without much effort.

Zanya's stomach fluttered.

Arwan paused and studied her. "Are you okay?"

She pursed her lips. "Yes. And stop reading me. It's not fair."

"I can't help it."

She sighed. "I know."

He grinned. "You could have left me some hot

water, though." He ran his fingers through his hair, smoothing down untamed strands.

She bit her bottom lip. "Sorry. I didn't realize we have only like twenty minutes of hot water."

He walked across the bedroom, his back and stomach muscles flexing with each movement. "I'll go on the roof tomorrow and see if I can adjust the angle of the solar panel. Maybe we can collect more power if we clear some of the overgrowth around the house."

Zanya nodded, unable to speak or tear her gaze from his olive skin and broad shoulders.

He picked up his hiking bag, looked inside, and then set it back onto the floor. "Where are my clothes?"

Zanya pointed to the dresser. "I figured I'd unpack while you were outside taking care of dinner."

"Oh." He stared at the drawers. "Thank you."

A flush of heat rose in her cheeks. She was such an idiot. They'd spent exactly one full day bonded, and she was already folding his socks and putting away his clothes. "Sorry if I..." She pushed a few damp strands of hair behind her ear, her fingers lingering on the curve of her neck. "I was just trying to be productive."

Arwan gave a low laugh. "Because being the one person who can save the middleworld isn't enough."

She smirked and shrugged. "There's that."

He laughed, louder this time. "We should get some sleep. It's been a long day, and tomorrow won't be any easier." He pulled down the blanket and sheets on one side of the bed.

Her heart skipped.

He froze for a split second, and then grabbed the pillow and tucked it under his arm. "I was thinking of sleeping on the couch, so I could keep an eye on things."

A streak of guilt tore through her, making her chest throb. It was obvious what he was trying to do. He promised not to push. Not to rush her. He promised he was okay with taking things slow, and he hadn't gone back on his word for even a second.

It was true, a part of her was nervous. This was all so new, and she had never been with anyone before. But another part of her yearned for him in a way that scared her half to death. It was as if her soul couldn't bear to stay away from him, and she would rather face her deepest fears and insecurities than sleep with him out of her reach, away from her touch.

That beautiful, terrifying thought was what won over her heart.

"No." She walked to his side and took the pillow, resting it back in its place. "Stay." She traced her fingers down the curves of his bare chest. His muscles tensed beneath her touch, then relaxed as she pressed her open palm to his skin. "I…" She swallowed and forced herself to look into his eyes. "I don't really know what I'm doing."

He wrapped his arm around her and pulled her in close, cradling her body against his. "I don't either."

She raised her brow. "You've never…"

He huffed, and a corner of his mouth arched into a grin. "Not many girls are interested in—" His grin disappeared, nearly breaking her heart.

She leaned in close and teased his neck with light kisses, leading a trail of kisses up to his ear. He coiled his fingers around the fabric of her sleeping shirt.

Her stone grew unusually silent, spreading a fog of peace over her shaken nerves. She kissed his jaw, then the crease of his mouth.

He parted his lips and met hers with more passion than she expected. She pulled in a sharp breath through her nose and wrapped her arms around his neck, embracing the warmth of his tongue gliding over hers and his hard muscle holding her close.

She'd found his gentle embrace more than once, but this was nothing like that. He kissed her with purpose, trading careful handling for strong intent.

He broke their kiss and pushed a wave of hair behind her ear, then caught the neckline of her sleeping t-shirt with his fingers and slid it over the curve of her shoulder. She drew in a shaky breath, her skin tingling.

"I feel like I have to ask…" He glided his fingers over her bare skin. "I don't have any protection."

Her cheeks flushed with heat. "Oh. Right." Her tone turned solemn. "About that." She lowered her gaze, unable to meet his. "We don't have to worry about that." She touched the inside of her arm with her fingertips. "In the orphanage they put an implant in all of the girls when they reached eighth grade. It was a…precaution."

"So…we're okay."

She nodded, too humiliated to say anything else.

The doctors at the orphanage had taken away so much—her childhood, her privacy, and her right to choose. Granted, she didn't want any kids. Not now. Not after seeing what her mother had been through. Still, deciding that for her somehow didn't seem right.

His gentle voice pulled her out of her thoughts. "Are you okay?"

"Yeah." She drew in a deep breath, savoring the warmth of his body near her. As long as they were together, she'd be okay. "I am now."

He ran his hand down her back and over the curves, then cupped the back of her thigh and lifted one leg while leaning her against the edge of the mattress. She followed his lead and relaxed back onto the luxurious sheets.

Arwan spread his fingers and traced his hand up her leg, stopping at the hem of her sleeping shirt. She gasped a tiny breath and pulled him closer.

He pulled back and searched her eyes. "I don't have to."

"I know." She rested her hand over his and guided him below the soft, cotton fabric. "I want you to."

CHAPTER NINE

Zanya

Zanya blinked open her eyes and stretched her hands above her head, savoring the warmth of the pillow top mattress and soft cotton sheets. She skimmed her hand over the cold sheets where Arwan had slept the night before, then glanced at the bathroom door, hanging open with the light off. He must have been up for a while.

She groaned.

He was a morning person.

Strike one.

She squinted at the fresh morning sunlight and slid her legs over the side of the bed, resting her bare feet on the floor. When her skin touched the cool stone, she pulled them up and cringed.

The floors here weren't nearly as warm as the natural wood in Renato's house. There she didn't need socks just to get out of bed. Here, in *their* home, things would be different.

She braved the floor a second time, winning the

battle with little more than a second round of chills. She dragged the top sheet off the bed and wrapped it around her, then silently padded to the windows and drew in a deep breath, taking in the amazing view.

She shifted focus to her own reflection in the window, showing her tousled hair and bare legs peeking out from under the sheer sheet.

Glimpses of the night she'd spent with Arwan reeled through her mind. She'd dreaded the idea of her first time. Now that it was gone, a streak of sadness burrowed deep in her belly. He had been so gentle and sweet. If every time could be that amazing, she'd never ask for more.

The bedroom door creaked open and Arwan walked inside. He stopped after a few steps and spent a brief, intense moment studying her.

Zanya's body flooded with heat, and she bit her lip, dropping her gaze to her bare feet. She brushed her legs together and clung tighter to the sheet.

Arwan closed the gap between them and pulled her close. "Good morning." He placed a kiss on her lips.

She couldn't hold back her smile. Just being near him made something inside her bloom. "Morning. How'd you sleep?"

"Better than ever." He trailed his hands down her bare arms.

Instead of her stomach fluttering, it growled—loudly. She raised both eyebrows and parted her lips. "I guess I'm kind of hungry."

"Good, because I have breakfast."

"I'm just going to slip some clothes on and I'll

be out."

He walked into the hall and grabbed the door handle. "Take your time." Before closing the door, he paused. "Are you…" His expression became solemn. "Are you okay?"

When she realized what he was asking, she quickly nodded. "Yeah. I'm…I'm fine."

He nodded, obvious relief relaxing his tense features.

When the door clicked shut, she showered, changed, and then joined Arwan in the kitchen. He stood behind the counter, pouring steaming water into a cup.

The earthy aroma of coffee infused the air.

"Oh. My. God." Her stomach growled again. This time she didn't care. "How did you get coffee all the way out here?"

"I didn't." He placed the cup on the countertops. "I found it in the cabinets. Manna from the gods?"

"More like compliments of Cualli, I'm sure."

"First, keeping the house in decent shape, and now coffee? She's not a goddess—she's a saint." She took the mug and sipped the hot brew. Her eyes fluttered shut. "Nothing could be better."

He grazed his fingers over the back of her hand. "I was just thinking the same thing."

Something cracked against one of the windows, making Zanya jump and spill hot coffee on her hand. "Shoot!" She set the cup back on the counter and watched the burn heal and vanish within moments. Healing was her favorite ability by far. "What was that?"

Another loud smack rattled the window,

followed by another.

She cautiously walked toward the window, peering at the small, colorful objects as they crashed into the glass and fell to the ground. "Are those birds?"

They kept coming, an entire flock of yellow and blue finch-sized birds, all following each other to their deaths. Zanya clutched her chest, her eyes wide as blood splattered and smeared over the glass.

Arwan stepped beside her. "What is happening?"

"I don't know, but…" She looked at Arwan. "That's not normal, right?"

Arwan shook his head. "No. That's not normal."

***

Arwan

Arwan walked outside to a graveyard of birds lying on the ground beside their home. Some were still alive, flapping their wings and spinning in circles. Others struggled and gasped for air. The rest, the lucky rest, were nothing more than tiny broken bodies.

Zanya followed behind him and covered her mouth. "My god…" She crouched beside a bird flailing its tiny feet in an effort to stand, but all it was doing was kicking violently in the air. "Can we help them?"

"No." He held out his hand to stop her. "Don't touch them. They could be sick."

She stood. "You think that's why they all flew into our window?"

It was possible, but not probable. "I couldn't say—" The thick layer of soil slithered and snaked to life.

Zanya gasped and leapt back. Arwan shifted, his eyes narrow as the jungle floor came to life.

What appeared to be tree roots broke through the soil and coiled around the tiny feathered corpses. The roots bored into the bodies and coiled around them, snapping brittle bone and tearing open each creature before pulling it underground, leaving red stains splattered over green foliage.

Arwan's heart raced as he stepped back, his hand extended to Zanya. "Come on. Come on, right now." She grabbed his hand, and he quickly guided her to the safety of the open bottom level of the home.

"What the hell was that?" Zanya panted, still clinging to his arm.

He searched every possibility, but came up with only one. Visions of Yaxche, the tree of life connecting all three realms, barged to the forefront of his mind. The tree served a wider purpose than to linger above the damned, trapping them in their eternal torment. It was a link between the underworld, the middle world, and the heavens, giving the dead a bridge for their journey.

Arwan tightened his grip on Zanya's hand. "My gods…" He recalled Contessa, the red haired vixen, once Sarian's lover, now his predecessor. She consumed the souls of men to stay alive in the middleworld, leaving their hollowed vessels to rot on top of the ground. Anything that witch touched was destined for evil, and with her in possession of the book of Popul Vuh, it was only a matter of time before the underworld would rise. "What have we done?"

"What are you talking about? What's going on?"

"It's our fault. We never should have left." He turned and studied the house on stone stilts, safe from reaching vines. "Wait…My mother built this house, knowing this day would eventually come. She knew…" He reached for more answers, but found none. "This doesn't make any sense."

"Hey." Zanya's sharp tone commanded his attention. Her eyes were piercing and her lips tightly pressed. "Would you please tell me what the hell is going on?"

"We have to get to the Temple of Inscriptions. We'll find answers there."

She tilted her head. "How do you know that?"

He touched one of the stone pillars, cool against his skin. The glyphs carved into the rock told a story. They spoke of the temple, where generations of history were etched into its walls. His mother used to tell him fables as he played outside. She said the markings would one day save mankind. "My mother told me so."

CHAPTER TEN

Zanya

Again, losing sight of her first rule only proved to blind her from the inevitable.

Zanya sat on the bed, watching Arwan shove supplies into his hiking pack. He worked feverishly—blindly, even—as if the rest of the world no longer existed. Sweat collected on his brow and his eyes were narrow while he carefully counted the rest of their protein bars and divided them into rations for the day's hike to the Temple of Inscriptions.

"Arwan..." She stood, lingering beside the bed. He didn't look up from the supplies, nor did he give any kind of indication he even heard her call his name. She took a hesitant step forward. "Arwan." She was careful to keep her tone gentle. "Are you okay?"

He finally looked up at her. "What?"

"I..." She bit the inside of her cheek. "Are you sure this is a good idea?"

"Why wouldn't it be?" He grabbed one stack of protein bars and slipped them into a small pouch in his pack, then zipped it shut. "You should get your things. We could leave tonight..." He paused, seemingly considering their options. "No. That's too dangerous. We need the daylight. More roots could rise, and we may not see them in time in the dark."

Zanya twisted her fingers. Maybe *he* was fine, but her gut wrenched over the fact he didn't notice *she* was absolutely *not* okay. "I don't know if I can do this." She shook her head, replaying the horrific scene of the birds being pulled underground. "I can't—" She choked on her words and lowered herself back onto the mattress. "How could this be happening?"

"It's happening." He stood and tossed his pack on the foot of the bed. "We need to be ready for it."

"I just..." She cradled her head in her hands, struggling for every breath. "It's all happening so fast."

Arwan walked toward her and sat on the mattress beside her. "Zanya..." He draped his hand over her leg.

She pulled away. "No." She buried her fingers deeper into her hair. "Just...give me a minute." She swallowed down the acid in her throat and pushed back tears, all to conquer the onset of a panic attack. It was just like when she was in the orphanage, except this time Tara wasn't there to talk her through it.

Her stone grew cold against her wrist, filling her with the peace she needed to steady her breath. She lowered her hands to her lap. When she finally looked at Arwan, his fingers were laced together with his forearms on his knees. He sat in absolute silence, his tense features and focused stare making it clear he had dived deep into thought.

She ached to know exactly what was trolling through his mind. Where his imagination had wandered and if he was thinking about her. But after a lifetime of knowing his mother was raped, then carried him for nine months in disgust, only to abandon him before subjecting herself to death—this new revelation proved there was more to his mother's story than he believed.

That *he* was more to *her* than he believed.

Zanya hung her head. How selfish could she be? "I'm sorry. It's just been a lot of change in a short amount of time, and I'm still wrapping my mind around it all."

He laced his fingers between hers. "I know. It's been a lot for me too." He squeezed her hand. "And I know you miss Renato and your mother."

Zanya pursed her lips. "I spent my entire childhood missing my mother." She huffed. "It's ironic, isn't it? She was gone all those years, and now that she's back, a part of me wishes she weren't."

"Don't say that."

"It's true. If she weren't here, we would still be in Belize with Renato, Tara, Peter, Jay, and Hawa..." Her stomach tightened, sending another pulse of bile up her throat. "I'd probably be training right now, learning how to use my abilities better. Especially now that the others are there—Eadith,

Beigarth, and Grima, and those two Arab windthrowers." She peered at her empty backpack lying in the corner of the room. "Now that I think about it, my mom hasn't just exiled us, but she killed any chance of me learning how to take her place." A coil of heat wound through her. She parted her lips. "Maybe that's it." She stood, letting go of Arwan's hand. "Maybe she's jealous."

"Jealous?"

Her eyes widened. "It makes so much sense now." It was the reason her mother hated Arwan being in the home. Why her mother discouraged her from wanting to learn Grima and Beigarth's petrifying ability. Why when she and Arwan bonded, they were forced to choose.

It was all jealousy.

Her mother regretted no longer being the Stone Guardian, and didn't want to see anyone surpass her own performance in that role. Even her own daughter.

She peered at the pack a moment longer, and then walked across the room and snatched it off the floor. "She's jealous of me—of us." She knelt beside the drawers and opened one at a time, shoving pieces of clothes into her bag. "She and my dad never bonded because he was human, and she hates that I got everything she never had." She stuffed the last piece of clothing in her pack and zipped it shut. "That has to be it."

"I don't know." Arwan stood and paced the length of the wall. "It does make sense."

"Hell, yeah, it makes sense." Zanya put on her pack. "But I'm not going to let her win." She touched the leather wristband with her stone held inside. "Let's go, before it gets too dark out."

Arwan stopped pacing. "Now?"

"Yes, now."

"But the tree. We have to be able to see its vines while moving through the jungle."

"You keep watch as we hike, and I'll use every ability at my disposal to keep us safe if something comes up." She walked toward the door.

Arwan hooked his hand around her arm, making her pause. "Are you sure about this? Because if you are, I'll follow you. I'll trust you, and your abilities."

Zanya tightened her jaw, recalling her mother's shrieking voice and trembling hands as she cast them out. As her mother, the one person who should have run to her defense, ordered her to choose—her family, or Arwan.

At one time, she would have chosen her mother over anyone. Now everything had changed.

"I'm the Stone Guardian, and I'm going to prove to you, my mother, and everyone else that I can do this—with or without *her* help."

***

Arwan

He followed behind Zanya, using game trails and breaks in the thick jungle terrain. He managed to keep up with her pace, though barely.

Something inside of her had changed.

She was stronger now. More capable. More

75

determined. Nothing she hadn't been since the moment he met her. Except now it came from a different place. A place he knew all too well, having lived in the same dark hole in his heart for too many years.

He scanned the jungle floor ten paces ahead, always keeping an eye out for movement under the leaves. Every hanging vine was suddenly a threat. The entire jungle had turned on them, and there was little he could do to keep her safe if the tree knew where they were and chose to strike.

He furrowed his brow.

Or perhaps it was being told where to strike.

"Zanya." He quickened his pace several steps and caught up with her. "I think Contessa knows where we are."

"Why do you say that?" Her eyes stayed focused ahead when she spoke, not shifting to him even for a moment.

"The tree swallowed the birds, but it didn't touch us."

"Because we ran to the house."

"Or…"

She finally glanced at him. "Or what?"

"Or it was *told* not to take us."

Zanya snorted. "Now trees are taking orders?" She seemed to contemplate his suggestion, and then slowed down for the first time since they'd left.

"This isn't an ordinary tree. You've seen what it can do. It tore those underworlders apart at Sarian's command. It could do the same in this realm if it's given permission from whoever possesses the Popul Vuh."

"Which is Contessa."

"Exactly." A gentle, humid breeze wove through the trees, carrying the stench of rotting flesh. His throat tightened. "Do you smell that?" The odor burned the back of his throat and filled his lungs. He covered his mouth, fighting the urge to gag.

Zanya lifted her nose in the air. "I don't smell anything."

Something must have died, and his keen sense of smell wouldn't allow him to overlook it.

When the stench grew more pungent, Zanya crinkled her nose. "Oh my god." She covered her mouth with her sleeve. "I smell it now."

"Stay close." He shifted in front of her and crept forward. Hundreds of years of fallen leaves and spongy moss cushioned each step. The rising heat seemed to intensify the funk, making it almost unbearable to his heightened senses. He coughed and closed his mouth, but it was too late. The full impact of it had coated his tongue and slid down his throat.

When the plant life thinned and the trees became sparse, he saw it—them—lying on the ground, consumed by crawling vines.

Tapir, rabbit, fowl, deer, all in a mangled, broken mixture of sunken-in bodies, drained of fluids. Blood stained the soil, guts stretched over cracks in the ground, and wide, empty eyes stared sightlessly. The animals' ribs pushed against thin layers of fur as if they'd been eaten from the inside out.

"If what I suspect is true," Arwan said in a low voice, "this is a message."

The light in Zanya's chest burst to life. "She's

watching us."

The distant snapping of branches caught his ear, though it was so far in the distance, Zanya didn't notice it. "We have to keep moving. The Temple of Inscriptions is only a few miles away, but it will take us several hours to reach, considering the terrain."

"Not with a little help." She stretched out her hands, and moments later, clusters of clouds rolled toward them. They gathered into dark, looming shadows, as if a tornado were forming overhead.

Zanya squared her stance, her face tilted to the changing atmosphere.

He'd only seen her use her windthrowing ability once, when he had unleashed his darker half, and she was out to kill him. He was fully aware of how treacherous this ability could be. Trees bowed to the fierce winds, and a dark funnel formed, reaching down from the sky.

Zanya pulled him behind her. "You may want to stay behind me."

CHAPTER ELEVEN

Zanya

Zanya squinted against the force of the winds, calling on the inner strengths she'd inherited from her bloodline. Her stone hummed loyally against her wrist, infusing her with more power than she could conjure on her own. As a team, she and her stone were unstoppable.

"If we appear to be a threat, Contessa may order the tree after us!" The roar of the storm reduced Arwan's voice to a mere whisper in the distance.

"I'm not going after that tree." She pivoted and extended her hands, directing the vortex straight toward the Temple of Inscriptions. "I'm going after the rest of them—all the way to the ruins."

Arwan's grip on her tightened. The winds intensified, stripping leaves and tearing off branches from tress that must have been hundreds of years old.

"Hang on, this is going to get rough!" She stretched her hands forward, pushing the storm through the jungle. The cracking of tree trunks was like claps of thunder. Winds sliced at the jungle, chewing anything green out of the ground and clearing enough of the foliage so they could complete their journey to the Temple of Inscriptions before nightfall.

Once the path was clear, Zanya lowered her arms to her sides, urging the light in her chest to dull. The winds faded until the sky stilled. Her muscles throbbed, and a deep fatigue washed through her, draining her face of heat. She examined the road of churned soil and grinned. "Well." She wiped her sweaty palms down the front of her jeans. "Not bad, if I do say so myself."

Arwan raked his fingers through his hair and grinned. "Not bad at all."

"We had better get moving." She rubbed her fingers together, measuring how much energy she had left after conjuring the storm. Unfortunately, the test revealed she had nothing. Completely tapped. Until she built up her endurance, it was important to pick and choose when she exhausted herself. That, or end up defenseless at the worst possible moment.

The rest of the hike to the ruin was uneventful. Arwan insisted on walking ahead of her to look out for any more signs of danger. All the while, she couldn't stop thinking about the scene of carnage they'd left behind.

She'd read about the tree a while back in a leather journal Renato had *borrowed* from Contessa's library. She frowned. That was before she and Arwan had braved the underworld to retrieve Jayden's soul.

Her heart ached at the thought of Jayden, back at home. She couldn't find him before she and Arwan left. He was probably worried sick.

Her mother may have wronged her, but the others hadn't, and she desperately missed Jayden's sarcasm and Tara's watery laugh. There was no telling when they'd see each other again.

She caught up with Arwan in the next few steps and stopped beside him, staring at the ruin. "Well, there it is."

Arwan shifted in silence. He seemed nervous or worried. Or maybe a little of both. Still, if his mother was right, they needed to know what was in that temple.

She took his hand. "Come on. We'll go up together."

***

Arwan

The temple was more enormous than he imagined. Hundreds of narrow stairs led up to a single room with an open door. As they approached the top, the stories his mother had told him as a child echoed in his mind. This temple was more than the remains of an ancient civilization. It was a chapter in history, with truth etched into stone tablets inside.

When they reached the top, Arwan leaned on one of the arched entrances, the stone cool and textured beneath his skin.

"Do we go inside?" Zanya asked between heavy breaths. Her normally flushed cheeks were drained of color, only accentuating the shadows that had formed under her eyes.

"I know you're exhausted, but we need light. Do you think you can provide some?"

"I don't know. I'm done in." She unclasped the pouch on her wrist and slipped out her stone. "But we can ask for a little help."

"Good enough."

She must have noticed the quiet hesitation in his voice. "Everything's going to be okay. I promise." She set her fingers over her stone. "Some light, please." It gleamed, and she looked up at him. "After you."

Arwan turned and faced the dark void. The glyphs could tell him anything, and he'd have to be willing to accept the truth—whatever that may be.

He stepped inside, followed by Zanya, who held the stone in front of her. It filled the room with a soft, white light.

He skimmed his fingers along the etchings in the large tablets, snapping fragile cobwebs and coating his hands in dust. The stories this temple held were thousands of years old, passed down by the elders of his people.

"My mother once told me the name of this temple means *House of the Nine Sharpened Spears*." His voice echoed in the space, bouncing off the stone walls. It had been many years since he'd read the language of the Maya, and even longer since he'd spoken it aloud.

"Can you understand any of this?" Zanya paused

and held the stone closer to the wall, examining the markings.

Thankfully, the skill of reading his language hadn't faded completely. He peered at the symbols, one after the other, sounding out the words in his head before translating to Zanya. "This speaks of the creation of the middleworld. It says, 'Here is the story of the beginning, when there was not a single bird, nor a single fish, or a single mountain. There is only sky. It is lonely. There is the sea. It too is alone. There is nothing more. No sound, no movement. Only the sky and the sea, lonely and silent. The three, known collectively as Heart-of-Sky, existed. And these are their names: Modeler, Star, and Hurricane.'"

"Who are they?"

"The gods of Tamoanchan—the heaven gods. The creation gods." He continued reading. "Then Heart-of-Sky says, 'Who is there to speak our name? How shall I create the dawn?' Heart-of-Sky only speaks the word, 'Earth,' and the earth rises, like a fog from the sea. They simply think of it, and it appears. They ponder on mountains, and they come. They ponder on trees, and they come as well, sprouting from the land. And so Heart-of-Sky says, 'Our work is good.' Then they paint creatures in the forest—deer, birds, snakes, and such. And each is given a home. But Heart-of-Sky is not satisfied. The creatures cannot pray or speak their name, so Heart-of-Sky tries again. They form a new creation with the ability to respect and give praise. Their new creation is made of mud and earth. It was pleasing to the eye, and it reproduced. So Heart-of-Sky allowed them to live and flourish on earth.'" He moved to the next column of glyphs. "'When Heart-of-Sky was pleased, they allowed their creation to populate the middleworld. But there was a flaw in their design. Mankind had the hearts of lions and were capable of love, but their flesh was weak. They perish from injury. They perish from famine. They perish from disease. Middleworld gods, those deemed to guard earth, pleaded with Heart-of-Sky to grant mankind a defense. They recognized the dark realm envied them, desiring the middleworld for themselves. Out of pity for mankind, Heart-of-Sky created a...'" He smirked and looked at Zanya. "You'll like this part." Zanya leaned in closer, waiting silently for him to continue. "'Heart-of-Sky created a stone, and in it poured the blood from Heart-of-Sky, giving it life and power.'"

Zanya's stone pulsed with light, as if it knew he was reading about it. Perhaps it did.

"What next?" Zanya's eyes widened like a child.

"Heart-of-Sky delivered the stone to a keeper, who was tasked with guarding it. Though man was stronger in brute strength, Heart-of-Sky agreed woman would be the guardian. Her passion, love, and fierce protectiveness far outweighed man, making her superior."

"Well, look at that." Zanya rocked back on her heels with her chest puffed out. "It says it right there. Women are superior."

"Who am I to argue with Heart-of-Sky?"

She glared playfully at him. "Smooth."

He winked and took her hand. "Come on. We have to go to the central tablet. There's more."

Once in front of the new slab of glyphs, he examined the symbol of a star etched at the top. "'While Modeler and Hurricane admired their creation, Star's soul was stricken with grief. Rather than linger in a haze of glory, she saw the truth. Mankind was doomed. Even with their blood in the stone, and a guardian to harness its power, it was not enough. Star watched for generations. Dark forces from the underworld grew in strength, striking at their fragile creation. Man's delicate nature could not be changed. Even with the guardian...'" Arwan touched the next column of glyphs. "There had to be more."

"More?"

"This section is titled something different—it's written differently too." He tilted his head examining it. "A premonition..."

"From the creation gods?"

He nodded. "Exactly. A premonition of the future. 'Star showed Modeler and Hurricane, whose pride was too great to agree. Star's heart bled. Guilt consumed her. She pleaded with Modeler and Hurricane to grant her release and allow her to protect man in the middleworld. They agreed, but with one condition—her reign as Star in Heart-of-Sky would be complete. She would be stripped of her crown. She would become mortal.'"

"Whoa. Talk about generous," Zanya said. "That's a big sacrifice in the name of being noble."

He stepped back. "I don't understand how any of this can help." He dropped his gaze. "Maybe she was giving me false hope."

"There's one more tablet." She nudged him

85

playfully. "Come on." She took his hand and pulled him aside. "We came all this way. We can't stop now."

He followed, and lingered in front of the final tablet before he continued reading. "'Star conceded to their condition. Her crown was torn from her head. She fell from the heavens, landing in the sea. Many days she lived hungry, cold, and afraid.'"

"A good deed never goes unpunished," Zanya mumbled. When he looked at her, she bit her lip. "Sorry. Keep going."

"'But Star was clever. There was a quality to being mortal she did not have as part of Heart-of-Sky. Now, as woman, she could become...'" Arwan tilted his head. "'*Pregnant*.'" The word slipped from his lips as the heat in his body spiked. "My gods," he whispered. He continued reading. "'Star walked day and night to a dark corner of the earth. There she found Yaxche, and journeyed to the underworld.'"

"So she gave up her place as a creation goddess, all to be cold and hungry, and then go down to hell? For what? And how, if she wasn't underworld herself?"

"She must have had help..."

"Help?" Zanya paused. "But...why?"

The darkness inside of him clawed at his chest, reminding him who he was. Though his legs began to feel weak, he forced himself to read on. "'The king of the underworld gazed upon Star's beauty. She...'" He blinked, his voice quivering as he read on. "'She seduced him and...lay with him.'" He swallowed the sick heat collecting under his tongue.

"'She gave her body to the king, and in that union…became pregnant.'" A single tear streaked down his face. "'The child was born under a full moon, unaware his creation was a union of heaven and hell. The son…'" He gulped in a breath. His legs quivered. "'The son of both Star and beast, a bloodline of royalty weaving together two realms, uniting powers of good and evil.'"

With a rush of nausea, he turned and dropped to his knees, then vomited on the stone floor.

"Arwan!" Zanya knelt beside him, her hands set on his back. "My god. You're shaking."

"This can't be—" The beast inside plowed into his heart, forcing him to collapse onto the cold ground. Heat drained from his face and the tips of his fingers chilled. Sweat slicked his skin.

"What's wrong?" She ran her hands over his body. "I can't sense anything."

He couldn't find the breath to respond.

"Come on, sit up. You have to sit up." She hooked her arms around him and hauled him upright, propping his back against the wall. She knelt in front of him, panic streaking her features. "I can heal you if you just tell me what's wrong. I don't know how to sense illnesses yet. I…" She cupped his face in her hands and searched his eyes. "*Please*."

He blinked, streaking a tear down his cheek. "Don't you see? How can you not see?"

"See what?" She ran her hands around his ribs as if searching for a wound. "I don't see anything."

He seized her hand, holding it tight. Too tight. "*I* am that boy."

CHAPTER TWELVE

Zanya

"'That boy?'" Zanya sat back on the cold stone floor. "As in, you're the son of Star and the underworld king? Like, some kind of half—" She choked on the word, and then parted her lips. "Oh my…" That must have been what Cualli had meant. He was special. A miracle, even.

And Cualli knew the whole time.

Her stone buzzed wildly against her skin, sending her into full-on alarm. She tightened her jaw and turned, searching the open entrance of the ruin. They were being watched. Whether it was Cualli and Balam, or Contessa doing the watching, she couldn't be sure.

"Come on." She draped Arwan's arm over her neck and held him against her hip. "You need to get up. We have to go home."

Arwan didn't move.

She pursed her lips. "Arwan. Come on." Her stone buzzed louder, making her heart race.

"Something's wrong. Someone's here. We have to go."

"What?" He dragged his gaze to her face with a blank stare, as if he hadn't heard anything she'd said.

If they were going to get out of there without risking a toe-to-toe confrontation, she had to snap him out of it. "Sorry about this." She rubbed her fingers together, building an electrical current over her skin. Energy buzzed over her fingertips, and she thwacked him on the ribs.

He gasped and his muscles stiffened. She secured her arm around him to make sure he didn't fall. He flinched, and the emptiness in his eyes vanished.

He blinked and looked at her—really looked at her. "Thanks."

"No problem. Now come on." She ground her teeth and pushed with her legs, hauling him to his feet. He slumped against her at first, but gradually gained his own footing until he stood without her help. "I don't know who it is or how close they are, but my stone is totally freaking out. We have to—"

Soft, padded steps silently carried Balam into the ruin.

Zanya let out a heavy breath. "Oh, thank God." She pushed strands of hair away from her face. Though she was happy to see him, she couldn't find it in herself to smile. If Cualli knew about Arwan's heritage, Balam most certainly knew as well, and that meant both of them had kept it from her.

Though…as a cat, it was impossible for him to say so. She rolled her eyes. Okay, he had a good

89

enough excuse.

The goddess, on the other hand…

Zanya glanced at the empty entrance. "Where's Cualli?"

Balam paused and peered at her with those familiar yellow eyes. Zanya stilled. "Is something wrong?"

The jaguar god quickly slunk out of the ruin. She looked at Arwan. "I have a feeling we should follow him."

"I think so."

Zanya traced Balam's path out of the temple and down hundreds of narrow steps, where the jaguar waited. Once they'd caught up, Balam continued down the path of destruction made by Zanya's storm.

She and Arwan exchanged a skeptical glance before pushing forward. Balam's tail swished and twitched, and every few yards he paused and shook off his paws, flicking mud and murky water into the air.

Finally, they rounded a curve in the path. Zanya slowed to a stop at the sight of Cualli in the distance.

The goddess's porcelain skin shimmered in the sun as she knelt on the churned soil, hunched over a tangled mess of uprooted plants. The tips of her golden strands skimmed over the ground, sprouting new, green ferns still in tiny spiraled balls.

Cualli reached out and touched the tattered leaf of a jungle palm. It fell off the plant into her hand. The goddess allowed it to slip through her fingers to the ground.

Cualli's statuesque figure stilled while she stared at the fallen leaf.

Zanya wanted to say something, but couldn't think of anything that would make it right. Under the circumstances, they needed a quick path to the temple, but now, seeing the goddess mourn over the very plants and flowers she was destined to protect, Zanya would have gladly hiked days to avoid the destruction she'd caused.

Balam stalked around Cualli and sat in front of her. The goddess turned, set her gaze on Zanya, and frowned. When she stood, Zanya took a cautious step back.

"What have you done to my jungle?" Her normally euphoric voice seemed sharp and dangerous.

"I'm so, *so* sorry." Zanya bit her bottom lip, searching for something more to say. "We had to get to the Temple of Inscriptions, and—"

"You found it necessary to destroy my jungle to find your way there?" She extended her hand down the path of wreckage. "As if you could not clearly see the temple from this very place, towering over the trees I have cared for, for generations."

"I..." Zanya swallowed. Every time she'd seen Cualli, the goddess had always been at peace. This was the first time she'd witnessed the pissed off version, and *she* was on the receiving end of the crap-o-meter.

After all, Renato had tried to give her a lesson in the consequences of using abilities once before—in his office—when she conjured a windstorm inside. He told her not to use her powers unless she was willing to clean up after them. At the time she thought he was playing the role of overbearing uncle. But now she understood.

"I did destroy your jungle." She stepped forward, looking Cualli in the eyes. "And I take full responsibility. It was an urgent situation. There was a tree—"

"Yes." Cualli glared, and Zanya could have sworn she felt the ground tremble beneath her. "There were many."

Zanya swallowed. "No. Not the ones I…" She wiped a tingle of sweat from her brow with her fingers. There was no good way to word it. "Not the ones I destroyed. There's another tree. Yaxche."

Cualli's features softened and her tightly pursed lips parted. "Yaxche?" The heat around the goddess seemed to fade, returning her to the familiar, gentle deity Zanya had always known.

Zanya's tense muscles eased. "I'm surprised you haven't noticed." Zanya closed her eyes and hung her head—resisting the urge to palm her forehead. "I didn't mean it like that." She exhaled and raise her gaze, then tried again. "*I mean*, it consumed a group of birds near our home, and then animals. A lot of them. It was as if they were—"

"Drained of blood."

Zanya nodded.

Cualli extended her hand, and Balam obeyed her gesture by walking to her side. Balam had always been her protector. The goddess calling on him to stay close wasn't a promising sign. "Then there are greater worries we must address. Yaxche is feeding on middleworld life." Cualli shifted her gaze to

Arwan. "And you, half-breed. Have you found the answers you seek?"

Arwan watched her without a response. He may have found answers, but they weren't what either of them had expected.

"I don't know what we should do," Zanya said, finally breaking the silence. "Contessa is definitely responsible for Yaxche reaching into the middleworld. That much we know. But how to fight it—fight her—is still a bridge we haven't crossed."

"The tree will destroy everything," Arwan said. "Animals, plants, humans. Once Contessa grants it permission, it will consume our world, allowing the underworlders to break through, and our realms will merge."

Zanya bit the inside of her cheek. She hadn't considered that as an option. But if Yaxche was used as a bridge—the way it was intended—that was exactly what would happen.

They'd fight a losing battle.

Cualli dragged her fingers between Balam's ears. "Then we must call on all of our strengths to be sure that does not come to pass." She trained her sights on Balam and gave a single, subtle nod.

A deep growl grew from inside his chest.

Balam bared his teeth, his ears pinned, and the fur on the back of his neck standing on edge.

Cualli looked at Zanya. "I suggest using your gift to call any reinforcements you may have."

Balam snarled and leapt forward, forcing Zanya to stumble back.

His legs quivered beneath him, and all at once, his jaguar form morphed into a towering man with bronze skin and bright yellow eyes. His face was adorned with streaks of blue paint, and bone earrings—what looked like animal teeth—hung from his lobes. A leopard loincloth covered the space between his lean, muscular legs.

It was the first time Zanya had ever seen Balam in his human form.

High, sharp cheek bones. Mocha skin. Dark lashes. Long, black hair hung down his back, tied with a thread of leather. No shoes, pants, or a shirt.

He was Cualli's guardian and friend, and he was glorious.

Balam must have sensed her fascination and looked away. He was obviously uncomfortable, so she'd do the best she could to not stare.

Cualli settled her hand on Balam's muscular neck. "While you ready yourself, Balam will stay by your side, in whatever form you need him."

"Ready myself?" Zanya shifted her weight. "For what?"

Cualli lifted her chin, her eyes gleaming with magic. "War."

CHAPTER THIRTEEN

The next day, Zanya sat on the sofa in her living room, struggling to gather her thoughts while she stared at the smears of mottled blood staining her windows.

Balam was lying in the corner—back in his familiar jaguar form. It would take time to get used to him being around, but when the goddess gave an order, she wasn't about to argue. Even if that meant listening to the jaguar snore half the day. How he was so relaxed, she'd never know.

Zanya hadn't used her seeking ability to find anyone from her group since she and Arwan fled the bonding ceremony. She blocked any effort Marzena made to reach out. She just wasn't ready.

But ready or not, it was time.

Zanya drew in a deep breath and closed her eyes, focusing on the smooth tone of Renato's voice and the warmth behind his chestnut brown eyes.

Flashes of light pulsed behind her lids, and her stone hummed excitedly against her skin. Then, silence. Zanya drew in another breath. The scent of tobacco from Renato's pipe tickled her nose and pulled her closer to his subconscious.

It was like making a phone call, and the person's voicemail picks up. But instead of talking to a machine, her thoughts filters through the recipient's mind, leaving them with a clear message.

Come to Mexico. Bring everyone. Hurry.

"How's it going?"

Arwan's voice broke her concentration. Zanya opened her eyes while Arwan crossed the room and sat beside her. "Did you get through?"

She nodded, and then swallowed the lump in her throat.

He took her hand. "It's going to be okay."

"I hope so." The idea of war was unsettling, but when it was between realms, it could mean the end of existence as they knew it.

Balam's ear flinched, and he lifted his head. The big cat pushed to all fours and walked across the living room until he was inches from the glass. A low growl simmered in his chest.

Zanya stood with a knot in her gut and walked to the window, squinting at the bright sun. "What..." She fixed her palm against the cool glass, watching what appeared to be a mass exodus of Mayan villagers, who were following a trail along the river. "Where did they all come from?" She stood so close to the window, her breath left a patch of fog, which vanished as quickly as it had appeared.

The villagers there wore similar clothing to those near Renato's home, which wasn't more than a simple loincloth and strings of hand carved beads. Women walked topless with baskets balanced on their heads. Babies were swaddled and strapped to their mothers' backs in a cloth sling that hugged the mothers' bodies. Though most of the men seemed older, they all still had long, black hair, which was tied in a braid, bun, or ponytail. They held an assortment of weapons, and flanked the traveling group on all sides.

Arwan walked to her side. "They came from their homes, in the jungle."

"I didn't see any of them when we were hiking here."

"You're surprised?"

"Well…" She pursed her lips. "I guess not. The villages pretty much blend into their surroundings, don't they?"

"And that's how they prefer it."

She frowned. "Until now."

Balam padded back to the spot he'd been napping, pawed at the floor, circled the area a few times, and then plopped on his belly, resting his massive head on equally massive paws. His bold, yellow eyes slid closed, and he settled back to sleep.

Zanya glanced at Arwan. "Well, Balam doesn't seem very concerned."

"Maybe he knows what's going on."

"Too bad he's not in his human form. He might actually be able to tell us something."

Arwan placed his hand on the small of her back, spreading warmth over her skin. "Just take care of your side of things, and Cualli will do the rest."

Zanya cocked her head, examining Arwan's relaxed features. "You have a lot of confidence in her."

"We have no reason not to."

"Yeah." Zanya gave a soft smile. "You're right."

Arwan leaned in close and whispered in her ear. "That's the first time you've said that since we bonded." He pulled her closer and placed a kiss on her neck. "Or maybe ever."

His hot breath prickled her skin. "It may be the *only* time, so enjoy it while it lasts."

"I intend to." He hooked his arms behind her legs and back, and scooped her up, cradling her against his chest.

She sucked in a breath and hooked her arm around his neck. "What are you—?"

He cut her off with a kiss.

Her muscles tensed, and she pulled back. "Whoa." She glanced at Balam. "What about…"

"What?"

Her cheeks flushed with heat. "You know." She gestured toward the jaguar with a nod. "Him," she whispered.

He chuckled. "I think he knows exactly what humans do when they're bonded and in love."

Her stomach fluttered. They were bonded, yes. But he'd never said the other thing aloud before. Neither of them had.

"Still, it's kind of…" Her throat tightened. "Awkward."

Arwan set her down. "Okay." He hooked his finger under her chin and teased his lips against hers, testing her willpower. "Tell me when you feel comfortable again. I'll be here." He kissed her again, harder this time. The tip of his tongue slid over hers, spiking her body temperature.

She coiled her fingers around his shirt, quick to notice the firm muscle under the soft cotton.

When he pulled away, Zanya bit her lip. "That's not fair."

"What?"

She arched a brow. "You know what."

He examined her with a crooked smirk. "You're beautiful."

She softened her tight lips. "I…" She squared her jaw. "Hey. You did it again."

"I don't know what you're talking about, *mi amor*."

She glanced at Balam a second time. "Jaguars are nocturnal, right?"

He grinned and then shook his head. "Sorry."

"Heavy sleepers?"

He arched a brow.

She blew out a puff of air and crinkled her nose. "It's probably not a good time."

"Whatever you say." He winked and placed a kiss on her forehead. "I'm going to shower. Let me know if anything else happens."

***

Arwan

He stood in their bedroom, leaning on the dresser that faced the wall. He had to get himself under control.

Since their first night together, Arwan had craved her touch. He craved her like thirst wrapped around his throat, every cell of his body on fire for some relief.

He never thought someone would love him—let alone be his soul mate. Now every moment he spent near her, all he could think of was the scent of her hair, the curves of her hips, and the power she harbored. She was a walking, talking, complex powerhouse of strengths, and she had complete control over him.

Her footsteps in the hall grew closer until she lingered in the doorway. There was no need to turn around to know she was there. He could hear her heartbeat, and smell the faint scent of her skin, teasing his need to be with her.

"Arwan."

He stripped off his shirt and tossed it in the laundry basket in the corner. "Yeah." He turned to face her and leaned back on the dresser, determined to appear like he wasn't going stir crazy like a caged animal. She was fragile, and he would force himself to respect her wishes, no matter how difficult it was.

She stepped inside, twisting her fingers. "You're mad."

"No." He ran his fingers through his hair. "I'm just…"

She watched him with a steady gaze. Her breath paused as she waited for his next word.

"Tired."

"I know the feeling." She ran her hand over her muscles, massaging a sore spot. "This whole thing has me pretty freaked out." She dropped her hands to her side. "I'm trying to be brave, but I have no idea what we're in for. A war between realms?

What will that even look like?"

This, he couldn't lie about. Not even if it would put her at ease. "It's going to be long, ugly, and terrifying."

Her gaze snapped up and her lips parted.

"But we'll make it through. I have to believe that."

She hugged herself and shifted her weight. "I didn't ask for this."

"You can't fall apart now."

"I know. I'm sorry. Just, those people leaving like that. They know something's coming, don't they?"

He walked to her and pulled her against his chest. "I don't know."

They could have sensed something, or Cualli could have warned them to leave before things got bad. Either way, they were more alone than ever.

She put her arms around him and pressed her cheek against his chest. Her fingers spread over his bare back. "You're all I have to keep me sane," she whispered.

He gently propped his chin on the top of her head. "You're all I *have*."

Zanya looked up at him, searching his face with those shimmering gray eyes. "That's how it's supposed to be, right?" She slid her hands over his back, across his ribs, and up his stomach. "Me for you, and you for me."

He shifted, his skin on fire where she touched.

She waved her hand, ordering a gust of wind to swing the door shut. Strands of her hair carried in the breeze

"Careful." He tightened his grip around her waist. "You may wake Balam."

She pushed onto her tiptoes and hovered her lips over his. "I don't care."

CHAPTER FOURTEEN

Arwan

Another day had gone by without a word from Cualli or the others. The atmosphere in the house had been tense, and Balam's nonchalant feline attitude had somehow heightened Zanya's anxiety. Arwan sensed it in her body language. Every time she tried to smile, her bottom lip quivered. She didn't seem to notice it. He did.

The moon was high in the sky, shining through the windows into their bedroom, washing everything in silky light. Arwan kicked at the sheets. The fan overhead spun in a blurred circle, doing little to cool him.

He pushed to his forearms and gazed down at Zanya, who was asleep beside him. He scanned the curves of her figure below the sheer white cloth. She was flawless—everything he ever wanted.

He lifted strands of her hair to his nose, inhaling her scent. He still hadn't wrapped his mind around the fact he'd enjoy the warmth of her body lying beside him forever.

She drew in a deep, sleepy breath. Her eyelids fluttered, though she didn't wake.

He placed a kiss on her bare shoulder and lowered his head back onto his pillow. Perhaps all the years he'd spent fighting for what he believed in had finally paid off. He was bonded with the love of his life, and his mother hadn't abandoned him without reason. The pieces were finally coming together, and the picture they painted was a bright future—if they could survive what was to come.

Zanya let out a tiny moan and rolled onto her stomach. Strands of wavy brown hair spilled over her face.

He drifted his hand down the soft ridges of her spine. When he lifted his hand, something wet slicked his fingertips.

A salty, metallic smell filled his nostrils, making his throat tighten.

He sat up and peered at his hand, covered in blood. "Zanya!" He yanked the sheet away from her body, uncovering roots clenched onto her legs.

"Zanya!" He grabbed hold of the invading tree and yanked on the roots with all of his strength. His muscles bulged and knuckles flushed white, though his efforts did little to separate Yaxche from her body. "Zanya, wake up!"

The roots coiled tighter and slithered up her torso as she slept. "No!" He snapped several thinner vines, but the others were too strong, and too hungry.

"Damn it, Zanya! Wake—"

Her eyes shot open, and a shrill scream tore out

of her chest. She pushed the top half of her body off the bed and stared at her legs in horror. "Get them off!"

"You have to use your abilities. I'm not strong enough!" He ground his teeth while yanking on one thick vine, snapping it in half. It went limp and fell to the floor, only for another one to take its place.

"Use your abilities!"

She screamed again, sharper this time. "It's inside me!" Zanya clawed at a root boring into her leg. "Get it off! Get it off!" Blood seeped from the gash, staining the sheet scarlet.

Arwan leapt off the bed, ran into the kitchen, and grabbed a knife from the drawer. When he skidded back into the room, Zanya and the entire bed were consumed by the tree.

Her screams were muffled inside.

"No!" He lunged forward and brought the blade down on the roots. Arwan froze when blood seeped out of the injured tree, onto the floor. The possibility of it being Zanya's blood was too real. If he cut into the vines, the knife could find her just as easily.

Zanya's screams suddenly stopped.

The roots stilled.

A blanket of silence covered the room.

Arwan's hands trembled, and the knife fell from his grip, clattering to the stone floor. He laid his hands over the tangled cage of vines, wedging his fingertips into any cracks or crevices he could find. "Zanya." He choked on her name.

Poor boy, a voice hissed, so quietly he questioned his own sanity.

105

He scanned the empty space, finding nothing but shadows, moonlight, and the lingering scent of Zanya's presence.

The darkness inside him flared, twisting his gut.

You cannot save her.

He turned his head, staring at the roots.

A light shone from inside the gnarled ball of slithering roots, making them glow red. Tiny blue veins stood out against the light as they pulsed with newly harvested blood.

Arwan leaned closer, peering through the now-translucent walls.

You cannot save her.

A root lifted from the mass, and Arwan stumbled back. The mass pushed up and coiled around one another, forming five fingers, then a hand and a forearm.

You cannot escape. The familiar voice was louder this time.

The roots lifted, gathered, and molded into a head, neck, and torso—like a creature spawning from its origin.

But it wasn't a creature.

Arwan snarled at Contessa's features as she grew from the tree.

The witch reached out, agitating the darkness inside him. It clawed and battered the walls of his chest, forcing him to his knees.

You cannot save her.

He clenched his teeth and fisted his hands against the stone ground. "I can." The words quivered in a breathless effort to speak through the sickening influence of his other half. His darkness coiled around his lungs like a vise, fogging his vision and winding his muscles tight until he struggled to breathe. "I can." He forced himself to his feet, trembling under the effort. "And I will."

Against his body's will, he stepped forward. "I know who I am." He squared his stance. "I know, and I'm coming for you." He glared. "Not even my father can save you now."

A flash of light exploded in the space.

Arwan gasped and shot up in bed.

Zanya sat up and placed her hand on his back.

He looked at her, touched her hand, and then her face. "You're here." He kissed her on the forehead, his lips lingering against her skin. "Thank the gods."

"What's going on?" She pulled away. "You're covered in sweat. Were you having a nightmare?"

He pushed his hair back and nodded. "Yeah. A very real nightmare."

"Well, if anyone can relate, it's me. Just...breathe."

He drew in a deep breath and threw off the sheets, the memory of her screams replaying in his mind. He stood and glanced out the window, movement catching his eye. He stepped forward and peered down at a sea of crawling roots spread over the jungle floor.

His stomach dropped.

Zanya shifted under the sheets. "What is it? More locals?"

He shook his head. "It's nothing." He swallowed, then lowered his gaze. "Go back to sleep. Everything's fine."

She lay back down and draped her arm on his side of the bed. "Come back to bed."

"I will. As soon as I splash some water on my face."

He walked into the bathroom and shut the door, pressing his back to it as he drew in shallow breaths. The tree was rising, and Contessa had become stronger.

He looked into the mirror at his own reflection. The witch had awoken something inside him in the dream—or vision, he couldn't be sure anymore—and if it could happen then, it could likely happen again. Next time, he may not be able to contain it.

His reflection in the mirror shuddered. Arwan blinked and leaned in closer, examining tiny shadows that danced behind his irises. His darkness was eager to escape. It was one tragic downfall to being half evil. The spirit of the damned fed off of other damned souls.

A wicked laugh carried through the air like a faint breeze.

It could have been his imagination playing tricks on him. Or maybe Contessa's power had bled into his mind. He glared at his own reflection. Either way, that part of him would never die.

When he returned to bed, Zanya had already fallen asleep. He lay awake beside her for the rest of the night, questioning himself over and over again.

Telling Zanya about the dream would only worry her, but telling her about the vines around their home would make her slip into panic. If the vines were still outside in the morning, he wouldn't be able to shelter her any longer.

After several hours had passed, crisp hues of yellow and orange pierced the darkness, shedding light into their room.

Three solid slams rattled the front door.

He sat up in bed.

Zanya yawned and stretched her arms above her head. "You okay?"

Arwan threw off the sheets and planted his bare feet on the stone floor. He stood and crossed the room, cracked open the bedroom door, and then stole a peek into the empty hall. He turned to Zanya and pressed his index finger over his lips, then slipped into the hall, silently creeping into the living room, where he glanced at the place Balam usually slept.

Arwan took a quick sweep of the space. He and Zanya were alone. Arwan tightened his jaw. The jaguar had left them by themselves, and he'd been too preoccupied to notice anyone who had approached.

He reached behind him and silently pulled open a drawer in the kitchen, taking a large chef's knife. The blade gleamed as the sunlight shined through the living room windows and cast over him.

Another set of knocks pounded on the door.

Arwan pressed his back against the wall and grabbed the handle.

If it were Contessa or one of her minions, he'd be lucky to slow them down before he was in real trouble. At least it would give Zanya enough time to escape. Neither of them could face Contessa alone.

He raised the blade and reached out to the brass handle. His breath quickened, and he gripped the metal knob.

A third round of pounding rattled the hinges.

Arwan flung open the door and leapt into the doorway, his knife poised to kill.

A heavy stick bounced off Arwan's forehead, rattling his teeth. "Foolish boy!"

Arwan staggered back and lowered the knife while pressing his palm to the lump forming on his head.

The old woman smacked him in the stomach with the homemade bludgeon and scowled. "Put t'at down before you hurt your own self, boy."

Zanya ran into the room, the light in her chest glowing brightly. She skidded to a stop. "Drina!"

The old woman's puckered features suddenly softened, and she displayed a full smile. "Zanya."

"What are you doing here?" Zanya ran to the Mayan soothsayer and hugged her tightly. Even Zanya, who was a solid four inches shorter than he was, was taller than Drina. Despite the woman's small stature, she was a force to be reckoned with, and her presence here could only mean one thing.

The others weren't far behind.

CHAPTER FIFTEEN

Zanya

"You have no idea how happy I am to see you." Zanya squeezed her one last time before stepping back.

"Me too, child." She patted Zanya on the cheek before her gaze shifted to Arwan.

Zanya glanced back at him. Arwan's mouth was still gaped open at Drina's surprise arrival—and surprise attack.

Zanya sucked in a hiss through her teeth. "Ouch. What happened to your forehead? I can heal it." She reached out to touch it.

He flinched away. "It's nothing."

Drina scowled. "You earned it." Her tone had turned harsh and her smile had vanished, replaced with deep creases in her forehead and a slanted brow. "Is not safe. You open a door armed wit' a hand knife t'at will not skin a tapir."

"Actually…" Zanya bit her lip. "Never mind." She examined the swollen knot on his head. "You know I can fix that if you let me."

"You shouldn't waste your strength on unnecessary healing. It's not a serious wound." He rubbed it again, peering at Drina. "I'll be fine."

"Oh." Zanya paused. "I didn't think about that."

"You need to." Drina grabbed her arm, and for the first time, her scolding was directed at someone other than Arwan. The woman let go and waved her wrinkled finger in the air. "You need to t'ink before you do, or you will get everyone killed. Is your job to lead. Be strong." Drina gave a single nod, as if declaring her statement to be law.

Zanya nodded along. "You're totally right. My mistake."

"No more mistakes." The woman stepped over the threshold, studying their home. Her tight lips parted. "Ohhh." Drina hobbled farther into the living room, skimming her fingers along the walls as she walked. "Is very nice." She clapped her hands together and turned toward Zanya with a broad smile. "Very nice indeed."

Zanya chuckled. "I'm glad you approve."

"T'is home needs to be blessed."

"Um…" She glanced at Arwan, who shrugged. "Okay. Sure. What did you have in mind?"

Drina's brows furrowed. "Blood, of course."

Zanya's slouched. "Of course."

"Where are the others?" Arwan asked, taking Drina's focus off the weird Mayan blood blessing thingy—thank goodness. She'd kiss him for that later.

"T'ey will be here soon."

"You didn't come together?" Zanya asked.

"T'ey flew on t'e arrow-plane." She drifted her flattened hand through the air, then dropped it to her side. "Man is not meant to fly. I came on bus, t'en kayak, and t'en Balam lead t'e way while servants carried me on *litera* t'rough much of t'e jungle."

"Servants?" Zanya looked at Arwan. "Wait, what's a *litera*?"

"One of those open chairs attached to wooden handles that servants carry someone on. Like for royalty."

"Oh, yeah." Zanya nodded at Drina. "That's totally less weird."

Arwan softly nudged her in the arm. "She is an ancient Mayan healer." he whispered. "Even higher than royalty with our people."

Zanya cleared her throat. "Right." Still weird. "Well, I'm just glad you made it okay."

A low chuff grabbed everyone's attention. Balam dragged himself through the door, his fur slick and his ears pinned back. The jaguar paused at everyone staring, bared his teeth with a quick snarl, and stretched out on the floor in the sun, licking his paw clean of mud.

"Where's Cualli?" Arwan asked.

Drina frowned. "She will be here soon."

Zanya stole a glance at Arwan, who looked equally worried over the vague response. "Okay. Well, you'll stay with us, in the spare room."

Drina shook her head. "I will camp outside, under t'e stars wit' t'e others."

"The hell you will." She snatched Drina's bag from the floor. "This is my house, my rules. You're staying with us in a comfortable bed."

113

Drina raised both of her bushy brows. "You *have* grown up."

"Yeah." Zanya smirked. "It happens to the best of us."

She led Drina into the second bedroom—what used to be Arwan's room as a boy. Since they moved in, she dragged the bed against the far wall, but left the wooden mask hung on the hook where it was. Anything to chase away evil was welcome to stay.

She set Drina's bag at the foot of the bed and shrugged. "This is it. I hope you'll be comfortable. Help yourself to anything in the kitchen, though there's not much. Balam's been hunting for us, and Arwan and I have been harvesting fruit from the local trees. I guess his mom had quite a garden going before she left. Cualli is taking care of the fruit and veggie-bearing greenery so we have food year round. Also, there's just one bathroom, but it has two doors. One in our room and the other in the hall."

Drina walked to the wall where the wooden mask was displayed, admiring it in silence.

"Beautiful, isn't it?" Zanya shadowed her. "Arwan's mom hung it there. This used to be his room."

"Yes." Drina touched the mask, as if recalling a memory. "Yes, it was."

***

The night had crept up on them quicker than she anticipated. Though they hadn't heard anything from Contessa, Arwan hadn't been himself since the night before.

He sat on the foot of the bed with no shirt and a pair of shorts. His hair had gotten longer. The longest layer framed his square jawline while loose strands fell around his face.

Zanya fluffed her pillow and sank into the down feathers. "You okay?"

Arwan glanced at her. "Just thinking."

"About..." He hadn't really elaborated on how he felt about this whole situation. Usually, she would be comforted with them having similar viewpoints. But this time, now more than ever, she needed him to be strong.

She leaned over, spotting the red, swollen lump on his forehead. "Would you *please* let me heal that for you?"

He grazed his fingers over the bump. "It doesn't hurt anymore."

"Liar."

He exhaled and lay down beside her, folding his hands behind his head. "If it makes you feel better."

"Finally." She pressed her hand over the lump, channeling heat and healing energy to her fingers. "There." When she pulled her hand away, the mark was still glaring at her. She brushed her fingers together. "Hang on. Let me try that again." It had been some time since she used her healing ability. "You know what they say—if you don't use it, you'll lose it."

"Who says that?"

She snorted. "Forget it. It's stupid." She positioned her hand over the mark again, concentrating harder this time. When she pulled her hand back, a smooth patch of flawless skin replaced the large bump. "See." She thwacked his earlobe and lay back down. "Told you." She flashed a smile. "Goodnight."

Once the room fell silent, another noise crept in—the rhythmic sound of what could have been a motor. "Is that..." She perked up and stared at the door. "Is that Drina, *snoring*?"

"Don't blame me. You invited her to sleep in the other room."

She groaned and wrapped her pillow around her head, muffling her ears. "Is she going to do this all night?"

"Unless Balam eats her."

Zanya giggled and snorted.

He wound his arm around her waist, pulled her close, and whispered in her ear. "*Te amo, querida.*"

She didn't have to understand a lot of Spanish to understand that. She bit her lip through a smile. "Me too."

It felt wrong to spoil the moment, but she couldn't help but wonder if he said it for the first time aloud now, before it was too late.

CHAPTER SIXTEEN

Zanya

The following night, Zanya sat across from Arwan in the living room, both of them watching Drina stare silently out the windows. Gusts of wind battered the trees, cutting through sheets of rain that drenched the jungle floor. Thankfully, rain meant the windows were finally washed clean of the aged blood smudged over the glass from the flock of suicidal birds.

It was one less reminder of the war to come.

Zanya tapped her fingers over her knee, bouncing her foot. "Do you think something happened to them?" She stood and walked to Drina's side. "They should have been here by now."

Balam yawned, displaying his canines, and stretched his front legs out in front of him, flashing a set of needle-sharp claws.

Zanya lightly rolled her eyes. "I'm glad someone's not worried."

"T'ey will be here soon," Drina said in a soft

tone, as if speaking to herself. "T'ey will come."

"I'm going to seek Marzena, just to be sure everything's okay."

Arwan shifted in his seat. "You really shouldn't—"

"I don't care." She glanced back at him. "Seeking doesn't take a lot of energy, and maybe Marzena can give us an update on their ETA. It's dangerous out there. Now more than ever." She closed her eyes and sought the seemingly young dreamwalker, focusing on Marzena's golden hair, fair skin, and fawn freckles dotted over her nose and cheeks. When they connected, a rush of cool energy flooded her veins. It took only a moment to get what she needed.

When she opened her eyes, Zanya peered out the window into the distance. She pressed her hand against the cold window, leaving an outline of fog where her skin touched.

Arwan stood. "Did you get through?"

Balam sat up, his ears rotating to the front. He chuffed and pushed to all fours, then padded to Zanya's side.

"Yes." A flicker of light pierced the darkness, showing like a tiny beacon of hope in the eternal darkness. "They're here."

Arwan walked to the back of the house, coming out moments later with bundles of gray wool blankets.

Zanya examined the linens. "What are you doing?"

"It's pouring rain. They'll be drenched and exhausted."

Zanya scanned the space in their home. "We don't have enough room for all of them inside."

"They'll set up camp on the stone platform outside. At least it's sheltered from the rain, and the tree's roots can't reach them there."

"Says who? Roots can crawl."

"Like I said." Drina clenched the leather pouch hung around her neck. "T'is house needs to be blessed."

Zanya noticed something gleam between the cracks of Drina's fingers. The woman removed a blunt dagger from the pouch and gripped the blade, sliding the sharp edge over her palm. When she was done, her palm flooded with blood that leaked out of her fisted hand, and down her wrist. "T'is house must be blessed."

Zanya rested her hand over her chest. She'd seen a lot of blood in her life—more than anyone should have. But to see Drina bleed took her breath away. "Are you sure—"

"Leave her." Arwan touched the back of her arm, as if reassuring her of Drina's knowledge. "Her blood carries magic."

"And it will keep t'e tree from crossing a protective circle." Drina turned and hobbled toward the exit. "We must hurry."

When she walked out the front door, Zanya turned to Arwan. "What do we do now?"

"Whatever you want. This is your home." He followed Drina's path out the door. Zanya was on his heels, down the small set of stairs, and onto the covered stone platform.

While Drina finished streaking smears of blood

over the stone floor, Zanya walked to the edge of the now-protected platform, the tips of her shoes hanging over.

Though the roots of the Yaxche had retreated back into the earth, the soil was churned and sucked dry of any life. It was clear Contessa was building its strength, helping it grow with any kind of nourishment—animal, plant, human, or minerals.

The humid night air caressed her cheeks, sending a shiver up the back of her neck. She pushed out her chest and peered through the foggy darkness into the tress, where a tiny orb of light flickered in the distance.

Zanya balled her fists and called on the light in her chest to illuminate, like a beacon for the others.

The distant orb grew in size, and a yellow haze cast light over the features of the group as they hiked forward in a single file line.

Zanya counted them in her mind as the group grew closer.

Cualli was the first to come into sight.

The group must have been protected by the middleworld goddess through their journey. Cualli's confident, smooth stride gave Zanya a bit of encouragement.

Her uncle, Renato, followed close behind, holding some kind of lantern. It illuminated the immediate space around them, giving just enough light for Marzena to follow without missing a step.

The normally child-like dreamwalker seemed older now, with her hair pulled back in a woven braid. When the light from Renato's lantern caught her eye, her sparking green irises seemed to glow in the night.

Then came the Arab windthrower twins, Ahmed and Yousef, both wearing their trademark hats propped on the crowns of their heads. Rather than the traditional white garb, the brothers hiked in pants, boots, and zip-up fleece sweaters—identical except for the color. Judging by their wide eyes and quick glances at every noise, they had never seen the jungle before, and weren't particularly excited to be there.

Hawa and Jayden were next in line. Hawa looked the same with her hair pulled back in a tight bun, making her eyes look almost feline.

A wave of relief washed through Zanya to see Jay again. She'd searched for him before fleeing the solstice celebration. When he was nowhere to be found, she and Arwan were forced to leave without saying goodbye. To know he was safe and well was enough to lift the thick weight of regret that had haunted her since that night.

Tears stung Zanya's eyes when her sights skipped to her best friend, Tara, walking beside Peter—the group's healer and Tara's boyfriend. Zanya shifted forward, but Arwan took her hand as if telling her to be patient and not step out of the protection of Drina's barrier.

Eadith, the French fire conjurer, was next in line. The burning red flames in her irises shone above her blonde hair and light complexion. Standing taller than most of the others, Eadith rolled a small flame in her palm, tossing it playfully from one hand to the other, making her own light on the hike.

Then, no one.

Zanya examined each face, accounting for them on her fingers. "There's three missing." She swallowed. "Beigarth, Grima, and...my mom."

Zanya glanced to either side of her, hoping for some kind of explanation.

Drina's gaze intensified. She waited without a word.

The pit in Zanya's stomach deepened. What if something had happened to them? She'd blocked Marzena from communicating with her up until recently. Sure, she needed space, but if something terrible happened to her mother, it could have been the single most selfish move of her life.

Balam butted his head against Zanya's hip, pushing her against Arwan's side. The jaguar god peered forward with inquisitive eyes.

Zanya scanned the jungle, pausing on another distant, flickering light.

The two petrifiers, Beigarth and Grima, stumbled into view, their huge frames and short legs so different from the others. Fur pelts were draped over Beigarth's massive chest, his red beard now braided into three thick strands.

Grima was Beigarth's cousin, and their kinship was more than a little obvious at a glance. Her strawberry red hair was woven into a single braid, displaying her round face, broad shoulders, and round waist leading to narrow hips, lean legs, and fur boots.

Zanya exhaled a nervous chuckle as the weight on her chest lifted. "Looks like Beigarth and Grima aren't huge fans of long-distance walks."

"In the jungle," Arwan added. "While it's

raining."

"T'ere is more to be afraid of t'an t'e rain," Drina said as she wrapped her hand with a shred of cloth.

"I can heal it if it hurts."

"No, child. Not necessary." She squeezed the cloth and then unraveled it, showing her palm without so much as a scratch.

She should have guessed. If Drina's blood was laced with magic, she was probably a quicker healer than any guardian—even with the stone's help.

As the petrifiers grew closer, the final person of their group emerged from the darkness.

Eleuia, Zanya's mother.

Dressed in all black, she would be invisible if it weren't for the lantern she too carried to light the way.

Zanya shifted, finding Arwan's steady hold to comfort her.

Balam was the first to brave the jungle floor. He leapt onto the soil and greeted Cualli with a thick, deep purr.

The group looked like a mob of drowned rats as they gathered in the safety of the protected stone platform, sheltered from the rain. Renato walked straight toward Zanya, only to be cut off by Tara, who threw her arms around her and hugged Zanya until she couldn't breathe.

Zanya held her friend for a long moment before Renato approached with a broad smile. "I cannot tell you what a relief it is to see you again."

Zanya coiled her arms around his lean frame and buried her face in his chest, inhaling the lingering earthy scent from his pipe. "I'm *so* glad to see you."

Peter dropped his pack to the stone floor and shivered. He acknowledged her with a head-bob. "Cool place."

Zanya took Arwan's hand again. "Thanks. It was his mom's."

"Now it's ours," Arwan said, standing tall, focused on her mother.

The Arab twins huddled together, chattering in Arabic, while Hawa pulled supplies out of her pack.

Jayden slicked back his hair as he approached, reminding Zanya of his shining moment in Victorian England when he attended the royal ball as *James Bond.*

"Never took you for the domesticated type." Jayden chuckled and looked at Arwan. "I guess even some women can be won over by the right guy." Jay extended his hand. "Congratulations, man. I never got to tell you both how happy I am for you."

Arwan examined Jay's gesture for a moment, then shook his hand.

Jay pulled him forward, holding his hand in a vise. "And since I'm dead and all, I'm not afraid to threaten your life if you hurt her."

Arwan yanked him closer and leaned in, staring him in the eyes. "One underworlder to another, huh?"

Jayden moved back, snatching his hand out of Arwan's. "That's not funny, man."

Arwan chuckled. "Just stating a fact."

Zanya tapped Arwan on his back, tearing him out of whatever weird bonding moment they were having. It was cute, but they'd have to pick it up later—when they weren't all so close to dying.

She examined the petrifiers, Grima and Beigarth, lingering on the soil. "You guys should come under the shelter."

"We aren't afraid of a wee bit of rain, lass." Beigarth pounded his chest with a fist. "We have mastered storms worse than this wee rain."

"It's not the rain I'm worried about." Zanya extended her hand. "It's not safe." Her tone had turned stern.

"Leave them," Zanya's mother said without looking at her. "They don't need a babysitter."

Zanya examined her mother's cold gaze cast to the floor. "Maybe not, but I'm telling them it's not safe, and you're just going to have to trust—"

"Blast you to hell!" Beigarth snatched a dagger from his side and sliced a root coiled around his leg.

"Get off the soil!" Zanya charged forward over unsafe ground, the light burning bright in her chest. Shouts from the group echoed through the air as she sped to Beigarth's side.

CHAPTER SEVENTEEN

Arwan

Arwan reached for Zanya, but she had already bolted out of his reach before he could hold her back.

More roots shot out from the soil, clenching onto Beigarth's calves, and anchoring the massive Viking to the ground.

Zanya conjured a bolt of electricity and launched it at a root coiled around Grima. The shock carried through the vine, attacking Grima in the same blast.

Grima's eyes widened, fingers coiled into fists, and limbs stiffened. When the shock ran its course, her muscles went limp, and she nearly collapsed onto the ground.

"Are ye trying to kill her?" Beigarth screamed. He scowled and slashed at another root.

Arwan examined the ground, now writhing with roots, just like earlier. It was as if they had appeared at exactly the right time and then...

"It was an ambush!" He turned to Renato. "I

should have known. Contessa waited for us all to be in the same place before striking. This is my fault." He glanced at the dagger strapped to Renato's side. "Stay here and guard the others." He snatched the blade from its sheath and sprinted toward Zanya, ignoring Renato's calls to come back.

Weak from the shock, Grima fell to the ground and struggled to chop at a vicious vine with a small hand ax. Arwan skidded to her side and finished the job with a swipe of his dagger. The root flailed and fell limp, only to be consumed by other limbs of the tree that broke through the surface.

Grima managed to stand, ax clenched firmly in hand. "Well, what are ye waiting for, lad? Go help the others!" She snarled and brought the ax down beside Arwan's foot, severing another of the tree's lifelines. "Off with ye, then!"

Arwan spun and spotted Zanya, her light burning ferociously in her chest. More whipping vines crawled toward her and Beigarth. One of the thorny roots wrapped around her ankle and yanked, nearly pulling her to the ground.

Zanya screamed and grabbed hold of it, then let out another cry.

Beigarth stomped on a smaller vine, obliterating it.

Arwan ran and positioned the knife in his hand for a downward strike. When he reached Zanya, blood ran down her leg as the tree sank its spikes into her muscle.

"Hold still!" He plunged his knife into it, but this one was hardier than the others. It recoiled, as if cringing from the assault. Blood oozed from the sliced vessels—most likely the blood it had just taken from Zanya.

The metallic scent shot up his nose, making his stomach lurch.

The tree had wounded her and had fed, continuing to gain strength.

He bore down with another jab of his blade, but this time Yaxche was prepared. A second root broke out of the soil. It seized Arwan's wrist and clenched his bones, forcing him to drop the weapon.

A firebomb exploded beside him, spitting soil and rock in every direction. The night flashed with warm light, and a wave of heat broke against his skin. The vine released him and retreated into the earth, but not without dragging his only defense down with it.

Arwan turned to Eadith, who nearly burned him alive with her latest assault. The French fire conjurer readied another inferno from the safety of the stone platform.

He turned back to Zanya. She'd been released by the tree and managed to limp toward Grima, who suffered from wounds of her own.

Now was their chance. The tree was hurt. If they could get to safety before it struck again, they would live to fight another day.

The earth shook, prompting Arwan to crouch in a fighting stance.

"Earthquake!" someone shouted from the distance.

Arwan sprinted toward Zanya, waving her to the house. "Run! Go with the others!"

A fault line split the ground, tearing the jungle

floor in half, and separating him from the others. He dug his heels into the soil and threw himself back just as the crater opened into a black, endless hole.

Hundreds of roots spewed from the crevasse, crawling over the ground like a cluster of angry serpents emerging from their den.

When the ground trembled and the gap grew, Arwan was carried farther from the group.

He caught a glimpse of Balam scrambling up a massive tree, hissing and clawing at the reaching vines.

Zanya's eyes widened when she spotted him. She bolted to his side without hesitation—the absolute last thing he wanted her to do. Her ability to travel quickly—like Hawa—had its shining moments, and this was one of them.

"Stand back!" She squared her stance and looked to the sky, gathering the storm clouds already looming overhead. When she raised her hand, a current of bright white energy traveled over her arms to her fingers, and a bolt of lightning flashed in the sky, striking the source of the tree.

A second fireball shot through the air like a meteor and detonated on the same target.

When the smoke cleared, the roots flailed and whipped in every direction. They snapped through the air like flaming whips, striking anything in reach.

"Ye bas!" Beigarth grabbed hold of a flaming vine and let out a warrior cry.

The tree's limb froze in his grasp.

Beigarth's features contorted as he pushed through the agony of holding fire in his bare hands.

The vine stilled, and then changed to a dusky gray before petrifying right in front of his eyes, all the way to the ground.

Beigarth's eyes turned red and glossy as he strained to keep the flow of his ability running freely through his hands. The petrifying traveled over the ground and under Beigarth's feet until the entire space around him was frozen in time.

Every leaf. Every grain of soil. Every fallen branch.

Everything in the area—except Beigarth.

Another strike of lightning crashed into the hole in the earth, tearing Arwan's focus back to Zanya. She lowered her arms. The light in her chest extinguished and she slouched in exhaustion. She panted and wiped her forehead with her palm. "Is everyone okay?" She asked in short, quick breaths.

Arwan tensed his own muscles as a quick body check, coming up with no more than a few minor lesions and ringing in his ears front the blasts.

When he scanned Zanya for obvious wounds, his gaze stopped at her leg. "You're still bleeding." She swayed and leaned into him for support. "Why aren't you healing?"

She shook her head, sweat collected on her brow. "I must have exhausted my energy with the storm again."

Zanya's mother was the first to march through the clearing smoke. "Are you all right?" She crouched and checked Zanya's wound, then hooked her arm around Zanya's waist and held her against her hip. Eleuia looked at him with sharp, cold eyes. "Back away from her. *You've done enough.*" The edge in her tone cut into him.

Zanya seemed too dazed and disoriented to protest, so neither did he. Her mother would care for her while he, Renato, and the others figured out their next move. Maybe it would allow Zanya and her mother some time to repair their relationship before this battle became any worse.

And it would become worse.

There was no doubt about that.

Beigarth limped past him, holding a gash in his arm. "When did ye plan on telling us thar is a tree out to eat us?" The large Viking paused beside him. "Or did ye plan on letting us all get killed?"

Grima walked past them and smacked Beigarth on his back. "Let the lad be."

Beigarth snarled, and then followed Grima to the rest of the group on the stone platform.

Renato caught his attention with a wave of his hand, gesturing for him to return as well.

With a step forward, the ground trembled a second time. This time vines did not rise from the ground, but instead, a noxious stink indicative of only one realm.

The underworld.

Arwan crinkled his nose, holding his breath so as not to gag on the funk. The tree had opened a path from the dark realm, and it would be only a matter of time before more than just Yaxche would rise.

"We meet again," Contessa said from behind him.

Arwan turned, spotting the witch only yards away.

Red waves fell around her, framing bright green

eyes and glossed lips. She sauntered toward him, each confident stride swaying her hips like the temptress she was.

To his surprise, she appeared healthy and whole. The last time they met she was bruised, starved, and nearly dead, working to convince him to trade—his dark half for a page of the Popul Vuh with the history of his mother written on its pages.

"Has no one told you a woman will most certainly swoon over a valiant hero?"

He stole a glance at the group, huddled on the stone platform, watching intently. If it were any other time, the rest of the group would have been beside him already, prepared for battle. But with the group wounded, exhausted, and Zanya nearly unconscious, there was nothing they could do—and they knew it.

She circled him slowly, sizing him up for whatever plan she had mapped in her head. "You are even more tempting than the first time I made your acquaintance. It really is unfortunate your father has given up on you. You would have made a fine king one day." She smirked. "And unlike my current marital duties, I would have enjoyed my role as your queen, in your bed."

The closer Contessa moved, the harder Arwan was forced to work to keep his other half under control. It fed off of her darkness, instigated by the commonality they held.

Renato was the first to disregard his own safety. "Get away from him, Contessa. I warn you." He strode toward them over the battlefield.

Contessa curled her lip. "How insulting." She

flicked her wrist, cuing the tree to weave a wall of roots, isolating herself and Arwan from the rest of the group. "How naive to believe I would be so easily intimidated." She met Arwan's gaze. "Though *you* know the truth, don't you?" She stepped toward him, studying his lips. "You can fully appreciate who I am—what I am." Shadows morphed and flashed behind her fair features. "For we are both spawned from the same origins."

Arwan narrowed his eyes. "I'm nothing like you."

"Oh, my dear boy." She reached out and pressed her hand over his chest. Both corners of her mouth rose into a sinister grin. "We are exactly alike." She leaned in closer. "The only difference between us is you have yet to embrace your true nature." She slid her hand up his chest and wound her fingers around his throat. She tightened her grip just enough to keep him from stepping away. His muscles stiffened under the clash of light and darkness battling inside him. "Unlike the others, who wish to fulfill only their selfish desires and watch you conform to their ideal perception of who you are, *I* merely wish to set you free." The witch leaned in and dragged her tongue over his lips. He cringed and turned his face. "Give me your darker half, and you will have the life you want." She flattened her palm over his chest, hovering her lips over his. "Give me permission to tear out your demons that shackle you. Release the cross you bear, and I will bear it for you."

The beast inside of him rammed against his chest, breaking down his will, one blow at a time.

"If I don't?" he managed to croak through clenched teeth.

Her glittering eyes darkened and bubbled with violet and black. "Then I will tear it from you, along with your beating heart."

The beast clawed at his ribs and flailed desperately for release. Bile burned the back of his throat, and he pushed down the urge to vomit.

"You forget that you need my permission."

"You will give it."

He snarled. "I will not. And you can't take it from me if I'm dead."

Contessa slid her hand up to his face, where she pinched his cheeks between her fingers. "Then I will make you wish you were." She pushed her body against his and slid her other hand up his shirt, tracing his abs. "It will consume you, you know." Her voice drew him into a trance. "Only after you are exposed to those you love—who you truly are."

That was the last thing he remembered before the darkness tore through him, and he turned.

CHAPTER EIGHTEEN

Arwan

The change took place in seconds, though it seemed more like hours.

Hours of terror.

Hours of underworld venom coursing through his veins, and his jaw clenched shut as he spat foam and saliva with every frantic breath.

Hours of heartache, knowing once the change was complete, Zanya and the others would see him for what he truly was.

Arwan collapsed on the ground, his fists clenched and his body shaking without control. The sounds of his form contorting broke him while his body took shape—first his shoulders and hips, followed by his knees and elbows. Each dislocation may as well have been a sledgehammer to his joints.

A spike of boiling heat spewed up his back as each vertebra popped out of alignment. His body stretched and bent in unnatural ways, morphing him into something unworldly. Into the beast he could no longer cage.

He scratched and clawed at the ground as his fingers became claws and his palms swelled with padding. He gaped open his jaw and gagged at the raw agony of a mouthful of predatory canines punching through his gums.

The scent of every tree, animal, and human nearby was suddenly discernible, and absolutely overwhelming.

The sounds were worse. His ears rotated and twitched at every minute noise. The birds, Contessa's laughter as it vanished back into the underworld, and the group's cries from the other side of the tangled wall of roots Contessa had erected.

Combined with his own deep huffs, racing heartbeat, and involuntary whimpers, it was nearly deafening.

"Arwan!" Zanya's scream was the first he identified above the rest.

"Don't go near the tree," Renato shouted, but it was too late. Zanya's footsteps grew louder as she rushed toward him.

There was no way around the wall. It was ten feet tall and stretched as far as the eye could see in either direction. But she would find a way. He had no doubt about that.

He scratched at the ground a second time, his wolf-like pads pressing imprints into the damp soil. Every muscle screamed in protest as he found his footing and stumbled from side to side as if he were a new fawn taking its first steps.

His legs shook beneath him, his black coat

matted with soil, bits of leaves, and debris.

"Don't you touch him, Contessa!" Zanya's voice carried through the air. The wall of roots shook from what could have been a wrecking ball, quaking the ground. The roots contracted—as if cringing from the assault.

An explosion of fire hit the barrier, sending shards of bark and plumes of smoke into the air.

A section of the wall blackened and fell away, leaving a hole just feet off the ground.

He would have given anything to tell her to go back. Not to look at him. She'd seen him like this just twice before—the time he tore Sarian's head off in the underworld and watched his limp body collapse to the floor. Then in the jungle, when she nearly killed him. If it weren't for Drina saving him when he didn't want to be saved, Zanya would have ended him that day.

He shook the soil from his fur and leapt into the jungle, slinking through trees with cat-like agility. His tail whipped in the air, helping him keep balance as he vaulted over fallen trees and balanced on the edge of a cliff, blazing his own path until he could no longer be detected.

His ear twitched and he halted, his body frozen in place. The apes and birds screamed their alarm calls before scattering and flying to safety, leaving him in silence.

He growled instinctively as clumsy footsteps grew closer, snapping twigs and tearing through low-lying plants. A cool wind drifted through the trees, carrying the scent of Zanya's sweat.

The others' shouts echoed through the jungle.

They were calling for her—crying for her to return to the safety of their home.

Of course she didn't listen.

She splashed through a puddle, and then must have grabbed hold of a low branch, shaking its leaves.

Zanya was close. She'd tracked him this far, and surely knew by now she wasn't looking for a man.

He lowered his body and lay flat against the ground, using the undergrowth to camouflage his presence. But being solid black with a tuft of golden fur on his chest wasn't the best camouflage in a world of green. He'd have to hope his silence and stillness would be enough.

Her footsteps grew louder and slower as she fell into a cautious pace. "Arwan?" Her voice shook when she called his name. "Where are you?"

He pinned back his ears and wrapped his tail around his body, quieting his breaths. If he ran, she would see him for sure. Not just that, but she could outrun him with little effort.

If she would just move in another direction, it would give him time to figure out how to morph a second time—this time back to his true form. Though change had always happened without consent, he'd eventually have to learn how to control it. Now was as good a time as any.

Zanya paused, her breaths quick. "Did she hurt you?" She took another step forward. "I'm so sorry I didn't get there in time. I was just so…" She whimpered, and a low sob rolled out of her throat. "I was so tired. I don't know what's wrong with me, but I couldn't push past it, and I left you out there alone."

Arwan peered at her through the greenery. She inspected the ground, then crouched and pressed her fingers into one of his tracks. "My God." She stood and scanned the jungle. "Will you please come out?"

He settled closer to the ground.

She walked several more steps, and then stopped. "Arwan." There was a pause. "I know you're here somewhere. I tracked you." Her tone became stern, and she perched her hands on her hips. "Goes to prove I was paying attention all those times you dropped tracking tips on our hikes." She stood in silence, listening, watching, and waiting for him to show himself. Her eyes narrowed. "Seriously? You're going to hide like I haven't seen you like this before?" She crossed her arms. "Shows how much you trust me. I thought we were past this. I thought you understood how..." She swallowed. "How I feel about you." The last words passed through her lips in a soft plea.

Arwan lifted his head just enough to spy over the plants. Her back was now turned to him as she searched the jungle in every direction.

"I'm not going to let you hide from me." She ran both hands through her hair, pushing it harshly out of her face. "Not this time." She dropped her hands to her sides and balled her fists. "So help me, I will tear this jungle apart, tree by tree." The light in her chest flickered to life. "Even if it drains me of everything I have."

He growled. She knew harming herself would lure him out. And he knew she wasn't bluffing.

"We are *bonded*." The last word came out of her mouth with more bitterness than he was prepared for. "I deserve to know who you are. All of you. I deserve that much!" A storm collected overhead. Raindrops fell from the sky, smacking against leaves and already drenched soil. A drop fell onto her cheek. Then another on her eyelash. She blinked it away, her face flushed with color. She pivoted, still searching for him in the trees. "You don't think I'll want you anymore." She pursed her lips and hung her head. "You don't think I'll still love you."

A strike of lightning flashed through the air, splintering a tree in half beside her.

The air seemed to ripple with power.

From her expression, the power scared even her.

Her sacred light continued to grow in intensity, piercing the air through the cracks of her fingers as she clutched her chest.

A cloud loomed above her, carrying an electrical storm. Veins of energy darted inside, building and flashing until the energy was too powerful to keep contained.

Zanya closed her eyes as the lightning storm grew brighter.

Something was wrong. It seemed as though she was not controlling her abilities, and instead, they had a mind of their own.

Her stone was not protecting her.

There was no one who would, except him.

Arwan pushed to his feet and snarled. He leapt forward and shoved her out of the way, just as the electrical charge released and struck the ground where she stood.

They tumbled to the ground. He was careful not to lay his enormous weight on her, now dwarfed in comparison. He scrambled and shot to all fours, and saw her sprawled out on the ground, mud streaking her cheek.

The light in her chest burned brightly for a few moments before it dulled, and finally vanished. She coughed and gasped in a breath, clawing at her chest.

Arwan nudged her with his snout. She was frozen to the bone.

Whatever happened to her back there had done more than drained her of her abilities.

It had nearly killed her.

He lay beside her and rested his head lightly over her chest. She needed the warmth, and without the others here to lead her back to the shelter of their home, this was the only way.

He wanted more than anything to cringe away. Flee into the jungle. Hide, as his instincts were compelling at him to do. Everything inside of him screamed at him to run. Everything but his unwavering devotion to her. That, and only that, was enough to make him stay.

She buried her fingers into his thick, black fur. "There you are." Her voice was raspy and barely recognizable. "I knew you wouldn't leave me."

He closed his eyes and relished the warmth of her touch.

"Can you talk to me?"

He lifted his head and stared down at her, his shadow shielding her eyes from the sunlight as it broke through the dispersing storm.

It was a fair question—one he'd never considered. He somehow met her gaze, finding it strangely easy to hold it, even in this form.

But with a fair amount of effort, he couldn't communicate. What beast could?

"It's okay." She ran her hand down his snout. "I guess I couldn't really expect it."

Her breathing had evened out, and her skin was no longer like ice.

"Zanya! Arwan!"

He looked to the left and let out a low growl.

"It's okay." She forced herself to sit up, swaying as her eyes fluttered open and closed. "The others are here. You can go."

She was so pale. So weak.

"Zanya!" It was her mother. Of all people, she would be the least tolerant. "Where are you?" Her voice grew closer. Too close.

"Go." Zanya gave a weak attempt at shoving him away. "Before she sees you."

CHAPTER NINETEEN

Zanya

Zanya opened her eyes to wooden beams running the length of the vaulted ceiling in her bedroom.

She carefully turned her head, unsure of the effect any movement would have on her muscles. But she needed to see if Arwan was there.

She frowned and slid her hand over the sheets to where he usually lay—now empty and cold.

She forced herself to sit up in bed, her head assaulted with pounding waves against her temples.

A deep throb spread behind her eyes.

"Headache?"

She sucked in a breath and squinted to the far side of the room where Peter sat.

He leaned forward, analyzing her from a distance. Even under the circumstances, it was good to see him again. "You were pretty out of it."

"Yeah." She strained to speak through the pain and slouched against the headboard. "What happened?"

Peter shrugged. "I was hoping you'd be able to tell us. When we found you in the jungle, I couldn't detect anything wrong with you. No cuts or bruises or concussions. You were just…passed out."

She rubbed the back of her neck, recalling the last moments she spent with Arwan. After he left, she must have lost consciousness. It was the only explanation that made sense.

"Do you want to talk about it?" Peter stood and walked toward her, then lowered himself onto the foot of her bed. The mattress sighed under his weight.

"Talk about what?"

"Whatever's going on with you."

She drew her brows together. "I don't know what you're talking about."

He analyzed her a moment longer, then let out a long, quiet breath. "That's too bad. Your mom and Renato are worried."

She bit her lip. The others. They were still here—though not inside the house. It was too quiet. "Did they want to leave after the tree attacked? Beigarth was pretty angry we didn't tell them about the danger sooner."

"He was pissed, but never mentioned leaving. They're all still here, outside. They made camp on the stone floor so they could guard the house."

"Oh." She relaxed her muscles. "You guys could crash on the couch and set up some blankets on the floor. I don't mind."

He chuckled. "Hawa was the first to volunteer to sleep on the couch, but Renato said we should all stick together. We have to keep you safe. Besides, your mom said you deserved some privacy, now that you're bonded and all."

"My *mom* said that?" She snorted. "Talk about hypocritical."

"Yeah, maybe. But it's true." He gave her a shy glance and grinned. "You're all grown up now."

"Oh, shut up." Her smile vanished when her mind wandered to Arwan. "Except he's not here."

"That's the other thing." Peter sat in silence, twisting a pulled thread from the seam of his sleeve.

He was just as readable as Tara—both of them unable to lie or keep a secret without their true nature showing through. "*What's* another thing?"

He pressed his lips into a tight line. "Everyone wants to know what happened out there between him and Contessa. They're worried. They're...talking."

"About what?"

Peter's silence said all she needed to know.

"Arwan isn't dangerous."

"Maybe that's true. But maybe not. He was out there with Contessa—alone."

"So what?"

"So, maybe..." Peter shrugged. "I never thought I would say it, but maybe she's rubbing off on—"

"*What the hell*, Peter?" She gripped the blankets and leaned forward. "Did you come in here to help or just piss me off?"

He raised his hands as if declaring defeat. "Don't shoot the messenger."

"Messenger?" She threw the blanket off, revealing the same clothes she had worn earlier that day. "I don't need a messenger. I'm right here, and if anyone has something to say, they can say it to my face." She pushed out of bed, rushed through the house, and barged through the front door to the camp outside.

The sun was bright and crisp, only increasing the humidity in the air. Nearly a dozen tents were pitched on the stone platform. A small fire-pit was set up in the center with kindling and branches of dead wood stacked on either side—some probably from Yaxche.

"Hey, listen up." She clenched and unclenched her fists, waiting as several of her comrades crawled out of their tents with sleep-glazed eyes and tousled hair. "I want to make something really, *really* clear, and I'm only going to say this once." She scanned the faces of everyone who had come to help. Her friends. Her family. The people she trusted most— or was supposed to, at least. "This is my house. Arwan's house. *Our* house. If anyone has a problem with that...well," she shifted her weight, "you're free to leave."

Marzena frowned. "Zanya."

"No." She'd never spoken harshly to the young dreamwalker before, but now was a time she needed to listen, not speak. "We need to stick together. We need each other now more than ever. I can't do this alone. But Arwan is one of us, whatever his origins are, and whatever you may think about him. *None* of you know him the way I do. So if you have a problem with respecting our home or respecting him," she looked directly at her mother, "you need to just suck it up and get over it—or get the hell out."

Her mother watched her for a moment before dropping her gaze without recognition or the slightest hint of emotion.

"Fine with me," Tara said. She finished crawling out from her tent and stood, wiping her palms down the front of her jeans.

A low murmur of affirmations hummed through the space.

All except her mother, who dug through her bag without a sound. Zanya would take that as a yes. At least until her mother gave her a reason to think otherwise.

The red curls framing Tara's face bounced as she walked to Zanya's side. The others resumed unpacking and chatting with one another.

Tara crossed her arms and leaned against Zanya's hip. "Where is Arwan, anyway?" Her tone was low and cautions.

Zanya gave a sideways glance, matching Tara's volume. "I don't know."

"Is that like a," she winked way too obviously, "kind of I don't know? Or you seriously don't know?"

"I seriously don't know."

The edges of Tara's mouth turned down. Frowning didn't fit her. She was always smiling, joking, or daydreaming.

"Don't worry," Zanya continued. "He'll be back."

"Oh, I'm not worried about him *not* coming back. I'm just not sure what's going to happen when he does."

Zanya tried to pretend her friend's concern didn't

worry her just as much. "What do you mean?"

Tara stared at Zanya's mother, who hadn't said more than a few words since she'd arrived. "She's losing it. I can tell."

"Should I be concerned?"

Tara shrugged. "I don't know. You think she'd actually try anything?"

"Did you forget when she tried to *shoot* him in Renato's house?"

Tara made an O-shape with her lips. "Yep. Forgot about that. Probably because I was with Peter when it happened."

Zanya inspected the crowded camp. "Which tent is yours?"

Tara gestured to a small green one set up near the center. "They made me be in the middle because I'm 'human,'" she quoted with her fingers, "and if anything 'happens,' I should be most 'protected.'"

Zanya tried not to laugh at her friend's triple-air-quote and bitterness at their good intentions. "I think it's a good idea."

Tara rolled her eyes. "At least I have a thin mattress, and with the fire going, it won't be so bad."

"You can stay in the house on the couch. I'd give you the bedroom, but Drina is already sleeping in it. I don't want you to be lonely."

"I'm not lonely. Peter keeps me company."

Zanya paused. "You guys are in the same tent?"

"Yeah, but you'll be happy to know we kind of committed to the whole celibacy before marriage thing, so don't worry."

"Celibacy, huh?" She exhaled, allowing the

weight on her chest to vanish with it. "That's cool."

Tara's face flushed pink. "Don't tease."

"No, I'm serious. He loves the hell out of you, and he's willing to wait. That's pretty impressive."

Tara fluffed her hair. "Yeah, it must be near impossible to stay away from all *this*."

Zanya chuckled. "If you need anything, you know where to find me."

Without warning, Tara threw her arms around her and hugged so tight, Zanya could hardly draw in a breath.

"What's this for?" Zanya grunted, tapping Tara on the back in a plea to loosen her grip.

"I never got to congratulate you." Tara squeezed her one last time, then let go and stepped back. "You're my best friend, and for all intents and purposes, you got married. That's a pretty big deal."

"Yeah. I guess it is."

Tara glanced down at her hand. "No bling, huh?"

Zanya dragged her thumb over her ring finger. "We didn't exactly have time to go shopping."

"It's all a bust anyway."

Zanya paused. "Wait, what?"

"You know. A ring, the white satin wedding dress. Fresh flowers in centerpieces. Round tables with silk cloths, not to mention those stupid advice cards where people write tips for a happy marriage. People are so opinionated. The whole wedding thing is totally overrated."

"Yeah." Her chest tightened. "Totally overrated." She'd never thought about it, but not having a wedding was a little like being robbed of a beautiful dream.

"Oh. I almost forgot. I brought you something from home."

It was the first time Zanya had heard her refer to Renato's place as home. Tara dug in her pocket and pulled out a round pendant made of wood, strung on a leather chain. "I thought you might want it." Tara dangled the wicker amulet Cualli had made her—the same one she'd fished from a waterfall with Hawa, back in Belize.

Zanya touched it with her fingertips. "This brought me so much comfort." She let it go. "You wear it. Maybe it'll bring you some comfort too."

"But…" Tara admired the gift. "Are you sure?"

"You're my best friend. There's no one I'd rather wear it than you." Zanya took it and slid the leather strand over Tara's head, carefully resting the pendant on her chest. "May it keep you safe and happy."

Her stone grew cool against her wrist, prompting her to shift her attention to the tree line. Her eyes widened. "Oh. My. God." She rushed toward Arwan as he stumbled out of the jungle without a shred of clothing. His hair was wild, his steps clumsy and staggered. One hand was cupped over his groin while the other shielded his eyes from the white rays of sun. "Are you okay?" She stripped off her sweater and tied it around his waist, then did a quick check of his body—no nasty bruises or bleeding. He seemed disoriented, but all in all, all right.

"I…" Arwan stumbled and nearly fell to the ground.

She hooked his arm over her shoulder. "Come

on. Let's get you inside."

The others waited in the distance, most of them averting their eyes.

Marzena was silent and still, as she usually was, standing beside Renato with her fingers laced in front of her and her eyes trained on the stone floor. "Should I come inside with you?"

Zanya paused beside the dreamwalker. "We'll be fine."

Marzena placed her hand on Arwan's arm, watching him intently, as if she were scanning him for something.

"Marzena."

The dreamwalker broke her focus to look at her. "We must be sure he is still himself. Your safety, above all else, must be protected." She gave him one more pause, and then stepped away. "Bring him inside. He must rest."

As soon as Marzena gave the okay, Drina hobbled to the door and pulled it open. "You heard t'e woman. Bring t'e fool into t'e house. I will make him some herbs."

While Zanya escorted him through the group, it was impossible to ignore her mother's glares. They pierced through the air and into her chest, making Zanya's heart race.

It was clear. Her mother's presence was a problem. Zanya had hoped it wouldn't be, but wishful thinking never got her anywhere.

She'd deal with it later, after Arwan was well enough to speak, and after they figured out what their next move was.

If she could keep the peace long enough to get

there.

CHAPTER TWENTY

Zanya

"So are you going to tell me what happened?" Zanya sat on their bed beside him, careful not to spill the basin of water infused with herbs that Drina had made. The mixture smelled a little like tea tree and chamomile, meant to calm him after the ordeal.

Arwan closed his eyes as she dipped a rag into the liquid and pressed it over his forehead.

"The others are worried." There was no point in saying why. It would only hurt him.

"They should be. I couldn't control it. Contessa's darkness, it..." He looked away from her, seemingly searching for the right words. "It's like her darkness brought mine to life. Like they fed on each other, and it was too much for me to hold in." He tried to sit up, but it was obvious he was still too tender to do much more than lie still on the bed.

She didn't remember him being this drained after his first shift in the underworld, or his second shift in the jungle—except she almost killed him then. "How did you turn back?"

He lifted his gaze. "I couldn't at first. I wanted to, but the beast was too strong."

"For being...changed, you seemed to still be yourself on the inside. I mean, you didn't hurt me. You didn't seem to want to, either. It was more like you were protecting me."

"Always." He set his hand on hers. "No matter what."

"So..." She bit her lip. Probing could cause him to pull away, but there were certain things she had to know. "Can you remember everything from when you're...changed?" That seemed to be the gentlest way to word it. "Are all of your thoughts your own? Like, do you know who you are, and who I am?"

"Everything's the same, except I can hear every sound, smell scents from miles away, and see ten times better than when I'm in my human form."

"That's got to be overwhelming."

"It almost drove me insane." He slipped his fingers between hers. "But it was you. You were what brought me back. In the jungle alone, knowing I had something to return to. That's what brought me back to myself. The bond we have is stronger than the darkness, and I knew you were waiting for me."

She leaned forward and pressed a kiss on his forehead. "Always."

He winced as the mattress moved when she sat back. "That bad, huh?" She set the bowl of liquid on the floor. "This remedy Drina mixed up isn't going to heal you as fast as I can."

"You need to keep your strength. Especially after today."

"And *I* need *you* to be at your best if Contessa or the tree attack again, so stop whining and hold still." She pressed her hands over his bare chest and channeled healing heat into his body. His tense muscles eased and his chest sank with a deep exhale. She lifted her hands and smirked in a *that-wasn't-so-hard-after-you-stopped-being-an-ass* kind of way.

He touched her cheek. "Thank you."

A stern knock on their bedroom door commanded Zanya to stand. She narrowed her eyes. Anyone knocking that hard better have a damn good reason. "Who is it?"

"Your mother."

The room fell silent. Zanya glanced at Arwan, who waited for her to decide what to do without giving his own preferences. He didn't argue not to let her in, or even grimace at the sound of her voice. He had every right to do those things, but chose to be a better man.

Yet more proof he wasn't who her mother claimed him to be.

Zanya walked to the door and cracked it open just enough to look her in the eyes. She tried not to seem bitter or cold. There was already enough tension to go around.

"Everything okay in there?"

Zanya bit the inside of her cheek to keep from saying something she'd regret later. "Do you need something?"

"Renato and I are setting up a training ring for

you outside."

"Now? I'm kind of busy with—"

"You need to train. That much is obvious from how you performed today."

"How I *performed*?" The light in her chest glowed as a result of her annoyance.

Her mother's gaze flickered to the luminance, and she frowned. "It must be hard to keep your mark as the guardian hidden when it's in such an obvious place." This time her words came out smooth and genuine, easing the heat in Zanya's gut.

"It can be challenging." Her light dimmed until it was once again gone.

"So…" Her mother stole a peek over her head, into the room. "How is he?"

"Not trying to tear my throat out, if that's what you're asking."

She snapped her jaw shut. "What should I tell Renato? Are you coming or not?"

"Go." Arwan's voice was raspy, but bolder than before. Zanya turned to see him sitting up, obviously stronger now that she'd healed him. "She's right. You need to train. I'm fine."

Zanya turned back to her mother. "Tell Renato I'll be down in five minutes."

"Use your powers and tell him yourself. You need all the practice you can get. Oh." She reached for something on the floor, sitting just out of sight. "I forgot to give this to you." She extended a small duffle bag. "Thought you might need it."

Zanya took it from her hand, and before she could ask what was in it, her mother had walked away. She shut the door, staring down at the bag. "I don't know if I can do this."

"You can do it," Arwan said.

"You don't even know what I'm talking about."

"It doesn't matter." He threw off the blankets and slipped on a pair of shorts over his boxers. "Whatever it is, you can do it."

A soft smile spread across her lips. "Thanks. At least you're confident in me."

Arwan walked to the dresser and took a folded t-shirt out of a drawer. "They need you. We all do." He pulled it over his head, and let out a small groan as he slipped his arms into the sleeves.

Moving around was a good sign, though he was moving slower and more cautiously than usual. Still, it was enough to make her feel okay about leaving him alone in the room for a while.

Arwan gestured to the duffle bag. "What is it?"

"Let's find out." She set it on the foot of the bed and yanked open the zipper. Her leather training gear was inside. She skimmed her fingers over the smooth surface, touching several scuffs and dents along the way. These were her mother's from years ago. Zanya had found them in Renato's house and worn them during her last training session, when she learned how to sprint like Hawa.

Here it was again, this time formally gifted by her mother.

The small bit of recognition was appreciated.

"It's my training gear." She lifted the top piece out of the bag.

"Are you going to wear it?"

"I don't know. Should I?"

Arwan walked past her and opened the door,

pausing in the threshold. "Maybe she needs to see you in it. For closure."

She set the training gear on the bed. "Where are you going?"

"I'll be there to watch you train. I just need to talk to Renato first."

***

Arwan

Arwan walked through the living room and past Balam, who was in his jaguar form, huddled beside the fireplace. Cualli had been gone since the group arrived, probably tending to her duties to the plants and flowers that needed her.

When he opened the front door, Zanya's mother was there. She stood up straight, watching him with narrow eyes.

He squared his jaw. "Waiting for Zanya?"

"Yep." She eyed him. "Feeling better?"

He nodded. "Thank you." He walked past her toward the group's camp.

"Don't thank me," she mumbled. "If it were up to me, we would have put you down like the dog you are."

He froze, heat simmering in his bones. He turned and faced her.

She raised a single brow. "Careful, *half-breed*. Don't let that anger get the best of you. It could turn you into a real beast." She grinned.

"I'm glad to see you are feeling well enough to be on your feet again." Renato's familiar voice rescued Arwan from the moment. He turned to his mentor, who paused, his gaze flickering between Arwan and Zanya's mother, Eleuia. "Is everything all right?"

Eleuia walked forward and bumped her shoulder against Arwan's as she passed. "Fine. I was waiting for Zanya to come out for her training, but she's taking a while to get changed. I'll go wait with the others." She peered up at the sky. "We're running out of daylight."

"Duly noted," Renato said. "I'll be sure to retrieve her if she's much longer."

Eleuia seemed satisfied with her brother's response, and joined the others, all waiting in a tight group.

"Did you know?"

Renato returned his attention to Arwan and slightly cocked his head. "What?"

"You know exactly what I'm talking about." He shifted his weight. "Tell me you didn't know all this time."

Renato had been by his side since he was a young boy. He was there when his mother left. He taught Arwan how to cope with his nightmares. He was even there the first time he turned.

Arwan would never forget the first night he transformed into something unworldly. How terrified he was. The unimaginable pain of that first shift. The years that followed, confused and panicked every time he felt the darkness within him flare to life.

"I knew you were different." Renato looked him straight in the eyes. "Your mother did not give me any history on you before she left. She did not tell me what your future would hold, or how painful it would be as a foster parent as I grew to love you like my own son, and was then forced to watch you face your darkest fears. It was only after Drina told me you were dark that I knew, and by then you were my family. By then, it was too late to turn you away."

A burst of fury tore out of Arwan, and he grabbed Renato by the shirt and slammed him against a stone pillar. His hands shook. His breath quivered as he fought to contain the beast. "Do you know who my mother is?"

Renato's eyes narrowed. "Your mother was a windthrower from the north. No matter her mistakes, she cared for you a great deal."

"A windthrower." Arwan loosened his grip. "Nothing else."

"Else?" Renato's features softened. "What else would there be?"

It was the defining moment he was looking for.

Renato did not know.

The front door opened and Zanya stepped out. She froze when she spotted Renato pinned to the stone beam.

Renato used a counterattack move and broke Arwan's grip, then spun him around and locked his arm under Arwan's chin. "And *that* is how you dissolve a threat even when your back is against a wall."

Arwan tapped on his mentor's forearm, cuing him to let go.

Zanya smirked and walked toward the group.

"Come on you two. Enough private lessons. We have work to do."

CHAPTER TWENTY-ONE

Zanya

"So where are we going to practice?" Zanya walked to the group, huddled on the protected stone platform. "We don't have a lot of space."

"I think we can be of some good." Grima looked at her cousin, Beigarth. "Ye up for a wee bit of work?"

"Aye. Let's give it a whirl."

The two petrifiers walked to the edge of the platform and crouched down, hovering on the brink of the protective circle. "If space is what ye need." Beigarth pressed his index finger on the ground. "Space is what ye'll get."

Grima pressed her hand to the soil and closed her eyes. The two sat still and silent, channeling their abilities into the ground.

Crackles and pops spouted from the earth as the ground turned a murky gray. The petrifiers pushed their ability out further, consuming whatever lay in its path, and turning it to stone.

Zanya's jaw dropped. Before her eyes, the soil, leaves, trees, and whatever was left of dead roots from Yaxche was immediately hardened and petrified.

When Grima and Beigarth stood, a large training circle stretched in front of them.

Beigarth pushed out his chest. "And that, lass, is how it is done."

Tara squealed with delight from behind her. "That was freaking awesome!" She pointed to another part of the forest. "Do it again, over there. Or there."

Zanya chuckled. "Do you want to be the one to explain to Cualli why half her jungle is rock?"

Tara froze, then lowered her hand. "On second thought…"

Zanya looked back at Grima and Beigarth. "That *was* pretty badass."

"Too bad we can't use it," Hawa said. "It's not protected like the rest of the house."

Everyone turned and stared at Drina, who stood beside a pillar. "It needs to be done." She retrieved her knife for the second time and mumbled. "Just when my last cut healed." Then hobbled toward the new training ring to create a fresh protective barrier with her blood.

"While Drina's taking care of that," she cringed, "let's figure out what I'm learning first."

Eadith, the tall, French fire conjurer, stepped forward. Her blonde hair was pulled back, making her face seem even thinner than usual, with high cheekbones and full, pouty lips. "Your fire conjuring skills are…"

163

"Non-existent." Zanya shrugged. "Seems like as good a place to start as any."

They waited a few minutes for Drina to finish, and when she was done, Renato signaled for the others to spread out. "Remember, stay inside the training ring and you will be safe. Venture outside, onto the soil, you are putting your life at risk."

"I think that's pretty easy to remember," Jayden said. "Don't get eaten alive by evil tree—check."

They all settled in place, and a tiny thrill ran through Zanya when Eadith's eyes sparked with light.

Zanya had never conjured fire before. It was an ability she'd read about in the scribes' journals at Renato's house, but the idea of making fire appear from nowhere was a little more than scary. She could have set the house on fire, or worse, herself.

"The key," Eadith said as she walked to the center of the ring, "is finding the fire within you first."

"Within me? How do I do that?"

"Some people feed off of their anger. Others use passion." Eadith held out her hand, palm facing up. She cupped her fingers. "Use whatever gives you the most energy and focus on that. Then, you start with a spark." Electricity rolled over her skin.

Zanya's lips parted. "I've been using the currents for a while now."

"Yeah." Jayden scoffed. "Mostly to zap me."

Eadith ignored Jayden's comment and continued without missing a beat. "Good, then you're halfway there. It takes a spark to make a flame. You must push yourself further and create more heat." She rubbed her fingers together until a tiny flame flickered to life.

Zanya lifted her hand and drew in a breath. "First a spark, then a flame," she whispered to herself. She closed her eyes, summoning a current of electricity to roll down her arm. The energy buzzed in her ears. Then she channeled it to her fingertips. The effort flickered, like a pop of static electricity, and then fizzled out. Zanya dropped her hand. "What do *you* use to channel your ability?"

Eadith's features hardened. "I remember my sister's laughter." From her expression, Zanya knew it was a bittersweet memory. The flame in Eadith's hand grew into a rolling ball of flames, reflecting in her teary eyes. She wound her arm back and pitched the flame at a nearby petrified tree, striking the trunk and splitting the hundred-year-old mammoth in half. The stone cracked and crumbled to the jungle floor.

Zanya knew little about Eadith's past. In fact, she didn't know much about any of the newcomers, except they were there to fight by her side and win this war. Even if it meant laying down their lives. Truth be told, she didn't need to know any more than that.

"Okay." Zanya squared her stance and tried again. She focused on the heat deep in her gut and channeled it to her right hand. The sparks came, along with a metallic taste in her mouth.

"Concentrate," Eadith said. "Command your abilities to work for you. Demand they do as you say. Build the heat until it threatens to explode out of you. Then envision that heat as *fire*."

Zanya held her breath and bore down. Heat crawled through her veins, making her body pulse with the need to set it free. The currents of electricity changed color, and the hair on her arms stood on end, followed by strands of her hair rising, ticking her scalp.

She needed to push harder. One last rush should be enough. She could feel it—deep in her bones. Zanya called on her stone for help, and when it answered, a succession of images scrolled through her mind—seeing her mother for the first time, and then the day she bonded with her stone. She dug deeper, and found the moment the lights of aurora touched her and Arwan, weaving their souls together forever.

A pulse of electricity shot down her arm. Zanya sucked in a breath when a flame sparked to life, wavering in the palm of her hand.

She smiled brightly and looked at Eadith. "I did it!"

"Now grow the flame. Find that memory and hold onto it. Channel that emotion into the fire."

Zanya reached for the memory of the exact moment they bonded. Her heart leapt and her mind jumped to the two of them on their first night together—his tight muscle packed under warm skin. His hot breath when it teased the curve of her neck. Their bond deepening—breakable only by death.

The heat in her hand grew until the ball of fire was the size of a grape, then an egg, and then a grapefruit. Soon the fire was too hot to hold close, and she was forced to stretch her hand away from her face.

"Now throw it," Eadith commanded.

Zanya's gaze scanned the faces of group. "Make a way." They clustered on one of two sides, leaving a gaping path in the center.

She chucked the flame like a softball—but it didn't get far.

The fire broke apart as soon as she threw it, scattering over the group and landing in tiny balls of inferno over herself and the jungle floor.

Zanya screeched and frantically flicked the flames off her clothing. The tiny burn marks healed within seconds. "What the hell!"

"It takes practice," Eadith said.

"Did that happen to you when you first started?"

"No. Never."

Zanya flicked the last of the flames from her clothes. "That's comforting."

"Practice. Don't give up." Eadith rejoined the group.

"Okay." Zanya shook it off and turned back to the others. "Who is next?" Her gaze landed on the Arab windthrowers. "I kind of already have the whole wind manipulation thing down, I think." Renato quickly translated for the twins. The two chattered in their native tongue before the short one, Ahmed, stepped forward.

She'd always known the brothers to be lighthearted, goofy guys. They appeared to be teenagers, maybe seventeen or so, and had always provided a bit of comic relief. But now, as the young man stepped forward, his already dark eyes seemed to grow darker as his youthful features sobered.

Ahmed slipped the string of prayer beads over his head and gave a crooked smile. He snapped his hands forward, pushing a gust of wind toward Zanya. It slammed into her like a train and knocked her to the ground, tearing the air from her lungs.

She coughed and wheezed, forcing herself to her feet before she was really ready to stand. She stumbled and caught herself, then stood, clutching her stomach. She ground her teeth and jutted her hands out, throwing a counterattack.

Ahmed's eyes widened, and the wall of wind slammed into him, throwing him back into the group. His twin brother, Yousef, caught him around the arms and squinted as dirt and leaves smacked into them, carried by the gust.

Peter chuckled. "Nice."

"It seems you have no trouble with that ability," Renato stated, his chest puffed out. "Very good."

Sweat collected on Zanya's brow. "It's tiring, though." She pushed stray hairs out of her face and stood up straight, recovered from the wind assault. "Who's next?"

"Perhaps you should rest," Marzena said, standing beside Renato. "You are young and gifted, but you have a weakness. Show *that*, and your enemy will prey on it, using it to their advantage."

"There's no time for her to rest," her mother said. "She has to push forward, tired or not."

It was tough to say, but her mother was right. "Like I said, who's next?" She looked at Grima and Beigarth, standing side-by-side. "I don't know how to do your ability." She waved them forward. "Come on down." Once she said it, she realized it sounded like the intro to a bad game show.

The two Vikings looked at each other and remained silent.

"I believe their ability is a bit...advanced," Renato said. "Perhaps you should wait until you're completely recovered."

Before her mother could speak, Zanya responded. "No. Contessa could strike at any time. It's now or never, right?"

Her mother stepped forward, a bit of humility in her gaze. "I think Renato's right. This one is too much."

"Weren't you the one who just said I had to push forward no matter how tired I am?"

"Yes, but not with this. I couldn't even perform their ability."

"Maybe that's because you didn't try hard enough."

Her mother lifted her chin, holding her gaze. "I know you think this whole thing is about you, but you staying alive is imperative to all of us. That's something you still haven't learned, because you're inexperienced and *stubborn*."

"Wonder where I get that from."

"This is not a productive use of our time," Renato interrupted.

"I think she should learn every ability," Hawa said. "The more weapons we have, the better."

"I don't get it." Jayden shoved his hands in his pocket. "What's the harm in trying?"

"Children." That word, coming from Marzena, caught all of their attention. "Wisdom in combat is perhaps the most vital weapon of all. If an ability is too powerful to master, using your strongest powers is a wiser option."

"What's up with everyone being so…scared?" Zanya gave Jayden a "please shut up" glare. He shrugged. "What? Am I the only one who sees it?"

Of course, he didn't shut up.

"I understand what you're saying, but how dangerous could it be? This is what I'm meant to do, right? If anyone should try to master all abilities, it's me."

Grima stepped forward. "Aye, lass. But it's a power ye cannot learn."

"Why?"

"Because we will not teach ye." Beigarth's voice contrasted Grima's warm, caring tone.

"Why not?"

"It's too dangerous, lass." Grima made an obvious effort to have a sweeter approach. "Listen to us. We are doing ye right. Ye just don't see it yet."

A long silence thickened the air.

Peter was the first to speak. "Well, if that's it for today, I think we should get the fire going." Peter took Tara's hand. "It'll be dark soon."

The group loitered a moment, and then dispersed without further discussion.

Zanya stood in place, watching as they meandered back to camp.

Arwan was the only one left standing in the new training circle. "Are you okay?"

"What the hell just happened?"

"I don't know."

"Why…" She touched her brow with a tinge of

sweat on it. "Why didn't they want to teach me? I don't get it. I need to know everything. The more I know, the better."

Arwan examined her. "Are you okay? You look pale." He pressed his hand to her forehead. "No fever."

"I'm fine. I heal, remember?"

"Yes, but if your powers are drained, they may not work."

Her focus shifted to Balam stalking out of the jungle with a dead boar hanging in his jaws. He dragged it to her feet and dropped it. Blood oozed from its blunt nostrils.

"Oh." Zanya stepped back. "That's..." *Disgusting.* "I mean...thank you."

Balam chuffed, and then slunk back into the jungle.

"I guess we're having ham for dinner." Zanya patted Arwan on the shoulder. "Have fun cleaning it. I'm going to rest."

Truth be told, she wasn't just tired. Exhaustion had settled so deep into her bones, and her legs were like fifty-pound weights as she dragged one foot in front of the other.

Near the entrance of the house, she caught a glimpse of Grima and Beigarth having what looked like a heated discussion.

Beigarth's lip was curled as he spoke harshly.

A spike of pain wrenched Zanya's stomach. The pain wound around her back and shot down her legs. Mixed with the fatigue, it was too much to bear. She paused, her legs shaking, and then dropped to her knees.

171

"Zanya!" Tara's frantic call cut through the air. "Peter, get over here!"

Arwan was beside her soon after.

Then the rest of them.

They gathered nearby while Peter crouched beside her and laid his hands on her back. "Tell me what's wrong. I don't..." He skimmed his hands over her arms and head. "I don't sense anything."

Pain coiled around her muscles. She ground her teeth. "I'm just...tired." She tried to push to her feet, but didn't have the strength to get off the ground.

"Get her inside," Peter ordered.

When Arwan scooped her into his arms, everything went black.

CHAPTER TWENTY-TWO

Arwan

Hours later, the entire group gathered in the house, all concerned about Zanya's condition—no one more than him.

Eleuia stood beside the fireplace in the living room. "We have to figure out what we know so far."

"And then what?" Jayden said.

"Then we will know best what our next step should be," Renato responded.

Arwan lingered by the window, staring at the vast jungle in the distance. The only one missing from the meeting was Balam, who stood sentry outside in case Contessa returned for another round.

"Shouldn't we wait for Zanya to wake up before having this discussion?" Hawa said.

Arwan looked at her. "She knows as much as I do about this situation, and I know more than *all* of you."

Eleuia glared. "Apparently so."

Arwan ignored the remark and continued. "We

know Yaxche, the tree of life, is being controlled by Contessa."

Tara coiled her arm around Peter's and leaned into him. "Why hasn't it destroyed everything by now? I mean, it would be easy enough, right?"

"Thanks to Drina's protective circle, as long as we're in the house or on the training platform, we're out of the tree's reach. But Contessa—I have no idea if she can cross."

"The question is," Marzena said, "why has she not yet tried?"

"I think she's too weak. The last time I saw her, she was falling apart. Now she stays in the underworld for the most part, only braving the middleworld when it's necessary."

"She certainly thought talking to you was necessary," Eleuia mumbled.

Denying Contessa's interest in him would only make the group more suspicious. He'd have to address this—right here, right now. "She wanted something from me. The same thing she wanted back in Moscow, when I went to her home to find out more about my mother." Arwan cast his gaze to the floor, too ashamed to look them in the eye when he said it aloud. "She wants the darkness inside of me."

The room was silent for a brief moment before Peter spoke up. "This may be a stupid question, but *why*?"

"She was dying. She wanted the darkness inside of me then, probably to fuel her."

"That makes perfect sense," Renato said, now pacing. "She gorged on the souls of men, but it wasn't enough. Your darkness would have given her everything she needed, and more."

"She's no kitten," Grima said. "That's clear as day. Why doesn't she just take it?"

Renato paused, shaking his finger as if chasing a thought. "Grima is absolutely right. Killing *you* should be no difficult task for a dark witch like Contessa. She has lived for thousands of years and consumed countless souls in her lifetime to sustain herself." He lowered his hand and watched Arwan. "Why are you different?"

"Because we're lucky," Jayden said, probably half-joking.

"No." Arwan's single word made the room fall silent. "She needs my permission to take that part of me, and I wouldn't give it."

Tara puckered her lips. "I don't get it. You don't ask permission to steal something. I mean—" she snorted, "not if you want to get away with it, anyway."

"He's royalty," Eleuia said, crossing her arms and examining him with a smug curl of her lip. "Prince of the underworld, and heir to the throne. No one can take from royalty without permission."

"Oohh," Tara said. "So, it's a hierarchy thing."

"You know the old saying," Jayden said. "Don't look the horse that someone gave you in its mouth, or something like that."

"Do not look a gift horse in the mouth," Yousef said, the taller of the twin windthrowers.

The entire group stopped and stared.

Jayden's jaw dropped. "Since when do you speak English?"

"Always." Yousef stood from the couch. "My brother and I learned when we were boys. Our father was a scholar from our people."

"You didn't think it would be helpful to say something sooner?" Tara said. "You know, just in case."

"I knew since the moment they arrived." Marzena pushed a lock of golden hair away from her tiny features. "But there is no need to share something someone wishes to be kept private unless it's absolutely necessary."

Beigarth cringed away from Marzena. "It's unnatural for a wee child to have such power. It's not right."

Marzena bowed her head politely. "I'm the first dreamwalker you have ever met."

"And my hope is you're the last." The stout Viking rubbed his beard and averted his gaze, mumbling in some kind of Celtic tongue Arwan didn't understand.

"We're thankful for your discretion," Yousef said. "To listen without speaking is the best means to gain knowledge. That is what our father taught us."

"I wholeheartedly agree." Renato smirked—not surprisingly. He and Marzena had been friends for as long as Arwan knew his mentor.

Ahmed, the other windthrower, stood from his seat. "Our father taught us our abilities are a gift to appreciate, even though they make us different from our clan."

"That's great," Hawa said sharply. "That's great. *Kumbaya* moment over with. Moving on. We know

Contessa is still too weak to attack." She counted the points out on her fingers. "And we know she's after Arwan's darker half to give her enough strength to make her pretty much unstoppable. We also know Zanya isn't exactly on her A-game."

"If Arwan never gives Contessa what she wants," Tara said, "we're safe, right?"

"But if Contessa is weak, she can't be controlling the tree alone. Who's backing her up?"

Eleuia chuckled.

Renato looked at her. "Is something funny?"

"I'm just thinking about how absolutely screwed we are."

Peter glanced around the room. "*That's* funny?"

"Who do you think is behind Contessa?" Eleuia studied Arwan. "Who is the *one* person in this *entire* universe who has enough power, and would be willing to back up Contessa's scheme?"

Arwan's stomach clenched and his lips parted.

There was only one. One who could, and who would support the destruction of the middleworld.

"Why are you staring at him?" Hawa said. "How is he supposed to know?"

"Oh, he knows." Eleuia pushed away from the fireplace. "He knows, because they happen to be very close." She scanned the faces in the room, commanding everyone's undivided attention. "Nobody wanted to listen to me when I warned you all against keeping him around. Maybe now you'll trust me when I say the *half-breed* shouldn't be trusted. He is his father's son. God only knows what really happened between him and Contessa that he's not telling us."

"*Ellie*," Renato scolded.

"No." She narrowed her eyes. "You are all dedicated to Zanya as the guardian, and he is a threat to everything we've worked for."

"Except…" Tara bit her bottom lip. "I mean, I'm only human and all, but Arwan and Zanya bonded. So…doesn't that mean we're all on the same team?"

Eleuia huffed. "What it means is he's deceived Zanya, and he will turn on us the first chance he gets."

"Ellie!" Renato stepped forward, his dark eyes focused on his sister.

Arwan stayed quiet. In all the years he had known Renato, he had only heard him raise his voice a handful of times.

"You *will* respect Arwan in his home. I will not tolerate anything different. Is that clear?"

She snapped her jaw shut and shook her head. "You're all fools, and it's going to get us killed." Before Renato could say another word, Eleuia turned and flung open the door, then walked outside.

Arwan drew in a deep breath through his nose, working to calm his nerves.

"I am truly sorry." Renato gripped the lapel of his dress blazer. "She has not come to terms with her daughter's bonding. Perhaps Zanya will be able to get through to Ellie once she is well."

"Aye," Grima said. "But ye have to know what is wrong with the lass before she falls ill a second time."

"I didn't sense anything wrong with her," Peter

said. "Her ability should keep her from getting sick, and should heal any wounds almost immediately."

"They do," Arwan said. "She burned herself during training with Eadith, and it barely fazed her."

Peter shrugged. "The only other thing I can think of is she's not used to using her abilities so often, and it's draining her."

"We can't let the lass rest," Beigarth said. "Not now."

"We can't keep pushing her either," Tara said. "If she falls apart, there's no one to take her place. I know Zanya better than anyone." She looked at Arwan. "Even better than you. When it comes down to it, she will come through. She always does."

"I'm glad to hear someone has faith in me."

Arwan turned to find Zanya standing in the hall, slumped against the wall for support.

He clenched his jaw. "What are you doing out of bed?"

"Showing you I'm not giving up." Zanya forced herself to stand up straight. "I won't let this—whatever it is—beat me."

"That's the lass," Grima said with a smile. "A true warrior, she is."

Zanya grimaced and gripped her stomach.

Arwan rushed to her side and hooked his arm around her waist. "You need to rest."

"I'm fine."

"Liar." Tara walked toward them. "Stop trying to be a superhero and get your butt in bed before you toss cookies all over the floor."

Zanya's lips twitched, and she gave a faint smile. "Fair enough."

Arwan led her back into the bedroom, onto the pillow top mattress. She eased onto the sheets, cringing under the effort. "I feel like I have the flu or something." She pressed her hand to her forehead.

"Peter says you don't."

"I know." She groaned as she leaned back. "I'm sorry I'm not out there with you guys trying to figure stuff out."

"We're doing fine," he lied. It was better she missed her mother's outburst. It would only cause her more stress.

"Will you lie down with me? I'd like the company."

Arwan grinned. "Absolutely." He rounded the bed and sat on his side.

She gestured him closer.

"I don't want to hurt you."

"I'll let you know if you do."

He turned and rested his head on her stomach. Being near her made him whole, and eased the doubts that haunted him.

She raked her fingers through his hair, relaxing his muscles. "Be honest," she said. "Everyone's freaking out, aren't they?"

He took her hand and kissed the inside of her wrist. "You shouldn't worry about that now."

"I have to do *something* while I'm lying in bed. I may as well worry."

He laced his fingers between hers, making small circles over the back of her hand with his thumb. "They're mostly worried about you, trying to figure out why you're so weak."

"I'll be back on my feet soon enough. All this training just has me feeling like crap."

He frowned. "They're also worried about me. They think I'll turn on them the first chance I get."

"I have a feeling *they* is mostly my mom."

He gave an honest nod.

"Figures. Don't let her get to you. You and I know the truth." She stroked his head. "Arwan, son of Star."

"Renato believes in me without even knowing who my mother is."

"Of course he does. He loves you."

Arwan couldn't hold back his smile. "If it weren't for him, I would have no one."

"He's incredible, I know. He took me and Tara in when he didn't have to. Gave Tara a place to call home for the first time in her life. He doesn't treat her any different. It takes a special kind of man to do that."

Arwan tilted his head and examined Zanya's face, paler than usual. "If you're tired, close your eyes."

"I am—" She covered her mouth and yawned. "Kind of tired." She blinked sleepily.

He touched her cheek while listening to her stomach make ungodly noises. He chuckled. "We'll have to get you something to eat soon."

She crinkled her nose. "Boar, I'm guessing?"

"It wasn't bad after Grima and Beigarth roasted it over a fire outside."

She shook her head. "I'll stick with fruits and veggies as long as Cualli keeps growing them for us."

He heard her heartbeat quicken.

She didn't have a fever. No virus. No infection.

The thud of Zanya's heart was like a nervous snare drum.

He sat up and pressed his palm on her chest.

A slow, steady rhythm beat under his touch.

Arwan paused. It didn't make any sense. He pulled up her shirt and positioned his head back to her belly.

The heartbeat ticked like a clock wound too tight.

He sat up, heat draining from his face.

Zanya must have noticed his sudden panic. "What?"

His limbs grew heavier by the moment. A thick lump formed in his throat. "Zanya."

She sat up straighter. "You're freaking me out. What's wrong?"

"You…" He swallowed, trying to push down the nausea. "How did this happen?"

"*What?*"

He looked into her eyes—those beautiful wolf gray eyes with generations of magic lurking behind them. "*Querida.*" He took her hand and rubbed it, his chest tight and his stomach now in his throat. "I know why you're so exhausted."

"Is it bad? Am I sick?" She squeezed his hand tighter. "Tell me."

"You're pregnant."

CHAPTER TWENTY-THREE

Zanya

Zanya snorted. "Yeah, okay." She lay back again. "Don't joke with me like that. You almost gave me a heart attack."

He planted his hand on her belly, his touch warm against her skin. The way he looked at her stomach—the soft amazement in his gaze. He leaned in closer and spread his fingers over the curves of her waist.

The only way she could describe it was pure, untainted infatuation.

Breath ceased to leave her lungs. "It's not possible. I mean, it could be if it weren't for my preventative implant, but it's still in my arm. I never had it taken out."

"Something's not right." He stood from the bed, walked through the room, and opened the door. He stuck his head into the hall. "Tara."

"Yeah?" Her voice was distant from the living room.

"We need you for a minute please."

"Coming!" A moment later, Tara walked through the door. Arwan closed it behind her. "What's up?"

Arwan crossed his arms, analyzing Zanya from a distance.

Tara's gaze flickered between them. "What's going on?"

"Um…" Zanya sat up in bed. "I just have a question about the contraceptive implant in our arms." She held her breath, still searching for a different explanation. "How long do they last?"

"Oh. Um…" Tara tapped her foot. "I think the nurse who put it in said five years. But don't quote me on that. We got ours when we went into high school. Policy." She looked at Arwan. "They had a couple of girls get pregnant and the institution almost got federal funds pulled because of it. So that was their solution."

"You have been here for nearly a year," Arwan said. "So—"

"Five years." Zanya counted on her fingers.

"Yeah." Tara shrugged. "I guess that's about—" She froze. "Wait." She stared at Zanya, her eyes widening by the second. "Why are you…?"

Zanya counted to five, then dropped her hand to her lap. A haze of panic made the entire world stand still.

"Oh. Em. Gee." Tara pulled wild curls out of her face and buried her hands in her hair. "You're *pregnant*," she whispered harshly. She gasped and did a little dance. "Shut the front door! But how do you know for sure? I'm assuming you didn't bring a random pregnancy test with you."

"I heard the heartbeat." Arwan tapped his temple. "Very good hearing."

"But…" Tara cocked her head. "I'm no doctor, but doesn't it take like six weeks or something before there's a heartbeat at all? Or…" She shaped her mouth into an O.

"It doesn't make any sense," Zanya choked out. "It hasn't been that long since…" Her face and neck rushed with heat.

"Maybe the development is faster than a normal human? With her genes and mine combined, I wouldn't rule it out."

Zanya's stomach slithered with sick heat.

Tara and Arwan's voices melted into white noise.

Her heart beat against her chest and her hands shook as she threw the covers off and swung her legs over the side of her bed.

Her fingertips turned cold and tingly.

She stood, swaying when she stepped forward.

Their muffled voices were like inkblots— abstract and unrecognizable.

Someone placed their hand on her shoulder.

She slapped it away on instinct, and then blinked and focused on her friend.

Tara yanked her hand to her chest.

"I'm sorry," Zanya said in a breathless whisper. "I'm…" Zanya's lungs constricted, and she struggled to draw in another breath. She clawed at her chest. "I can't breathe."

Arwan guided her back onto the bed.

"Peter!" Tara flung open the door and ran into the other room. She returned a moment later, Peter following behind her.

"Is it a panic attack?" Peter knelt beside the bed.

"I think so," Tara shrieked, "but I don't know for sure."

Peter cupped Zanya's hands. "She's ice cold." He looked to Arwan. "Go get some blankets while I try to calm her down." When Arwan dashed out of the room, Peter looked at Tara. "What happened right before her symptoms? Anything out of the ordinary?"

"Yeah! She just found out she's pregnant."

Zanya gulped in a breath. "Tara!"

"What?" She gestured to him as if putting him on display. "He's a healer. It's like a doctor. Patient confidentiality and all that."

"Pregnant?" Peter continued to rub her hands to warm her chilled skin. "Is that true?"

Zanya shook her head, still not willing to admit it aloud.

"Her birth control lapsed. They just found out."

Zanya choked on a sea of spit. "Tara!"

Arwan came back into the room holding a thick blanket.

Renato followed behind him, Hawa on his heels. "What the hell is going on?" Hawa said. "Is she okay?"

Zanya scanned all of the faces, all of them staring at her, waiting for an explanation. She pulled away from Peter and bolted out of bed. "Get out. Everyone. Please, just get out of my room."

Peter touched her arm. "You have to calm down."

"Calm down?" she screamed. Tears blurred her

eyes. "How am I supposed to calm down? This is not what I wanted." Her frantic voice was unrecognizable, even to herself. "I shouldn't be..." A sob dribbled from her throat. "I don't want to be!"

Arwan spilled the blanket onto the bed and stepped toward her. The hurt in his eyes was more overwhelming than the news itself.

A tear slipped down her cheek. "I'm sorry. This is my fault. I should have been more careful. I'm so sorry."

He wiped away her tear. "We will figure this out."

"There's nothing to figure out. We can't have a baby. I'm not ready. We're not ready."

"A baby?" Renato's voice cut through the moment like a knife. "Do you mean to tell me you are expecting? *That* is the cause of your symptoms?"

"So much for patient-doctor confidentiality," Tara murmured.

Zanya shook her head, as if doing that would silence the voices and deflect the probing stares. "I need some time." Zanya stepped back, distancing herself from Arwan. "Please. I can't do this right now." Arwan reached for her. She pulled away. "I *can't.*"

She rushed through the group, snatched her shoes from the floor, and bolted through the living room—past Drina and the others who hadn't barged into her bedroom—out the front door.

Hot tears scalded her cheeks as she passed Balam and her mother, who stood guard outside.

"Zanya." She stepped in her path. "What happened?"

"Leave me alone." Zanya stopped to shove her feet in her shoes.

"You're crying."

She sniffled and wiped the tears from her eyes. "What do you care?"

"If this is about earlier—"

"It's not."

"Then what—"

"You can't do this!" Zanya shouted, jabbing her finger in the air. "You can't reject everything about my life and then suddenly try to act like you care when something's actually wrong." She ran into the jungle toward the only place she knew.

The Temple of Inscriptions.

***

Arwan

Eleuia stormed into the house and honed in on Arwan. "What the hell did you do to her, *half-breed*?"

Renato stepped forward, his hands extended. "Ellie, there's something—"

"You have to stop protecting him! If you want him to stick around so bad, he needs to be accountable for his actions. Now what the fuck did you do to my daughter, you son-of-a-bitch?"

Arwan gripped his mentor's arm. "It's all right." He faced Eleuia. "Zanya's fine. She's just...confused."

"What the hell are you talking about? She was crying, and then ran into the jungle. *The jungle!* Whatever you did to her made her choose risking her life out there instead of staying here, where it's safe!"

Every muscle in his body went rigid. He didn't intend for everyone to know. Not like this. But now that it was out, the news was best coming from him.

Eleuia snarled and stepped toward him. "If you laid a hand on her, I swear to—"

"Zanya's pregnant."

Eleuia stopped mid-stride. "What?"

"We just found out. It explains her sudden fatigue and inability to have complete control over her powers."

Eleuia half-stumbled back. "She's..."

"We're all shocked, but she'll be okay. I'll make sure of it."

He expected her to lash out—try to kill him, even. It wouldn't be the first time. Instead she pressed her back against the wall, then slid down to the floor. "A baby," she whispered. Eleuia dragged her hazy gaze to him. "You got my daughter pregnant."

Arwan's body flushed with heat. It wasn't until now he felt a pang of shame. He should have taken further precautions. He should have done more to protect them from this. "She won't do this alone."

Eleuia looked away without saying another word.

"Where do you think she went?" Tara asked.

Arwan rubbed the back of his neck. "I don't know, but Eleuia's right. It's definitely not safe for her to be out there alone."

"Aye," Beigarth said. "Ye better go find the lass before some harm comes to her and the wee babe."

The thought of something happening to them nearly ruined him. "I'll bring her back as soon as I find her."

"Do you want me to come with you?" Hawa said. "For backup? I can run back here faster than you if something happens."

"No. I don't want anyone else's life on the line. It's better I go alone."

Hawa nodded.

"Be safe." Renato followed Arwan to the door, watching as he walked out to Balam.

"If Zanya comes back," he said to the jaguar deity, "be sure she doesn't leave again."

The cat chuffed and flicked his tail.

That was as definitive a response as he'd get from an animal. "Thank you."

He examined the ground outside of the petrified training ring. Shoe prints in the mud stretched down the path Zanya had made with her storm—toward the Temple of Inscriptions. Of course. It was the only other place she knew.

He followed the tracks. She'd be far ahead of him by now, and it would take him hours to make it to the temple. She was probably already halfway there if she used her sprinting ability at all. And if she had, she'd be weaker than when she left.

He broke into a jog with his eyes set on his goal—the temple on the distant hilltop. His breath quickened as he picked up his pace, implementing the years of training on the beach in Belize.

Green streaked by him on either side as he sprinted forward.

Clouds ahead gathered into a looming shadow, and a drop of rain fell onto his cheek. More spattered over his shoulders.

Zanya would be caught in the storm. She'd be cold and alone.

He pushed harder, ran faster—dirt flinging behind him with each step.

The clouds opened, letting sheets of rain pour over the jungle. The soil became mud and turned into tar, clinging to his shoes and the bottoms of his cotton pants. It would slow him down, but it wouldn't stop him.

Rain smacked him in the face and drenched his hair, weighing it down and spilling random strands over his forehead. He blinked through water in his eyes and ground his teeth, leaning forward as he started up a slow incline.

Without notice, a crack ran down the path ahead and the ground gaped open. Arwan turned and skidded, digging into the mud. Roots whipped out and grabbed his legs. He clawed at the ground, his fingertips raking through the murky soil.

There was nothing he could do.

He was pulled along the slick jungle floor until there was nothing left for him to hold onto, and he was pulled under.

CHAPTER TWENTY-FOUR

Zanya

Zanya ran up the temple steps, through the entrance, and into the dark tablet room. She summoned the light in her chest, which gave just enough to cast a glow over all four walls—and not take up too much of her abilities.

She balled her fists and paced from one end of the temple to the other, inspecting each tablet as she passed. "This wasn't supposed to happen," she spat. "This wasn't the plan." She stopped in front of the tablet with the star carved above the text—the story of Arwan's conception, and his mother's self-sacrifice to regain immortality.

She touched the markings and closed her eyes. His entire history was carved into this stone, but there was nothing of his future. Of their future. She let out a tiny whimper. "I want to go home."

Home.

What a strange concept that had become.

Once it was an institution for castaways.

Miserable and oppressive, *it* was home.

Then an estate on the beach in Belize. It was in Renato's house she found herself. It was there she became free, and *it* was home.

All of it was torn away when she and Arwan bonded under the lights of aurora. They were forced to flee to a strange house in Mexico. A house long abandoned, left empty and cold.

Now Arwan was her home.

But now, no matter where they lived, she would never have a chance to fulfill her role as the Stone Guardian. Her reign would be cut short by an accident with a heartbeat—a mistake too catastrophic to repair.

A familiar melody carried through the air, easing her heartache. Zanya wandered toward the sunlight just outside the temple's entrance, half-hidden behind dark storm clouds still heavy with rain.

She searched the temple steps but found no one.

Cualli was close. It was the goddess's angelic voice that lured her out of the darkness, and her lullaby Zanya recognized.

She walked down the steps, scanning the area until she caught a glimpse of Cualli's long, golden hair. The goddess sat on the ground with her legs stretched in front of her, skimming her fingers over tiny green buds of new growth.

Zanya wiped her face clean of tears as she approached. "What are you doing here?"

"Waiting for you."

"How did you know I was here?"

"I followed you by wing." Cualli examined Zanya's face and tilted her head—ever so slightly—

as if she were confused. "You are saddened."

Zanya sniffled, determined not to cry in front of a goddess. Her throat closed, trapping in a sob.

"Mortal women have always fascinated me." Cualli stood and touched a bare branch on a nearby tree. Green leaves bloomed and opened in seconds. "Mortals carry such responsibility and withstand great deals of pain, yet never lose the ability to love."

"Not all of us," Zanya said.

Cualli skimmed her hand over another branch, sprouting more green. "You speak of your mother."

Zanya didn't respond.

"I knew your mother when she carried you in her womb. She cradled her swollen belly as if the universe lay inside." She stroked a plant, giving its wilted flowers new vibrancy and life. "While in labor, her screams shook the air. It was then I wondered why any mortal woman would willingly endure such great pain for another human."

"You knew my mother before...all of this?"

"I watched her, though she did not know I was near. It was my duty—as it is my duty to protect you now."

"What if not every woman wants to make the same sacrifice? Do you think that makes her a bad person?"

Cualli scattered colorful blooms between blades of grass. "I have roamed the middleworld for many years, young guardian, and I have yet to find a mortal woman unwilling to sacrifice her own flesh for that of her child."

The goddess's words dug deep into her soul.

Zanya hung her head. She could lie to herself and say she wanted this baby, but it would be a terrible lie.

When she lifted her head, the goddess was gone.

Zanya sighed.

There were two paths for her future, both of them impossible and heartbreaking.

Abandon her child and leave it to be raised in ignorance like her mother had done to her, or keep this unexpected baby, and hide in order to protect it from the terrors that would soon overtake the middleworld.

***

Arwan

The tree dragged Arwan down through layers of earth and clay. The closer he grew to the underworld, the stronger his dark side became, and the more vicious it turned.

There was no way to be sure if he could control his other half in the underworld. This realm had torn the beast out of him last time he was there. But he was determined not to lose his humanity. He'd been to this damned kingdom before, and he knew what to expect.

He'd fight away his darkness until he had nothing left.

He groped at the wall of solid earth and searched for a ledge or rock to cling to and climb his way back to the surface—but there was none.

The vines crawled up his torso and squeezed,

wringing the air out of his lungs. His throat burned, and every cell of his body screamed with the need for oxygen.

He grabbed hold of the tree and bore down, tearing at roots with all of his strength.

They tightened, snapping a rib.

He had no air to shout.

Dirt and rocks scraped at his skin as he was yanked further into the earth, and then slammed to the hot, dusty ground.

When the tree loosened its grip, he gasped in a desperate breath.

The air was scalding and noxious, burning his lungs.

He rolled onto his stomach and pushed to all fours, saliva stringing from his lip as he heaved in several more gulps of air.

It was the first time he had gone to the underworld by means of the tree, and it was no better than drowning in the lake with Zanya.

"Get up." Contessa's order was like a military commander talking to a rookie in training.

Arwan scrambled to his feet and stumbled back, squirming under the influence of his darkness. It filled him completely, threatening to explode out and force him to turn.

He clenching his side as the beast rammed into his throbbing ribs and ricocheted off the splintered bone, driving spikes of searing pain down his spine.

"It has become quite clear, half-breed, you will not give me your darkness willingly." Contessa signaled the tree with a flick of her wrist. Roots broke through the ground and wound around his legs, anchoring his feet in place. "You and your clever comrades have discovered my one weakness." She wrapped her fingers around his throat. "I need your darkness to thrive in the middleworld if I wish to fulfill my vision of conquering both realms, and I will give you one final opportunity to cooperate. Yield, and I will return you to the middleworld to spend your final days with loved ones before the cleaning begins."

Arwan ground his teeth as sweat rolled down his hairline and over his temple. His dark half seemed to be attacking him from all angles, prying and pushing to be freed. "You would use my strength as a weapon of mass destruction."

"Yes. A weapon like no realm has ever seen and never will see again, in this life or the next."

Saliva pooled under his tongue, and he resisted the urge to gag. "Then you will have to kill me first." He spit onto the cracked soil, his saliva tainted red with blood.

Contessa stared down at the ball of saliva and crinkled her nose. "No." She returned her focus to him. "It is not *you* I will end." She squeezed his throat tighter. "*Yield,* or the guardian's life will be taken only after a slow, torturous death."

He fought against the tree's hold, but there was no use. "I won't let you touch her."

Contessa's irises rolled with violet and black magic. "You are powerless to stop me." She leaned in closer, poising her lips above his. "And her death will not be merciful. It will also be in vain. I will tear her apart, one fragile piece at a time, until she begs to die." Contessa brushed her lips over his. He cringed away, but with the roots coiled around him and her fingers wrapped around his throat, he couldn't move far. "I will scoop out her eyes and tear out her tongue, then I will sever her fingers one at a time, and she will be blind and dumb, drowning on her own blood as she screams." Contessa placed a kiss on his lips. She hovered her mouth beside his ear and whispered, "All while I force you to watch."

Arwan clenched his eyes shut, pushing away the images that played in his mind.

Contessa would stop at nothing. Nothing, until she was stopped. Although every prediction and ancient record deemed Zanya to be their savior, he was the one piece missing from the legends.

"You forgot who I am."

Contessa grinned and stepped back.

He had a secret weapon he had never used.

One he had never acknowledged until now, when he had no other choice. "Whether you're the queen or not, *I* am the *blood* heir to the throne. I am rightful ruler of this kingdom after my father, and I say *you will not harm her*." A blanket of peace washed over him, and the beast inside of him submitted.

Contessa's eyes narrowed as she examined him.

He stared down at the roots keeping him captive. "Leave me." They obeyed, and retreated back into the soil.

Contessa took several backward steps, her heel scuffing over several stones along the way.

Arwan lunged forward and gripped Contessa by the throat—returning the favor. His hands shook as he held her like a lifeless doll, dangling in his grasp.

She was pathetic, really.

After all these years, he just now realized it.

He and the group of Riyata had spent time and resources fighting Sarian in the middleworld, only for the general to meet his demise in the underworld.

Now Arwan was here again, in his native realm, facing yet another enemy who thought she could overpower him in his own kingdom.

Not now.

Now he understood.

He was not Riyata. He never had been.

He had spent his entire existence denying his true bloodline and rejecting his royal status.

No more.

He was home.

Contessa's lips parted and a muffled laugh gurgled out of her throat.

He tilted his head, examining her with a morbid fascination.

"It is freeing, is it not? Allowing your darkness to rule you." She stopped struggling to escape him and let her arms hang at her sides. "I see it in your eyes. You have taken command of the beast within, and the darkness has spread into every fiber of your soul."

Chapter Twenty-Five

Zanya

Zanya raced back to her home to escape the storm. She didn't want to face the loneliness after Cualli left her at the temple, even if that meant facing everyone's stares and the humiliating questions instead.

Worse would be facing Arwan.

He didn't seem happy when he discovered the baby, but he wasn't upset, either. Maybe he was just in shock. That made two of them. She'd give it a few days to sink in. Then they could talk about their options.

A huge crack in the ground forced Zanya to slow her pace. She approached the hole and leaned over the edge, peering into the void. A foul stench coated her tongue—the unmistakable trademark of the underworld.

Zanya searched the ground for any sign of Yaxche but saw none. Her attention was stolen by slide-marks in the mud. Someone—or something—

had fallen, or worse, been dragged into the void.

With the villagers gone, it was likely an animal of some kind. Yaxche's newest victim.

Zanya carefully navigated around the hole and completed her journey home. Balam paced along the edge of the protected stone platform with his ears pinned back.

The camp was vacant, and the front door to their home hung wide open.

A weight settled in Zanya's stomach.

If Contessa attacked while she was gone—if Drina's protective barrier didn't work against the witch's powerful magic—she'd never forgive herself.

Zanya ran past Balam and through the door, up the stairs, and burst into the living room, where the entire group was crowded in a circle.

Everyone turned and looked at her.

Panting, she scanned their faces. "Is everyone okay?"

Tara crossed her arms. "Other than the fact you ran off and worried us all half to death—yeah, we're fine."

"Sorry. I needed some time alone."

"Alone?" Renato stood from the chair beside the fireplace. "Did Arwan not find you?"

"Should he have?"

"He went after you," her mother said. Her tone was normally spiked with contempt when she spoke about Arwan. Now her voice reflected the worry in her eyes.

That made her worry. "I didn't see him—" Her breath caught in her throat. "Oh my god. The void."

"What are you talking about?" Peter asked.

"There was another crack in the ground, and slide marks." It was the only explanation. He wouldn't have left their home and not returned. He wouldn't have left her out there alone. How could she be so selfish? Of course he would go after her. "Arwan was pulled under."

"Pulled under where?" Tara said.

Drina frowned. "Home."

"Home," Zanya echoed.

"I guess I'll be the one to ask," Hawa said, standing on the other side of the room. "Are we going after him?"

Zanya nodded. "We can't leave him down there. God only knows what they're doing to him."

"There is no way to gain access to the realm," Renato said. "Arwan is the only one of us with underworld blood. He *is* the key."

Zanya looked at Jayden. "That's not entirely true."

Jayden shook his head, his hands raised as if already declaring defeat. "Hey, I've spent time there, and it's not a place I want to vacation."

"But you're the only one, Jay. Like you said, you've been there. Your blood could be the only way."

"You can't bleed a rock." He shrugged. "I've been dried up since I came back."

"What do you mean dried up?"

"As in, he doesn't bleed," Hawa said. "I know. I pulled a knife out of his side. Nothin'."

"A knife?" Zanya tilted her head, examining Jay.

"Don't ask," Hawa said. "The point is, you're

not going to get a blood sacrifice from him any time soon."

Zanya pinched her lip between her teeth. There had to be some way. Something she was missing. She couldn't let him stay there alone.

"Zanya." Her mother's voice tore her out of her panicked thoughts. "Even if you could reach him, do you think he would want that?"

"What is that supposed to mean?"

Her mother's gaze flickered to her belly. "Your condition isn't exactly prime to go touring his realm."

"My condition?" Zanya balled her fists. "My *condition*? I never wanted this baby to begin with. I didn't ask to be trapped with some kid to take care of." She scoffed. "I thought you of all people would understand."

Her mother's face flushed. "*Zanya*."

"It's true. You had to hide like a coward while the world went on around you, and you did nothing about it. You couldn't because you chose having your baby over fulfilling your responsibility."

"That's exactly right," her mother said—nearly shouting now. "I chose you, and whether you know it or not, if you don't honor the life inside of you, you will regret it forever. And trust me. You'll have many, many years to regret."

Something inside her snapped, and she said the one thing she never thought would come out of her mouth. "My only mistake would be choosing this half-breed baby over…" Zanya stopped and pressed her hand over her mouth, gagging on her words.

Tara set her hand on Zanya's back. "It's okay.

It's normal to have these thoughts."

"How could I have said that?" Zanya rubbed her hands down her face, grateful Arwan wasn't around.

"We know you didn't mean to call your baby a half-breed. You're just stressed and—"

Zanya looked at Tara, stopping her mid-sentence. "What?"

"I'm just saying, you're tired and—"

"No." She looked down at her belly.

Drina touched her own lips with her wrinkled fingers. "*You.*"

***

Arwan

The darkness consumed him, rushed through his veins and seeped deep into his soul—just like Contessa had claimed.

His mother had created something she could not control. A beast that could choose which side it would fight for.

After a lifetime of refusing to embrace his dark lineage, he'd been forced to face the inevitable.

This was it.

He was, after all, his father's son.

He was, after all, a monster.

He released Contessa's throat, clenching and unclenching his fists. Power like he'd never experienced poured through him, making his veins swell and his muscles bulge.

Contessa touched the swollen marks on her neck.

He blinked, now peering through a shroud of darkness with bright violet fogging the edges of his vision.

"You're beautiful," Contessa whispered, her voice still raspy. The marks on her neck morphed from bright yellow to blue.

A growl rolled in his chest.

The beast—once a combating force inside him—now made him complete. It shared his body with his mind, both of them one piece of a whole, reunited after a lifetime of being pitted against each other.

"This is mine." He scanned the first realm of the underworld, desolate of any followers after the tree had had its fill. "Where are my slaves?"

"They are still here, my lord." Contessa settled her hand on his chest, and then slid it up and cupped the back of his neck.

Her touch no longer sparked with his other side. Instead they meshed in the most perfect harmony. "*Where*?"

His hard tone must have startled her. She bowed her head, subservient to his authority. "In the realms below us, my lord. There are eight more, each layer with its own prisoners."

Perhaps if he had embraced his rightful place sooner, he could have saved the middleworld from years of anguish.

Generations of fallen soldiers.

Lifetimes of pain.

"There is so much more for you to see. So much more for you to experience." The way her lips formed that last word grabbed him from the inside.

He leaned in and kissed her, long and hard.

When he pulled away, he tilted his head, sensing the change in the temptress. She was no longer a threat. Instead, she was an ally.

She pressed her cleavage against him. "You, *my lord*, are the answer to our woes. Your realm is threatened by the inaction of your father, the king. Your return is our saving grace—our chance to overthrow not only the middleworld, but the heavens as well." She raked her fingers through his hair. "With your married bloodlines, we could rule them all."

"We?" He grabbed her wrist, bending the delicate bones until he felt them grind together. She flinched but did not pull away. "You are my father's mistress."

"You speak as if it were my choice."

Arwan eased his grip.

She snarled. "Your father, the king." The way she said his name—so tainted with contempt. "He is far from a king. Far from the ruler you could be." She yanked her wrist out of his grasp and wound her arms around his neck. "I had no choice but to join him. He never would have allowed me to seek refuge in his realm and complete my bidding otherwise. And it is only because he believes I do all of this for *him* that he allows me to stay. Otherwise..." She pressed her body against his again. Arwan's nostrils flared as the scent of her perfume tickled his senses. "I would have perished. And if I had perished—" The witch licked her thumb, then streaked it over his mouth. "You and I would have been robbed of this...opportunity."

He ran his tongue across his lips and tasted the

bitter tinge of her saliva.

He had never been so attracted to the witch before—so absolutely entranced by her beauty and the way her lips formed each word, spoken by her sultry voice.

The noxious aftertaste of her mouth reminded him of who she was, and what she did to remain alive in the mortal realm.

She was a temptress—a stalker of souls. She was a parasite with an arsenal specialized to snare men in her trap—and he was falling into it.

He shoved her back.

Contessa stumbled and fell to the dry, cracked earth. Her perfect red waves spilled over her shoulders, and she glared up at him.

"Kneel," Arwan commanded.

The witch watched him for a moment, then obeyed and pushed to her knees. He approached, the darkness still motivating him.

Once he stood in front of her, Contessa reached up and wrapped her fingers around the buckle of his pants. "I can please you. I can be the queen you so badly desire."

Arwan pulled back and struck her across the cheek, slapping her to the ground. She pushed onto one hand, holding her face with the other.

"You are *not* who I want."

Contessa scrambled to her feet, her cheek puffy and red. "I will forgive you for laying a hand on me, though just this once."

"That's too bad." Arwan pushed up his sleeves. "Because I intend to do it more than once."

CHAPTER TWENTY-SIX

Zanya

Inside her home, with a cup of herbal tea in her hands, Zanya couldn't let her mind rest.

Arwan was in the underworld, and it was her job to get him out. They were bonded, and her soul wouldn't be whole until he was back where he belonged.

"How's the tea?" Her mother poured a steaming mug of herbal brew while the rest of the group was outside in their camp. She'd prefer almost anyone else to be there...

"Fine." Zanya sipped the hot drink. Hints of sage, mint, and ginger rose with the steam and infused her senses.

"Good. You'll need your strength for the baby."

Zanya frowned, refusing to linger on the subject. She wanted to be comfortable talking to her mother about it, but the mother-daughter bond wasn't there anymore—not like the first time they met. And not when Zanya was ashamed of her own contempt over the pregnancy.

So for now, until things changed, they'd talk business and keep it at that. "I need to figure a way to get Arwan out of there."

Balam lay in the corner, dozing. His presence was barely detectable, except when he twitched or flinched in his sleep.

Her mother turned on the electric stovetop and put the water to boil. "I don't think you're in much condition to go anywhere—let alone the underworld."

"My *condition* has nothing to do with it. It's not a question of if, it's a question of when, and how."

Her mother walked into the living space and sat on the chair across from her. "Zanya…" She laced her fingers and leaned forward.

"Please, don't." Zanya sipped her tea. "I really don't want to hear it."

"Sometimes what we want and what we need are two different things."

"I doubt you're the person who should be telling me that."

Her mother leaned back in her chair and sighed. "Do you think he would ever forgive you if you went to get him, and something happened to the baby?"

Zanya cringed, a spike of annoyance stiffening her muscles. "I don't think that's any of your business."

"That's my grandchild."

Zanya snorted. "Says the woman who tried to kill the father of *your grandchild*—twice. Why do you care so much about this? Just leave it alone.

Please."

Her mother examined her for a long, silent moment. "Okay, then what happens when you go there, and your abilities fail you at the wrong time?"

"They won't."

"Because you have so much control over it, right? Like outside when we trained—you chose to collapse on the ground and scare everyone half to death."

"That's different."

"You're right. Because in the underworld, if your abilities fail, you'll die. Do you think he'll forgive you then?"

Zanya stayed quiet. Her life was one of the only things Arwan would sacrifice himself to save. If she was at risk, he would do whatever he could to save her—no matter the cost.

"And what about the stone?"

Zanya glanced at the leather bracelet with her stone hidden inside.

"What will happen to it if you're gone, and you have no heir to pass it to?"

"You're here."

"But I passed the stone to you. There's no *takesies-backsies*. You're the Stone Guardian now, and it's your job to protect it."

"So what are you suggesting, exactly? Not make any effort to get him back?"

Her mother shrugged. "That's home to him, Zanya. If he wants to leave, I'm sure he could. Maybe he's choosing not to. Ever consider that?"

"No." Zanya clenched her jaw. "And I won't. He belongs here, with me." She was never so sure about anything in her life.

***

The next morning Zanya got dressed and met the others outside.

Jayden was the first to notice her. He tapped Peter's arm while staring, the gesture catching everyone's attention. "Wow." Jayden raised is eyebrows. "You're uh…" He froze and glanced at Hawa, then cleared his throat. "You're finally ready. About time."

Hawa rolled her eyes. "Smooth."

Her mother nodded in approval. "The gear fits you perfectly." She flexed her arm. "You've filled out."

"Yeah. I guess that's from all the raw foods, hikes, and training."

"Good. You'll need the strength for the baby."

Zanya frowned, unwilling to linger on the subject. "I've been thinking about this all night, and I have a plan." Everyone gathered in a tighter circle in silence. "We'll go to the opening where Arwan was pulled under. I'll give a blood offering, and the tree will give us access to the underworld. We go in, we get out. That's it. It's the four of us, and only us." She gestured to Jayden, Renato, and Beigarth. "Hawa, you can escort us there and back since you can sprint back once we're in. You'll be the safest one to travel alone. Everyone else stays here and waits for us."

"What about me?" her mother said.

Peter raised his hand. "And me. What if someone

gets hurt? I should be there."

"We don't know if your powers will work in the underworld, Peter. And even if they do, I need you to take care of everyone here. While I'm gone, you're in charge."

"Damn right, he is," her mother said. "Because I'm coming with you."

Zanya ignored the comment and continued to address Peter. "If anything happens while we're gone that you can't handle, you have to get them out. Do you understand?"

Peter nodded without a hint of protest.

Marzena and Drina stood together, watching from a distance. It was typical for Marzena to be short-worded, if she spoke at all, but not Drina. It was strange she hadn't protested or rooted them on. Nothing except sadness showed in the deep creases around her mouth.

Marzena narrowed her eyes, focused on Zanya. *If you should meet the witch and have the chance to kill her*, she transmitted with her mind, *take it. Do not hesitate to steal the life from her body, because she will surely not hesitate to steal yours.*

Zanya nodded, knowing she was the only one who heard Marzena's words.

"How do you know this'll work?" Tara said. "I mean, the tree could let *you* in, but what if it doesn't let the rest of them through?"

"Arwan and I had no problem when we traveled through to get Jayden back. And *then* I didn't have underworld blood coursing through me."

"There is one rather large problem with this plan," Renato said. "The tree was designed to sense underworld blood. It is not like the lake. It is not an inanimate object or a placid body of water. It is very much alive, and if it senses anything but underworlders in its grasp, it will reject them—with extreme prejudice."

The group fell silent.

"If I end up going alone, so be it." Memories of her last visit to the underworld flashed through her mind, sending her nerves on edge. She wiped a bead of sweat from her brow. "I get that you guys are scared. I'm not exactly excited about being dragged back down there either. But I can't leave him. He wouldn't leave me."

Renato nodded. "Then it's settled. We go as far as we can, together."

Zanya mirrored Renato's nod, thankful for his resilience where others faltered. He would be the one to stand strong. He had raised Arwan, and no matter their bloodlines, they were family.

When the group dispersed, Eleuia grabbed her arm and stepped close, speaking in a low tone. "What the hell is going on?"

"What are you talking about?"

"You don't want me to go? How dare you treat me like that—especially in front of all of these people? *My brother*. They'll think you don't respect me."

Zanya silently stared into her mother's face.

She let go of Zanya's arm and pulled back, her eyes slightly widened.

Besides raw anger and contempt, it was the first genuine reaction she'd seen from her in a long time.

"I don't want you to go because you wouldn't

sacrifice for him." Zanya squared her stance and faced her mother—a little like looking into her own reflection. "You want him gone, so if things get bad, you wouldn't even try to save him."

Eleuia paused, as if considering Zanya's words. "You're right. I wouldn't try to save him. But I'd do anything to save you."

A stretch of silence lingered between them, and before Zanya could find words to respond, Eleuia joined the group who would brave the deadly journey alongside her.

Her mother leaned in to Hawa and whispered. Hawa nodded.

Zanya sighed.

She knew her mother meant well, but it was too little, too late.

Once they'd said their goodbyes, it didn't take long for the small group to arrive at the tear in the earth. Stench continued to saturate the air, suffocating the plants until they turned a murky brown. Zanya covered her nose, doing her best to ignore the funk that coated her throat and scalded her lungs.

"What now?" Jayden asked.

"Now…" She slid a knife out of its sheath attached to her belt. "I bleed." She extended her wrist over the hole and poised the blade over the flickering pulse in her vein.

"Wait." Her mother grabbed her hand. "Are you sure about this? I know I couldn't stop you even if I wanted to, but there's more at risk than just me or you."

"I know what you're worried about, but it's not

real to me. Not yet. You can't put something in danger that doesn't even exist." They both knew she was talking about the baby.

Her mother stepped back in compliance.

"Now hold on," Zanya said. "When the tree comes, it'll come fast and it won't be gentle. If you're not holding on, you'll be left behind. Jayden, you stand in the back. With underworld blood in the front and rear, the tree may have less chance of denying us access." Renato coiled his arms around her waist, and the others clung to him in a too-close-for-comfort hug train.

She looked at Hawa, who willingly gave Eleuia her spot in the mission. "We won't be long."

Hawa nodded. "Be careful."

Zanya drew in a breath and ran the blade across the blue shadow under her skin, splitting it open.

Blood poured from the vein, pumping scarlet down the curve of her wrist, and into the gaping hole.

After a few moments, the wound began to heal.

"Where is it?" Jayden said from behind her.

"I don't know." It should have come for her the moment it sensed her blood. Maybe Contessa had somehow ordered it not to come, but nothing could completely ignore the purpose of its existence. Maybe if she just got the tree's attention. Zanya stomped on the ground. "Hey." Her shout echoed through the air. "Come on. Where are you?" Her wrist had healed completely, so she sliced it again, flinching under the burn of the air licking her raw, open wound. She pumped her fingers, calling on more life to flow out of her. "I have every right to enter. I have underworld blood in me, and this is my sacrifi—"

Roots exploded out of the hole and seized Zanya's legs. The rest of the group clung to her when it yanked her under.

Renato had his arms coiled around her torso, her mother behind him, then Beigarth, and then Jayden.

The tree yanked them down through layers of soil. The back of Zanya's head smacked into what felt like a rock. Her teeth rattled in her mouth and impact rang in her ears. She shouted and held her head as tight as she could to protect it until it healed—if it healed. There was no telling how the underworld had changed.

One last yank pulled them into the dark realm. With the vines still tight around her legs, she flailed her arms back and slammed against the ground. She wheezed and clawed at her heart that rattled and skipped before beating again.

Groans from the others filled the air. Zanya kicked at the tree until it released her and retreated back where it came from. She sat up and took a headcount.

Renato. Jayden. Her mother. Beigarth.

Everyone was alive. For now.

"Everybody okay?"

The petrifier stood and dusted off his clothes while squinting under the relentless sun. "A true Viking never sits aside like a maiden when there's a battle to be fought."

"I'm wishing I stayed put right about now." Her mother gagged on the air and then covered her nose with her hand.

Beigarth's eyes widened. "No time to worry on such matters now, lass." He pointed in the distance. "There's a true good fight with yer lad and that witch, and I have a gut feeling we should take cover."

A hideous scream tore through the air. Zanya followed Beigarth's prompt and turned around. Arwan stood in the distance, clutching a handful of Contessa's hair. He dragged her back, throwing the witch off balance. She kicked at the soil while holding onto his forearm, desperately trying to break free.

"He's going to kill her," Zanya said.

Jayden snorted. "Good."

She gagged again. "We need to go." She clenched her stomach. "I forgot how rancid this place smelled."

It wasn't until that moment Zanya remembered her mother's history with the underworld. In the past, after they traveled back in time and she bonded with the stone, her mother had been taken prisoner by Sarian and kept here—tortured—and possibly even raped. It was here her mother learned about Sarian's darkest plans, and even who Arwan truly was.

No matter how she felt about her mother, returning to this realm was more of a sacrifice than she should have made—even for her own daughter.

"We need to find cover," Renato said.

His voice must have caught Arwan's attention. He froze and turned his head, staring at the group with blank eyes. He stood absolutely still while Contessa thrashed in his grasp, as if her attempts to break free didn't faze him in the least.

Renato took Zanya's arm. "Something is not right."

"Yeah." She shifted her weight. "I get that too. He doesn't seem…normal."

"That's because he's not normal," her mother said. "Maybe now you get it. He belongs here."

"That's not true," Zanya snapped. "He doesn't belong here. He belongs with me, and I'm taking him home."

She walked ahead, leaving the group at her back. The blood that had once stained the ground was no longer there, the faded marks now fully absorbed into the cooked soil. It was as if there had never been thousands of underworld captives, beating drums and cheering when a bloody sacrifice was made.

Now there was nothing except abandoned ruins, a few scattered boulders, and them.

Zanya shielded her eyes from the punishing sun of the damned realm and peered at Arwan's face.

Renato was right. Something had changed in him. He was different now. Someone she didn't recognize.

The closer she walked, the less sense it made.

Why was he not happy to see her? Why wasn't he running to her?

Now only several yards away, Zanya stopped. He remained like a statue with Contessa still trapped in his grasp.

And his eyes.

His eyes were vacant of warmth—like empty, black coals.

"Help me," Contessa screamed. She dug her nails into Arwan's arm. He didn't even flinch.

The others in the group flanked her on either side.

"Arwan." She stepped toward him. He pulled away. Zanya reached out to him. "What's happened to you?"

"He's dangerous," Contessa pleaded. "Help me and I'll get you all out of here."

"Shut up," Zanya snapped. "You deserve everything you get."

"Perhaps. But what will become of your comrades? He is no longer the man you once knew. You can see that for yourself. He is going to kill us all."

"*Aye*," Beigarth said in a soft tone. "I wouldn't be one to agree with the *hoor*, but he isn't the same lad, now, is he?"

"Arwan." Zanya bit her lip. "I know you're in there. I know you are. It's just this place…"

"This is where he wants to be," her mother said. "Don't you get that?"

"No!" Tears stung her eyes. "I don't believe that. I can't."

CHAPTER TWENTY-SEVEN

Arwan

Arwan tried to focus, but it was nearly impossible with the storm raging inside him. Contessa was in his grasp, lying at his feet. He was going to end her here. Now. Just like he did Sarian. This time, he didn't need to change into a beast to do it.

Then Zanya appeared and his entire world came undone.

Heat rose from the scalded ground, forming a distant mirage of the sea in the distance. Was *she* a mirage? Or perhaps Contessa had conjured her to break his focus.

Arwan glared and tightened his grip, making Contessa screech and coil into a ball. That was it. Zanya couldn't be real. Not in this realm. There was no way for her to gain access without him when Jayden didn't bleed. And the others…they couldn't have made it.

"We should go," her mother said. "We can't stay

here much longer. The heat." She peered up at hell's sun, trapped under the roots of Yaxche. "It's too intense."

Zanya shook her head, sending stray hairs to feather around her neck and cheeks. "Not without him."

Her mother cringed away from the bright light above them. "He doesn't want to come with us. We need to leave."

"Zanya is right," Renato said. "We cannot give up on him."

Arwan stepped aside. Everyone in the group leapt back as if they were terrified of him. Maybe they were.

Everyone except Zanya.

Her feet were mounted in place, her gaze never wavering. "Come home with me." She stretched her hand out. "We need you." Her throat visibly tightened. "*I* need you."

Arwan examined her hand. He'd seen it a thousand times—memorized the lines in her palm and the warmth of her touch.

But *his* Zanya would have touched him without hesitation.

They had to be an elaborate hoax.

"Yo, jungle boy." Jayden's voice was like a flute playing off key, scratching at his ears. "We're here to break you out, but you have to make a choice." He tried to shelter Eleuia from the full force of the sun. "And quick, because most of us won't last long. We put ourselves in a shit-ton of risk to find you."

"You're not real." Arwan glared. "None of you.

You can't be." He yanked Contessa to her feet, pulling a scream from her lungs. "Make them go away."

"It was not me who brought them here. It was you."

"Liar." He threw her back to the ground.

Contessa held her scalp. "No, my lord. Not this time."

"*My lord?*" Zanya shifted toward her. "What the hell did you do to him?"

"I did nothing he did not desire." Contessa's body shook as she struggled to stand. "Do you not see, young guardian? Your love, your soul mate, he is mine now. The underworld has claimed him."

Arwan cocked his head, admiring Zanya's soft smile. Even though she wasn't real, he would take this brief moment to enjoy her beauty, and remember the moments they had together—when he was still the man she fell in love with.

"He's free to go where he wants," Zanya said in a soft, gentle tone. "But no matter where he is," she reached out and touched his cheek, "he'll always be mine."

A rush of breath escaped his lungs and his vision cleared of the violet fog. Her touch, her warmth—it brought him back to reality. She'd found his humanity for him, and brought it back.

He rested his hand over hers, splayed over his cheek. "Zanya. How…?"

She took his hand and led it to her belly. "It has its advantages."

Arwan had nearly forgotten. Their baby.

Contessa was right. If it weren't for him being

there, Zanya never would have come after him He blinked, as if clearing cobwebs from his mind. "What am I doing here?"

"I don't know, but it's time to come home."

Home.

His mother's home, in the middleworld, with the ones he loved—and who loved him. That was where he truly belonged. Heat simmered and bubbled in his gut. "*You.*" He turned to Contessa. "You commanded the tree to force me here."

"Perhaps." She stood up straight and smoothed the creases in her dress. "But it is you who wanted to stay."

"Can we just kill this bitch and get out of here?" Jayden shouted. "Please?" Jayden looked at the others. "Seriously. I'm okay since I'm already dead, but I don't know how much longer they'll last in this heat."

Tiny, fluid-filled bubbles rose on Renato's arms and forehead. Red and angry, his skin would begin to peel if he didn't escape soon.

Arwan tilted his chin to the hole overhead that led to the middleworld. "The tree can take us back if I order it to do so. We can all go—"

Zanya's scream sent a shockwave through the air. Arwan looked to see Contessa's arm wrapped around her, holding a jagged rock to her throat. "You will not leave," the witch spat.

Arwan stepped forward, the darkness flooding his veins once again. "Let her go."

"Stay with me. Stay and I will allow her to leave with her life."

Zanya's eyes were wide as she stood perfectly

still, gripping Contessa's forearm with one hand and protecting her belly with the other.

Arwan scowled. "If you do not release her, I will *end you*."

Contessa's expression changed. The color drained from her face, leaving her like a pale doll.

He would tear the witch apart with his bare hands before he let her hurt Zanya. That was what it had come to. Arwan balled his fists. "As you wi—"

Before he could finish his sentence, Contessa pushed Zanya toward him and dropped the blade.

Zanya stumbled forward and clung to Arwan.

Contessa's lips trembled with a smile. "My lord." She bowed, spreading her dress, displaying a low curtsy.

Arwan growled. "Stop calling me that."

"What makes you believe I am referring to you?"

A slither crawled through Arwan's gut. He grabbed hold of Zanya and poised his mouth beside her ear. "Stay behind me. Do you understand?"

She nodded, terror streaked through her features.

Arwan turned to face the one man he despised more than anyone.

His father, King of the Underworld.

"After all these years." The king stepped forward. "After all of my efforts. You are home." He was a massive man with a dark, full beard and eyes burning like red embers. Hellhounds flanked him on either side. Muscular and bare of any fur, their jaws dripped with white froth. One dog growled and snapped at Jayden, who leapt back.

Zanya's mother clung to Renato. Boils from hell's sun had blemished her skin. Arwan had never seen this reaction to the underworld, but then, Zanya had the ability to heal, and he was native to that realm. Perhaps all Riyata were not immune to the severe conditions.

He'd be surprised if she stayed on her feet another minute.

It was a mistake for them to come.

They would all die.

The king examined the failing group, his sights stopping on Zanya. "Why have you come here?" His voice was baritone and rough. "What are you doing in my realm?" His royal cape dragged behind him, leaving flames streaked over the ground in his wake.

"He's come to sabotage our mission," Contessa said in a rush, hurrying to the king's side. She wound her arm around his and took her place beside him, as if she belonged there.

As if she weren't just trying to seduce Arwan into taking her as *his* queen.

Contessa locked eyes with him. "He's come to overthrow you, my lord. I stopped him by holding his love—the Stone Guardian—captive beneath a blade."

His father observed the group for a long, silent moment, then examined the rest of the realm—quiet and vacant of underworlders. "What has happened here? Why are there no damned souls in this realm?"

"You didn't know," Arwan said, almost under his breath.

Arwan stole a glance at Zanya, who seemed to be holding up well enough. The effect of the sun did little damage before her healing ability kicked in and mended her wounds. As for the others, they continued to fade.

The king turned his head and looked Contessa in the eyes. "Explain."

Her hand shook as she pointed at Arwan. "Your son has traveled here to rob you of your crown. It is mutiny, my lord. He is desperate to save his pitiful comrades from our plot to seize the middleworld. He is here to put an end to our reign. You must destroy him."

His father's eyes moved to Arwan.

They never wavered.

Never faltered.

"Why are you really here?" The king let go of Contessa and walked toward him. The closer he was, the more heat radiated from his body.

Arwan examined his features. He had inherited the king's sharp jawline.

"I was brought here," Arwan said. "Your queen tried to seduce me and convince me to overthrow you."

"Is that so?" He ran his hand over his beard while nodding.

"Lies, my lord. I would never do such a thing."

"Says a damned whore," the king snarled.

Contessa did not dare respond.

The king stopped in front of him, nearly toe to toe. Barely taller than Arwan, the raw power he possessed dwarfed him in comparison.

"You must act, my lord." Contessa's eyes rolled with violet magic. "Do not appear weak. Do something!"

The king tilted his head, examining Arwan. "All I have ever wanted is for you to return and claim your rightful place as my son, prince of this realm. Have you come to fulfill my wish?" His features turned to stone, and the heat around him flared with intensity. "Or have you come to die?"

The hellhounds bared their teeth and growled, sending strings of froth to the floor.

"I do not belong here."

"You belong *only* here. This realm runs through your veins. This is your home."

Arwan looked back at Zanya, who worked to heal the others from their burns.

Arwan shook his head. "No. I belong with her."

When his father turned, Arwan used the moment of distraction and commanded the tree to take the group to safety. Roots exploded from the ground and coiled around their bodies. A collection of screams filled the air.

The king raised his hand, stopping the tree from moving any further. He turned back to Arwan. "You may be the rightful prince, but I am the king. Your word does not trump mine in my own realm." He clenched his fists, and the roots tightened around each person.

Beigarth grabbed hold of the tree limb imprisoning him and turned it to stone. With one mighty blow of the Viking's fists, the dead remains shattered and scattered to the ground.

The king grinned, as if amused by the show of strength. "A petrifier. How clever."

"Not clever, ye bas." Beigarth rolled up his sleeves. "The end of ye is what I am."

227

"Beigarth!" Zanya screamed.

The king flicked his wrist, sending one of his hounds after its first target. Beigarth crouched and poised his hands like a football player. When the hound leapt, the impact took Beigarth down with a heavy thud.

With the king once again distracted, Arwan commanded the roots to bring the others to the safety of the middleworld.

"I'll kill you! I'll take everything!" Contessa's shrill scream was the last thing he heard before a blade tore into his flesh.

CHAPTER TWENTY-EIGHT

Zanya

The tree yanked her mother through the air and out of sight, back to the middleworld.

Jayden was next. His arms flailed as the root carried him through the passage above.

She couldn't leave Arwan behind. Zanya shocked the roots, loosening their grasp enough for her to slide out of their hold and fall to the solid ground.

Beigarth still struggled with the hellhound. The beast was on top of him, snarling and snapping at Beigarth's face. The Viking grabbed the hound's upper and lower jaw, his muscles bulging as he forced the beast's mouth open. The hound thrashed and screeched until there was a loud snap. It let out a high-pitched whine, still struggling to escape. Beigarth scrambled to his feet and laid his hands on the underworld beast, and transformed it to stone.

The Viking picked up the petrified hound and launched it through the air at the second beast,

229

which leapt out of the way before its stone companion crashed to the ground and shattered into dust.

"Help Renato," Zanya shouted. She'd healed him already, but Beigarth seemed to be more resilient against the unrelenting sun than the others.

"Aye!" The Viking ran to his side, but Renato pushed him away.

"Get back," Renato ordered, struggling with the vines wound around his torso. Renato snapped one of the roots in half, but more replaced it—more than he could fight off.

Zanya scrambled to her feet and ran toward Arwan, who was now bleeding on the ground.

Contessa loomed behind him with the pointed, scarlet-stained rock still in her hand.

Just feet away, the witch's gaze flickered to Zanya, ordering roots to grab her ankles. When it snagged her, she lurched forward and smacked to the ground.

Contessa stared down at Arwan with a wild gleam in her eyes. "If you will not grant me your darkness, I will at least take your soul!" She plunged the blade into his back a second time. He shouted and arched his spine, contorting his body as he desperately attempted to reach the wound.

She brought the weapon down another time, tearing into his neck.

Blood splattered over her face, raining scarlet on the dusty ground.

She dropped the pointed rock and straddled him, grasping his face in her hands, digging her nails into his skin. She pinned her lips to his, then opened her mouth wide and forced him down to the ground.

Arwan fought against her, but being wounded and bleeding, was too weak to push her off.

A high-pitched hiss screamed out of her, accompanied by a fog of darkness seeping from her nostrils like a smoking gun.

Arwan flailed, kicking his legs and digging his heels into the ground.

"No!" Zanya conjured electricity in her hand, turning it to a ball of inferno. She pitched it at Contessa, but missed.

Blood pumped from Arwan's wounds as Contessa's attack continued.

"Stop!" Zanya kicked at the tree, but it was too strong. She reached out to him. "Stop, *please*." The last word dribbled from her throat in a watery sob. She pulled at the roots coiled around her ankles and delivered another shock, but after all of her efforts, her abilities were weakening.

There was nothing she could do to reach him.

A root from the tree rose near Arwan and slithered toward him. Zanya's eyes widened. "No, no, no!" The tree would consume him while Contessa did the same. He'd be eaten from all angles, from the inside out and the outside in, leaving nothing for her to bury.

When the root reached him, it paused and moved away from the gash in his neck.

Zanya exhaled.

It moved away…

The root projected up and punched a hole in Contessa's gut.

She let go of Arwan and gasped, letting out a

gurgled scream. She scratched and slapped at the vine while still straddling Arwan.

The vine pushed deeper into her core. Her eyes widened.

Blood dribbled from the corner of her mouth.

The king walked toward Contessa, his remaining hound at his side. "You dare to martyr my son?" His eyes flashed red.

A wave of heat smacked into Zanya from the king's anger.

He pounded his chest. "You dare strip my only heir away from me?"

"My lord," Contessa wheezed.

"Stop speaking, you betraying whore." The king lifted his hand and twisted it in the air, directing the tree further inside her.

Contessa convulsed and groaned, her mouth gaping. He grabbed her by the hair and pulled her back, throwing her off Arwan. She screamed the best she could as her breaths quickened.

Her lips quivered.

A thin vine crawled out of her nose and felt its way across her face.

"I do not need you by my side," the king said. "You were mere entertainment—a plaything for my pleasure." He looked down at Arwan, half-dead and lying in a pool of his own blood. "You dare steal his soul, as if he were one of the many mortals you consumed in the middleworld to keep your pathetic body alive?" He craned his neck and stared down at her. "Time for play is over." He gestured to his hound, who leapt forward and tore into Contessa. More roots from the tree crawled from her mouth, filling her throat and cutting off her air. Her eyes grew wide as tiny capillaries burst, turning her entire eye red.

The hound yanked and peeled away her flesh, thrashing its head, pulling wet clumps of twisted innards onto the ground.

Zanya turned her head and closed her eyes, but couldn't block the sound of the hound feasting on Contessa's organs.

She struggled against the roots again, but her energy was draining faster than she could compensate. Her healing ability protected her from the sun's scalding heat, but with the life growing inside of her, healing Renato, and using a mixture of her other abilities, she had nothing left.

***

Arwan

Every breath sent a sharp stab to his lungs. Life continued to drain from his neck. He was fading…

Arwan lay on the ground, watching Zanya just feet away. He managed to reach out to her, streaking blood over the dusty soil. All he wanted was to hold her in his last moments.

The king crouched beside him and examined the wound on Arwan's neck, then let out a low huff. "You do not have much time left."

Arwan never took his gaze off Zanya. Regret drilled into his bones. The child she carried would never know him, and he would never spend another night with Zanya, with his arms draped over her body under satin sheets.

"Boy." The king slapped his cheek. "Look at your father."

When Arwan refused, the king grabbed his chin and turned his head.

"There is no one more inclined to save you than I. All I want—all I have ever wanted—is my heir to return to his rightful place beside me." He leaned in closer. "Do this, and I will not only spare your life, but I will withdraw my attack on the middleworld."

His fingers were cold as ice. Arwan coughed, then swallowed down the metallic taste coating his tongue.

"It is the one gift I can give before you part ways with the fragile humans you have grown so close to."

"If I refuse?" Arwan whispered—though barely.

"You will not leave my realm with your life."

Arwan swallowed a mouthful of his own blood, and then gagged.

"If he stays, you'll let him live?" Zanya said. "You'll save him?"

The hellhound barked, making her flinch.

The king raised his hand, sending the beast into submission. "Yes, he will live to one day take my throne."

"Then take him," Zanya said. "Save him, and let the rest of us go back to the middleworld."

The king stood and turned to examine the others.

"*Arwan.*" The pain in Renato's eyes was frightening. "Fight. You must fight to stay alive." Renato choked on his words, and a tear slipped down his cheek. "I know you have light in you. I've known since you were a boy. I saw it in your eyes."

The king tilted his head. "You care for the boy."

Arwan grabbed the king's ankle. "Leave him alone." He coughed a hot fountain of blood that dribbled down his cheek.

Zanya strained to reach Arwan. Her fingertips barely touched his. Shadows crawled into the edges of his vision and his heartbeat thudded in his ears, slowing with each passing breath.

A sob trickled from Zanya's chest. "He's fading." Her voice was muffled in his ears.

The king grabbed him by the shirt and yanked him off the ground, sending a streak of pain through his body that jolted him awake.

"Make your choice," the king demanded.

"He can't," Zanya said. "I won't make him choose." She curled her fingers around Arwan's as tightly as she could. Her touch was so warm compared to his. "He'll stay. Let him stay. Let him live."

"He's nearly dead," Renato shouted. "Help him, for god's sake, help him!"

The king looked back at Arwan. "You must choose yourself. Say so, and I will return your comrades and leave the middleworld in peace."

Arwan blinked slowly, with little energy left to speak. He squeezed Zanya's hand tighter. He'd never see her again. He'd never have the chance to hold their child, or hike through the jungle he'd come to love so much. He would never breathe the fresh air of Belize, or walk along the beach outside Renato's home.

But Arwan knew the king enough to know the

truth.

If he did not stay, the king would kill them all, and there would be no one left.

Arwan parted his lips and struggled to push out his consent. "I agree."

The king waved his hand, and the tree snatched them all from the ground, pulling them to safety.

Everyone but Renato, who was left behind, still trapped in the roots.

Zanya's scream faded into the distance. Arwan looked at Renato.

"You said everyone," Arwan whispered, fighting to stay conscious. "You said you would save them all."

"Yes, but you are beyond hope." The king pulled a knife from his sheath. "A life for a life. That is the cost."

CHAPTER TWENTY-NINE

Zanya

The tree regurgitated Zanya onto the ground and quickly withdrew, filling the passage that led back to the underworld.

Zanya lay on the ground, leaves scattered under her body and a cool breeze drifting over her skin. Her heart ached so deeply, she'd never recover.

Zanya grabbed a handful of soil and crushed it in her fist while grinding her teeth.

He was gone, and he was never coming back.

"Zanya." Jayden's voice was tender, almost as much as his touch. He laid his hands on her arm. "Are you okay?"

"Where's Renato?" her mother said.

Zanya closed her eyes tightly and curled into a ball. It was as if a hole had been punched through her chest. A massive, gaping wound that tore out her heart and scorched it to ash.

"Where is he?"

Zanya forced her eyes open and scanned the

area. "He…" She swallowed against an aching throat. "He's not here?"

"No, he's not here!" Her mother circled the passage in the ground. "They blocked our way back." She stopped. "Will it bring him like it did us?"

"I…" Zanya stared at the tree, its roots coiled tightly like a barrier, "don't know."

"Where is he? When is the tree bringing him?" Her voice turned fanatic. She looked at Zanya and buried her fingers in her hair. "Where is he, Zanya?" Her screams made the nearby birds flee from the trees.

Zanya's heart pounded and her fingertips went numb. She'd just lost the one man in her life she would ever bond with, and now her uncle was missing. It was all too much.

Zanya pulled her legs to her chest and wound her arms around them, burying her face between her knees. "I don't know. I don't know. I don't know." The repetitive whispers did little to calm her. Nothing could ease the pain of the tether in her soul being severed from Arwan forever.

There was a thud. Zanya picked up her head to see her mother dropped to her knees beside the roots. The bitter woman she had known since her return was now stripped down to that of a child, desperate for the sanctuary of her family.

Her mother shoved her fingertips between the vines. "We have to get him out. We have to get him out." She yanked and pulled at the tree, though it did no good.

Beigarth walked behind her, his eyes sad. He

watched her in silence for a moment, then reached out and set his hand on her back. "Ellie."

She slapped Beigarth's hand away. "Don't call me that! Only Renato calls me that."

The Viking stepped back, more pity flooding his gaze. "Aye," he said in a low voice. "Aye."

"Renato!" Her mother screamed at the blockade of roots. "Renato!" She looked at Beigarth. "Do something! Petrify it. You can do that, right?"

"Yeah, that's a good idea," Jay said. "We can break through rock. We can use explosives or something."

Beigarth shook his head. "If the tree is still holding to him, he will be petrified the same. It's too dangerous."

"But if it's not," her mother said, "it'll work, right?"

Beigarth frowned. "The tree is too large. It spans the realms. I can't do it alone."

"With Grima," Jayden suggested. "I mean…" He shifted his weight. "I know me and Renato didn't start off great, but he deserves for us to try."

"Even with me and Grima, lad, we aren't enough. It's not going to be enough."

Her mother looked at Zanya, tears building in her eyes. She didn't speak. She only stared with wide, empty eyes, as if part of her soul had left her, leaving her cold and terrified.

Zanya grimaced and stared down at her belly. If it weren't for this baby, she would have had enough power to escape the tree in the underworld. She could have reached Arwan and saved him from Contessa's attack. She could have saved them both.

"I hate you," she whispered to herself. To the unwanted baby inside her. To the gods who created such a damn mess to begin with.

She hated them all, and she'd never forgive herself.

Her mother stood, her hair carried in the breeze. "We should get back." There was a slight tremble in her voice. "Back to the others so we can tell them and prepare." She dragged herself past Jayden and Beigarth, her arms hanging limply at her sides.

Zanya watched her mother walk back toward the house. "Ready for what?"

Her mother stopped. "Renato is gone. We have a proper Mayan burial to prepare."

"Gone?" Jayden stepped forward. "But we don't know that. Not yet. Not for sure."

"Listen to me." Her mother lifted her index finger, her hand trembling. "When you've been on this quest as long as I have, you learn along the way. One, your life really is at risk, and that becomes inherently clear the first time you watch someone you love die in front of you, and there's nothing you can do about it. Two, you can't spend any time hoping to get them back. Hope is the most dangerous emotion to cling to because it'll slow you down." More tears shined in her eyes. "He is *gone*—in that damned realm with the king, and that *monster* you all trusted so much." She quickly wiped a tear from her face. "Renato wouldn't want us standing around here like a herd of lost cattle waiting for slaughter. He'd want us to lay him to rest and move on."

Beigarth walked to her mother's side. "Aye. I

say we get back to the others before someone else gets hurt."

Jayden watched Zanya, maybe waiting for her response. "I…" Zanya whimpered. "I guess that's our only choice."

Jayden spit on the roots and pursed his lips into a snarl before walking back toward the house without saying a word.

Zanya lingered behind, watching as the tree constricted and then eased, as if it were breathing.

It had to be by the king's order they were blocking the entrance, and if that were the case, no amount of brute force would tear through them. The tree would have more reinforcements waiting, even if Beigarth petrified the top layers.

She turned toward the others, who stood quietly, waiting to go home.

Zanya felt sick as the word passed through her lips. "Home."

Where was that without Renato or Arwan? Her home was with the man she had bonded with. The men she loved. If they were both torn from her life, what more did she have to live for?

"Don't." Her mother's sharp tone tore her out of her thoughts. "Don't think like that."

Zanya knitted her eyebrows. "What do you—?"

"You don't think I've seen that look before? Mostly in the mirror. I have, and I know how it can consume you. Don't let your mind go there. Not now. Not ever. Do you understand?"

Zanya nodded.

Her mother's features softened and she stretched out her hand. "Come on. Let's go."

Zanya walked toward her mother, who still had some minor burns over her arms and face. Peter would heal her when they got back.

Her mother grabbed Zanya and hugged her against her side. "You did good."

"I tried." Zanya pushed down tears. "I really did."

"I know." She combed her fingers through Zanya's hair, which was strangely soothing. "If I knew everyone wasn't getting out, I never would have agreed to leave."

"You didn't have a choice. He knew exactly what was going on, and he chose to let it happen."

"He was half-dead."

"That's exactly why he did it, Zanya. You saw the change in him—the complete darkness in his eyes."

"He came back."

"Maybe, but for how long? The evil overtook him and he couldn't control it. If you can't admit that, you're blinding yourself from the truth." She sighed. "After you told us about the baby, I hoped he could be different—for your sake. But a rock is a rock. A tree is a tree. They can't be anything different than what they are, and he can't choose to be something he isn't, no matter how much you wish he could."

Zanya draped her hand over her belly. It was true. When they found him in the underworld, the Arwan she knew was gone. His eyes were empty. It was as if an unknown shadow had consumed his soul.

She curled her fingers around her shirt.

What would this baby be like?

Would it be human, or something…else…?

A powerful explosion erupted, and Zanya crouched as the land below their feet trembled. "What was that?"

Another blow rammed into the layers of soil. The roots guarding the underworld bulged, some of them snapping in half. One whipped into the air and flailed for a moment before falling limp to the ground.

"The king," Beigarth said.

"No." Zanya extended her hands, hoping her gesture would keep any of them from running toward the passage. "The tree would open for him."

Another explosion, this time so close the vibration hummed right under her feet. "Get back," Zanya said. "Get back!"

Vines from the tree trembled and morphed to a dusky brown.

Another blow snapped several of the vines. One vine whipped the ground beside them, tearing a hole in the dirt.

Deep scratches tore at the vines—visible from where they stood.

"We have to get out of here," Jayden said.

"Aye. Go!"

The group turned and ran, but Zanya couldn't move. Her feet were locked in place, her gaze focused on the vines as they strained to keep in whatever was working to escape.

The clawing grew louder, slicing at her eardrums like a metal rake over rocks.

Her mother grabbed her arm. "Zanya, now!"

Zanya jerked her arm out of her mother's grasp, not saying a word.

"If ye don't come on yer own, I'll carry ye over my shoulder!"

Zanya extended her hand. "Just...wait." She couldn't explain it, but a flicker of familiarity rushed through her. Like the magic that bonded them was coming back to life.

The scratching stopped.

Silence filled the air.

The only sounds were that of her own pounding heart, and the rapid breaths of the others behind her.

Zanya tilted her head, watching the vines change from dusky brown to mottled gray, as if they were dying.

The ground trembled, carrying small sticks and rocks over the soil. The vines cracked, and a massive, dark shadow exploded from the underworld.

Zanya shielded her eyes, and her mother seized her arm.

Arwan, now in the form of the beast, scraped and scratched his way through the remaining vines, tearing them to shreds with his massive claws. He thrashed his head, snapping at Yaxche with a feral look in his eyes.

Once he'd broken his way through, he pulled himself onto the middleworld and scrambled to gain his footing, then circled the entrance, growling as he waited...

For what, there was no way to be sure.

Arwan couldn't speak to her in this form. She just had to trust he knew who he was—who she was—and wouldn't hurt them.

When nothing followed him through the portal, Arwan tilted his massive head to focus on Zanya and the others.

Still panting, Arwan shook out his fur, and then let out a massive roar.

His jaws gaped, displaying prehistoric canines and a bright pink tongue with fleshy curved spikes like a lion.

His roar was not an ordinary sound. Even as a beast, Zanya sensed it was full of pain and fury. It was a scream. That of loss. Of sorrow.

"He's gone," Zarya said softly. "Renato is without a doubt *gone*."

When there was no response, Zanya turned to see her mother standing between Jayden and Beigarth, her face drained of color.

CHAPTER THIRTY

Zanya

"Get away from it," her mother screamed. She yanked Zanya back several steps.

"It's okay. Don't be scared."

Beigarth stomped forward, a small ax clutched in his hand. "I'll do away with the beast."

Zanya braced her hand on his chest. "No."

"We need to get out of here," Jayden shouted from behind. "It's not attacking. Maybe we can—"

"Stop calling him *it!*" Zanya shifted her feet over the damp earth, her focus on Arwan. He was massive, with onyx fur and a gold tuft on his chest. But she still saw him—the glint of humanity in his eyes proved he was still in there.

"Him?" her mother said in a near whisper. Her brow rose while her gaze darted between them. "Him, as in, *him*—him?"

"Yes, but something's wrong."

"No shit, something's wrong!" Her mother's face flushed with color. "That," she jabbed her finger at

246

Arwan, "is the father of my grandchild! That is definitely wrong!"

"Shut up!" Zanya clenched her jaw. "Don't you ever know when to just…*shut up*?"

"Jesus, Mary, and Joseph," Beigarth murmured. "What on the god-lovin' green earth is that?"

Zanya looked back to Arwan, her attention split between him and a lighted figure walking toward them—Cualli.

With every stride, newly sprouted grass sprang from the earth, hosting an array of wildflowers in a rainbow of colors.

Her mother stepped to Zanya's side. "What is she doing?"

Zanya smiled. "She's greeting him."

Cualli walked to the entrance of the underworld and sprinkled a handful of soil into the gaping hole, then blew the remaining bits from her palm. A cluster of trees and bushes bloomed and sealed the hole, making it as if it were never there.

She turned to Arwan and gave a slight bow. "Welcome, half-breed." This time the term didn't sound so terrible. In fact, it carried an air of prestige in the goddess's tone. "I welcome you to my realm."

Arwan stopped pacing and watched the goddess.

His breathing calmed, and his fur lay flat and smooth.

He bowed his head.

"I don't believe me own eyes," Beigarth said.

"That is bad-*ass*," Jayden whispered.

"I don't understand." Her mother shifted forward, as if investigating the situation. "Why are

247

you welcoming him?" She spoke to the goddess as if they were good friends. Her mother was probably in shock. It was the first time she'd seem him in his beastly form.

Cualli glided toward Arwan and settled her hand on his head. Her delicate fingers sank into his fur. "Forgive them," she said in a gentle tone. "They know not who you are."

Arwan tilted his head and inspected the goddess.

"You must find it within yourself to return to us. Find it within yourself to return to *her*." She looked back at Zanya.

Arwan bared his teeth and gaped his jaw—this time in more of a yawn. He shook his body like a wet wolf, then lay down and curled into a ball on the ground.

He let out a high-pitched whine when the change began.

There was a thud after Beigarth's ax slipped out of his grasp.

By now, Arwan was already half-morphed. His muscles convulsed. Paws leaned out into fleshy fingers, his fur retracting into smooth, mocha skin.

His snout crumpled down, bones snapping and joints popping into place. When his beautiful face finally shone from beneath layers of teeth and fur, he was back.

Cualli removed the feathered garment covering her body. The goddess's hair hung down her back, shrouding her nude curves. She covered Arwan and ran her fingers through his hair. "Wake."

Zanya walked to Cualli's side and looked down at the feather garment, shimmering in the moonlight. She thought standing beside a nude goddess would be awkward, but it wasn't so much. It was like standing beside a live form of The Birth of Venus—a truly timeless piece of art.

"Perhaps he is in need of a familiar voice," Cualli said, gesturing to Arwan. "Speak to him. Bring him back."

Zanya crouched beside him and cupped her hands on either side of his face. She hovered her lips beside his ear before speaking softly. "Come back to me."

Arwan twitched and gasped. His eyes flew open and he grabbed hold of Zanya's throat, his fingers clamped around her airway.

"Hey!" Her mother's footsteps grew louder until she was beside them. She snatched a stick from the ground and struck him once, twice…but Arwan didn't seem to feel the blows. "Let her go!"

Jayden and Beigarth were there within seconds. The stout Viking clenched Arwan's arm and strained to loosen his grasp, but even his efforts were in vain.

Zanya searched his face, but the man she knew was not there.

She grabbed hold of his forearm, her lungs burning for air. She raised her other hand and sparked electricity between her fingers.

Cualli covered Zanya's hand with hers, extinguishing the pulse of energy. She leaned down and placed a kiss on Arwan's forehead. When she pulled away, his grip softened, and Zanya was able to pull in a breath. She slipped out of his hold and touched her throat, staring at Arwan as his eyes fluttered shut and his cheek fell against the cool earth.

In mere moments, he was asleep.

***

Arwan

The long, curved blade gleamed under hell's sun. Arwan lay on the ground, gulping in breaths like a landed fish. Life was slipping from his body and spilling onto the burned soil.

His heartbeat thumped in his ears.

Slower…slower…

The King of the Underworld vanished from sight, too far for him to follow. His vision blurred. His lips turned cold, even in the scorching realm.

"Be still," the king ordered from the distance.

Arwan fought to open his eyes. When he did, the sun nearly blinded him. A distant shadow was all he could see, cast by a large, looming figure—that of his father.

"I have fulfilled my destiny," said a familiar voice. A voice that had educated him, comforted him, and scolded him, sometimes all at once.

"Your sacrifice will allow him to live," the king said.

There was a short pause. "I will not plead for my life, nor will I fight you."

Arwan dragged his arms closer to his body and tried to push himself up, but had no strength to spare.

Fatigue wrapped around him like a warm

blanket.

He could close his eyes and sleep so easily...

"You would give your life for the boy?" the king said.

No, Renato. You can't—

"I would. He is my son."

"There is only room for one father. He is my right by blood."

Arwan's fingers and toes tingled. Darkness took over his vision.

"Perhaps," Renato said in a steady voice, "but he is my right by heart."

After a moment of silence, blood spattered over the ground and a stream of blood flowed toward him.

Arwan bolted into a sitting position, his stomach slithering with nausea. He touched his mouth and ran his fingers over the tip of his tongue. It took everything he had not to vomit the remnants in his stomach, fearful of what he might find.

"Hey, there."

He jumped and looked to the far side of the room.

Zanya leaned against the doorway with a mug of tea cupped in her hands. "How are you feeling?" She walked inside and set the tea on the bedside table, then sat beside him. She lifted her hand to touch his forehead.

He caught her wrist. "Don't."

"Don't, what?"

"Don't touch me." He slowly released his grip.

She propped her hands in her lap and twirled a

string pulled from the seam of her sleeve. She pinched her bottom lip in her teeth, probably wondering what had happened in the underworld. She had the right to know, but he couldn't say it aloud.

"I shouldn't be here." Those were the words he managed to push out. The only thing he could say to her after everything that had happened.

"Then why did you come back?"

He closed his eyes, unable to block the memory. "I had no choice."

"Everyone has a choice."

Those were the same words Renato echoed his entire life. *"You always have a choice."*

As a boy, he believed it. Then, when his dark side grew stronger, hope slipped away. Now there was none to be found.

A metallic flood pooled under his tongue. He curled his top lip. "The king wanted me to stay. I left against his will."

"You mean your father."

"*No.*" Arwan swallowed, his throat still raw and sore from the ordeal. "Renato was my father." A spike of bile crawled up his throat. He pushed it down and drew in a shaky breath.

Zanya pressed her fingers over her quivering lips. A tear slipped down her cheek. She squeezed her eyes shut, clearly trapping in a sob.

Losing Renato had all but punched a hole in his chest. But Arwan had been so entangled in his own grief that he didn't recognize—until now—how deeply hers ran.

She wiped away a tear and composed herself.

"Then he's really gone."

Arwan nodded. "If it weren't for me, he would still be here."

"You know that's not true."

It was true. As much as neither of them wanted to believe it, Renato would still be alive if Arwan had died at his father's feet.

"Did he suffer? Was it fast, at least?"

Arwan turned his face away from her. If she only knew what the king had forced him to do, while he was half-dead, lying on the ground like a cooling corpse.

He fisted his hand and pressed it against his mouth, fighting the urge to gag. He could still feel the warmth of Renato's blood sliding down his throat, and the salty coating it left over his tongue.

He would never tell her.

He would tell no one.

Hobbled footsteps grew louder until *Tia* Drina's stout form lingered in the doorway. Her small brown eyes and wrinkled skin crinkled with a smile. "I am glad to see you have returned to us, you foolish boy." But the smile lasted only a moment, and a blanket of silence covered the room once again.

Drina hobbled through the room and reached with her crooked fingers to touch his face. Arwan pulled away, but Drina pressed her palm to his forehead anyway. The old woman's features softened and she nodded. "Good. No fever."

He examined her empty hands. "No stick this time?"

She offered a crooked smirk. "Not t'is time." She

reached in her pouch and pulled out a handful of crumpled herbs. "Keep t'is close. It will help you sleep." She piled the offering beside the mug of tea Zanya had brought in. "And t'is." She held up the wooden mask from his old bedroom. "It will do as your mot'er promised. It will keep t'e nightmares away."

He stared into the wooden carving, as if it would speak to him. As if it would tell him all of this was a bad dream, and now it would all go away.

But as he watched the mask, it said nothing.

Deep in his soul he knew, not even his mother's magic would help him forget.

Drina handed the mask to Zanya with a nod. "Now I must go with Eleuia, Cualli, and Balam. We have much preparation to do."

Arwan lifted his head. "For what?"

"We must prepare to guide Renato's soul to his next life. T'ere is no body to rest in a tomb. We will gat'er offerings, and send him wit' *maíz*, jade, and fire." Drina left the room, closing the door behind her.

Zanya set her hand over the blanket covering his legs. "I'll help them with whatever they need." She stood and hung the mask on an old, crooked nail sticking out of the wall. "There." She stepped back and gave a half-smile. "Now try to get some more sleep."

"I should be involved."

"You will be, but if you're not rested, you'll barely be able to stand during the ceremony. You're lucky you made it back at all. Don't push it."

CHAPTER THIRTY-ONE

Arwan

Arwan coughed, nearly drowning on the dose of hot, metallic liquid. His mind hazed over, his senses confused and weak. The sun continued to pour down, blinding him every time he opened his eyes. He pulled in a breath and rolled onto his side, his entire body trembling. "What did you do to me?"

"I spared your life." The king grabbed Arwan's face with one hand and squeezed his cheeks, forcing his lips to part. More warm liquid filled his mouth and leaked down his throat.

Arwan heaved and pushed the king away. "What is that?"

"Drink." The king grabbed him again, but this time his hold was more powerful. Arwan tried to escape, but there was no strength left to fight. "Drink until your belly is full with life." Arwan's eyes rolled in the back of his head. He did as he was told, taking one deep gulp after another until the bowl that was pressed to his lips was empty.

"Good." The king moved away, his shadow providing relief from the unrelenting sun. "You will heal. You will live."

Arwan rolled onto his belly. Liquid sloshed in his gut. He wiped his mouth with the back of his hand, streaks of red painted his knuckles. "What is this?" The ache in his back where Contessa had torn into his flesh began to ease. "What did you give me?" The veins, cartilage, and skin on his neck burned as they knitted together. Strength returned to his muscles. Arwan pushed onto all fours, staring at the puddle of blood spilled on the ground. Arwan ground his teeth. "What have you done?"

"A life for a life. That is the cost."

Arwan narrowed his eyes, still trying to collect his thoughts. He turned his head, his gaze landing on a pile of half-eaten organs on the ground. He scaled up Contessa's body that was propped upright by the tree in a morbid display of death. Roots wound in and out of every orifice, still squirming as they fed.

Arwan blinked and shook his head, casting the sight out of his mind.

The beast inside him woke, providing the energy he needed to stand. He swayed on his feet and shielded his eyes, peering at the underworld realm. For a moment he had forgotten where he was.

"Welcome back from the dead, my son." The king stood beside the limp body of a man wrapped in roots.

A man in a pressed suit, with thick, black hair. Displaced strands hung in his face.

Arwan's chest restricted. "Renato?" Arwan

stumbled toward him. "What did you do?" He braced his hands on Renato's shoulders, then tilted up his mentor's head to find his pale, dusky complexion, and a gaping wound in his throat.

"It was a small sacrifice for the greater good."

"No." Arwan's stomach clenched and his head spun, blurring the world around him.

"Now you will take your rightful place, my son, as the prince of this realm."

"We had an agreement." Arwan balled his fists, his body shaking. "You broke it."

For his entire life he had chained his beast deep inside him, never allowing it to see the light of day. But with Renato lying limp in front of him, there was nothing left to hold him back.

Arwan dropped to his knees and raised his face to hell's sky, then let out a massive scream. The beast tore through him in an instant. His entire body seemed to ignite as the monster took over, tearing cartilage and bending bone into odd, ungodly shapes.

When it was over, Arwan faced the king and bared his teeth.

"Do you believe you will kill me?" The king stood his ground. "Take my realm prematurely, perhaps?" He withdrew a blade from its sheath attached to his belt—likely the same blade used to slash Renato's throat. The king's eyes flashed red.

Arwan leapt forward and swiped the blade out of his hand, tearing deep wounds in the king's arm. The knife clattered to the ground and skidded over the soil until it hit the base of a rock.

The wound on the king's hand healed

immediately. "You are confused. Mourning. These are mortal emotions you have adopted. You must release them. Release these humanistic weaknesses, and you will be set free."

Arwan gasped and sat up in bed, clutching the blankets. Sweat drizzled down the back of his neck, his body coursing with so much heat he could barely breathe. It was as if the sun of the underworld never left him, even after he woke from his dream.

He threw off the covers, walked into the bathroom, and flipped on the shower. Standing under some cool water could help calm his nerves. When he was finished, he slipped on some clothes and combed his hair back with his fingers.

Zanya cracked open the door and walked into the bedroom, her eyes red—likely from crying. "I wasn't sure if you'd be up." Her voice was cracked and hollow. "Drina sent me to wake you and tell you to get ready."

"For what?"

Zanya's bottom lip trembled. "Renato's funeral."

He paused, and then sat on the bed. "So fast?"

"Drina said it's tonight at sunset. She says it's a sign of disrespect to wait, even with no body." She pursed her lips as if a bitter taste were on her tongue. "Anyway…" She cleared her throat and walked to the dresser, where she pulled open several drawers and rummaged through them. She threw a handful of clothes back in the pile and exhaled. "I don't have anything nice to wear. No little black dress." She turned toward him and crossed her arms. "I can't do much about that, but I'm sure I could find some flowers. Maybe some of the blue ones from out back." Her tone built in intensity with each passing word. "Or maybe Cualli could grow us some. Maybe some red ones..." A tear streaked down her cheek. "Or maybe orange..." She pressed her hand over her mouth. A sob broke through the cracks of her fingers.

Arwan walked to her and wrapped his arms around her. "Shhh." He carefully propped his chin on top of her head and cradled her against his chest. "Just breathe. It's going to be okay. We're going to be okay."

"No." She hugged him and twisted her fingers around his shirt. "None of us is ever going to be okay again."

Arwan clenched his jaw. As much as he wanted to comfort her—tell her there was a reason Renato was taken from them too soon—even *he* didn't believe it. Renato was his one constant in his life before Zanya. The first person besides his mother he had trusted, and now he was gone.

"I'll make it right." He pulled her closer. "I'll make this right."

***

Zanya

They'd send his soul to rest with water for ease of transition, and fire to light the way.

Drina said normally they would make him a tomb and bury him with *maíz* in his mouth, pottery around him, and valuable kernels of jade scattered in the catacomb. But as there was no body to adorn in farewell gifts, they would send his spirit instead.

Cualli walked in front, holding a torch overhead. Her golden hair glowed under the flickering, warm light. Each of the goddess's steps sprouted beautiful wildflowers, leaving a carpet of colors for the burial procession.

Zanya walked beside her mother, Arwan, and Marzena, who had been Renato's long-time friend. It should have been Drina in her place, but the Mayan elder insisted. It was the seemingly young dreamwalker who had kept Renato company during his lonely years—after her mother had left and while he was raising Arwan on his own. Marzena was there, giving the fallen hero what no one else could—friendship.

They walked down a thin path toward the river while the evening sky prepared its display of orange and red, and the sort of bright rays only shown just before sundown.

Zanya balanced a clay tray in her hands, holding neat stacks of shucked corn—or *maíz*, as the Maya called it. From what Drina had told her, the *maíz* was the most valuable of the burial items.

Her mother carried strings of beaded jade around her neck.

Marzena marched with a mirror. The sun reflected from its surface, shooting flashes of light back into the sky as if they were communicating with the gods.

Arwan walked beside her with a basket in his arms. Tucked inside were pieces of marble, mushroom figures, and a sack of vermillion red dust made from ground cinnabar.

All of these items carried a heavy significance in a traditional Mayan burial.

Zanya glanced over at the rest of the group.

If Renato only knew how many people loved him...Perhaps he did. She had to believe he knew...

Zanya heard the roaring of the river before she could see it. The air became more humid. A chill rolled down her arms.

When the group broke out of the jungle thicket, they stood at the river bank. The water was clearly powerful, yet there were very few white rapids. It was a flowing vein of life through the jungle. Perhaps that was why the ancient Maya showed so much adoration for water. It gave life to the earth and everything on it.

Cualli stilled by the edge of the bank and continued to hold the torch overhead. As the rest of the group gathered, Zanya's gaze was pulled upstream. There was movement in the bushes—flashes of figures darting between trees.

Zanya glanced at Arwan. "Is someone else here?"

"I think so." He searched the tree line. "It looks like villagers."

"I thought they all left."

"Not all," her mother said. "Some of the men—probably those who were ill or injured—led the women and children to new lands before the battle reached their homes. The rest are here. They're here for him."

Drina hobbled through the group and stopped by

the edge of the river. The priestess raised her hands, as if greeting them. *"Kíimak 'oolal."*

Zanya had heard the Yucatec language enough to know that Drina was greeting the villagers.

As Drina continued to shout in the foreign language, the natives emerged from the tree line with leather straps over their shoulders and a pouch cradled against their bare chests.

All of them were men, wearing nothing but loincloths adorned in feathers or strips of fur. Smears of blue, white, and red ointment were streaked over their faces. Some had on headdresses. Others wore thick bracelets made of black stone and large rings through their noses and ears. Their chests were painted in elaborate patterns of black dots and colorful highlights.

When Drina finished speaking, she turned to the group and signaled for Zanya, her mother, Marzena, and Arwan to step forward.

The four of them did as they were told.

Drina looked to the sky. "T'e sun sets in t'e west. T'e time has come."

CHAPTER THIRTY-TWO

Zanya

Cualli's voice broke the silence. She hummed a tune—the same soft lullaby she had hummed before.

Zanya secured her grip on the offering tray. She didn't know anything about Mayan funeral traditions, but this seemed somehow...different. Special, like Renato.

The natives inched closer to the river while bouncing on the balls of their feet.

Cualli lowered the torch to the water and skimmed the flame over the rippling surface of the river.

The red and orange blaze danced over the water, and when she lifted it, a small flame was left behind, burning on top of the reflective surface.

Zanya peered at the fire as its colors changed into a deep green, and then flowered into a large, tropical lily. Blue and purple petals with a bright orange center—it was the loveliest flower Zanya

263

had ever seen. When she looked at it closer, the middle of the bloom wavered, as if the flame were alive inside.

Beneath the flower grew a large lily pad.

Drina gestured to the river. "Put t'e offering beside t'e flower, on t'e lily pads."

While Zanya balanced the tray in one hand, Arwan took her other hand and led her down the mud-slicked riverbank, into the water. It wasn't nearly as cold as she anticipated. In fact, the current was warm as it rushed around her ankles, then up her calves, and over her thighs until she was waist deep. She dug her feet into the riverbed, slick with pebbles and shoots.

She laid down the offering where she was told, unsure if the lily pad would hold the weight.

One by one the others followed with their offerings, until all of them were arranged around the flower.

Marzena was last. The tips of her golden hair dragged through the current as she touched each item and spoke. "*Maíz*, to give Renato sustenance for his journey to the heavens. Jade to pay his way through the realms, and statues of the great deities to aid Renato in finding…" The dreamwalker paused, tears glistening in her eyes. "To aid in finding his way through the spirit world. A mirror to deflect evil spirits." She picked up the sack of red dust and untied the grass knot, letting the burlap fall open in her palm. She took a handful of powder and blew it over the offering, coating it with a thin layer of vermillion. "And ground cinnabar, to symbolize death, and rebirth."

Marzena looked to the villagers who stood silently on the riverbank.

When Cualli waved the torch in the air, Marzena gestured to the flowing water. "Now go. Give the offering to the river."

Zanya looked to her mother, who smiled softly. "It's all right. You're the guardian now. He would want you to do it."

Arwan, her mother, and Marzena returned the shore. This shouldn't be happening. Renato should have been there, with them, where he belonged.

She gripped her chest as it constricted, unintentionally streaking red powder over her skin.

A single flower petal drifted past her, bobbing on top of the water. Then another—this one dark purple in color.

Zanya looked upriver at the blanket of colors swirling and drifting toward her. While Cualli's humming grew louder, the villagers reached into their leather sacks and pulled out handfuls of petals, casting them to the wind. The flame in the center of the lily flower grew brighter, sending a plume of heat into the air.

Zanya looked to the shore, where everyone stood with their arms interlocked.

Zanya hesitated to leave the offerings, but gave them one last moment of admiration before her stone buzzed from inside its pouch, mimicking her heartache.

"I'm sorry. I almost forgot." Zanya retrieved the stone and held it between her fingers, turning it in the sun. Inside was something peculiar—a flickering, blue light. It pulsed so quickly, not indicative of its normal swirling patterns. It must have been a sign it was mourning like the rest of them. They had all lost something when Renato died. "I'm going to miss him too." The stone gave a dull flash of light, which she felt throughout her body. "Yeah, it's time to say goodbye."

It glowed from its core with hues of bright blue, white, and green, all spiraling around each other in a whirlwind of color.

The flame inside of the lily burned hotter and larger, growing into a small torch.

Zanya stepped back, making sure not to drop her stone into the river. Just as her mother had said when she first bonded with it:

Once you bond with the stone...it will feel your pain, and you will feel its pain. When you are sorrowful, it will show compassion. When you are joyful, it will celebrate your happiness. It becomes a part of you, since you are, in fact, a part of it.

And now, as always, her stone sensed she was heartbroken.

With a rainbow of colors covering the river, the lily flower closed and extinguished the fire. The flower's bright colors dimmed until it wilted. The edges of the lily pad buckled and swallowed the offering, pulling it underwater with a low gurgle and a burst of bubbles.

The water flashed aqua blue with a burst of light, and it was over.

Zanya turned back to her friends and family. Tara sobbed into Peter's chest, while Hawa stood with her arm still interlocked with Jayden's.

Her mother lingered with her arms wrapped around her torso, staring helplessly into the water, as if some part of her were missing.

When Cualli's humming faded, the only sound was the distant wind dancing through the trees.

Zanya waded through the water back to shore, skimming her fingers over the cool current as the remaining flower petals vanished into the distance.

Arwan held out his hand. She took it, and he pulled her onto dry land, into his arms. He placed a kiss on her forehead. "I don't know what we're going to do now that he's gone."

"We must prepare for what is to come," Marzena said. "This was only the beginning."

"Do you think we stand a chance?" Jayden asked.

"Aye." Grima nodded. "We will, if we stick together."

Ahmed and Yousef stayed in the back of the group—Ahmed with his small, white hat crinkled in his hands, and Yousef silently counting prayers out on a string of beads.

Hawa drew in a deep breath, watching the river carry away what was left of the petals. "With him gone, everything seems kind of hopeless."

"Nothing is hopeless," Marzena said. "I will not allow Renato's life to have been taken in vain."

"We will rest tonight," Drina said. "We will rest, and start again wit' t'e new day."

CHAPTER THIRTY-THREE

Zanya

That night, Zanya lay in bed with her eyes wide open, staring into the distance while she listened to Arwan's uneven breaths.

The room was dark except the glow of her stone. It sat on her nightstand, mimicking the luminance of a firefly, but with a tiny blue light flickering in its center.

Arwan groaned and kicked at the sheets, then rolled onto his side, facing away from her.

Since returning from the underworld, he hadn't slept without having a nightmare. So much for the mask. It was supposed to keep away bad dreams, but so far had done a pretty shitty job.

While Arwan drifted to sleep, she was forced to sit beside him and watch as he grabbed handfuls of blanket while he contorted in pain. Maybe not physical…The pain came from somewhere else.

Arwan rolled onto his back again, sweat dotting his forehead.

She picked up her stone and held it close, rolling it between her fingers and watching the flickering light. "What are you?"

Her stone hummed quietly, sending vibrations of comfort and warmth down her arm.

"You've changed."

The tiny pulse in its center flickered brighter and faster.

Arwan's breathing suddenly slowed. Zanya turned her head and looked into his face.

He was awake now—his eyes wide open and his throat tight. His arms were still flexed from the mental onslaught. That wouldn't wear off for a while. She knew from experience.

Zanya exhaled, the room otherwise silent. "Are you okay?"

He didn't respond.

He never did tell her what had happened in the underworld—how Renato died, and what his father, the king, had said or done after she was pulled back to the middleworld by Yaxche.

He hadn't told her, and she wouldn't dare ask.

The answer might be more than she could bear.

She returned to admiring her stone. "What do you think it is?"

He sat up and threw his legs over the side of the bed, giving her his back. His shoulders rose and fell with each breath. His head hung low.

"It's flashing so fast," she continued, hoping to tear his attention off of the images reeling through his mind. She knew all too well how difficult it was to shake the aftermath of a nightmare—especially when they weren't just dreams, but memories. "My stone hasn't told me what it is. I can feel when it's afraid or happy. Right now it just seems…warm."

There was a long moment of silence.

"Warm?" His voice was raspy, but at least he was talking. He smoothed his hair down and faced her.

"Yeah. Literally." She held the stone out to him. "Touch it."

He watched its light waver and mix into clouds of light. "Will it let me?"

"I don't know. Why don't you ask?"

The creases in his brow softened and he gazed at the stone. "May I?"

It flashed with a soft glow.

Arwan carefully pressed his fingertips over its smooth surface. Sparks of electricity popped between them on contact, as if it were a plasma sphere.

Arwan pulled back. "Do you know why it's flashing?"

Zanya shook her head. "I guess maybe it's trying to tell me something, but I haven't figured it out yet."

He leaned down and pressed a kiss onto her bare shoulder, and then slipped his hand under the seam of her shirt, hovering over her belly. "How do you feel?"

Talking about the baby still made her wildly uncomfortable. It was like she was a knocked up teenager every soccer mom gossiped about, and she'd do just about anything to hide her dirty little secret until she figured out what she was going to do with it.

She looked away from him.

Do with it—what a shitty thing to think about her own baby.

She was more screwed up than she thought.

"It's okay if you're scared." His voice brought her back. "I think that's normal."

"What do *you* know?"

He stopped tracing circles around her bellybutton and laid his hand flat over her stomach. "I don't know anything except…" He watched his hand, as if he could see the tiny life inside her.

"Except what?"

"Except this baby is us." He looked into her eyes. "I never thought about having a family. It was out of the question, so I pushed it out of my mind. Even after I met you…I knew it would go all wrong, but you kept pulling me in."

"If I remember right, you were the one pulling *me* in."

He smirked. "Maybe we needed each other more than either of us knew. Maybe this baby was meant to happen." He spread his fingers over her skin. "I can feel it." He looked up at her stone. "Now, thanks to your stone, so can you."

Zanya's mouth went dry, and she examined the tiny, flickering light. "You mean…"

"The heartbeat matches. They are the same, just like you and the stone are the same."

"Like me and our baby are the same," she whispered.

A strange flood of emotion gripped her heart. Just like when she bonded with the stone and was taken by a fierce protectiveness, the same instinct seized her now. She rested her other hand over his, over her belly, and wove her fingers between his. "I could have hurt her by going to the underworld."

"Her?"

"All Stone Guardians are women. It has to be a girl, or I'd have no one to pass the stone to."

He gave a brilliant smile. "I forgot." His face flushed with color. "A girl."

A new worry washed over her. One she barely had time to consider past her own distress. "Are you happy? I mean, are you okay with this?"

He chuckled. "I wasn't exactly expecting this to happen—ever, let alone right now. But—"

"Please don't feed me some cliché line like *it's a blessing*, or *everything happens for a reason*. I'll slap you."

He laughed again. "I was going to say, I'm happy because it's you. If this were happening with anyone else, I don't think I'd be. But with you..." He kissed her belly. "I'll be here every step of the way, whatever you need, forever."

***

Arwan

The next morning, Arwan was first to get out of bed. The sun was barely rising, but they had work to do, and there was no telling how long the king would wait before he brought his minions into the middleworld for the fight of their lives.

After getting dressed, he left Zanya to sleep, and walked through the house. The door to the spare bedroom where Drina slept hung open, with the patterned blue and red quilt folded at the foot of the bed.

When he continued into the living room, Balam lay in the corner, in his usual spot. Arwan's presence woke the jaguar deity, who yawned, letting his tongue curl out of his mouth with massive canine teeth on display. His snout crinkled and Balam licked his paw, then blinked lazily at Arwan.

"Good morning." He took a quick account of what they had left in the kitchen—a few fruits and vegetables, but no meat. Arwan gathered the rations on the countertop and crossed his arms, taking a mental headcount of the people camped outside. "We have a lot of mouths to feed. I think you'll have to step up your hunting if we want to keep everyone from starving."

Balam let out a low, lazy growl and plopped his head back onto the floor.

"We're counting on you." Arwan waited for the deity to budge, but he didn't. "Zanya will need her strength now that she's eating for two."

Balam's ear twitched, and he blew a huff through his nostrils. He pushed to all fours and dragged one large paw after the other toward the front door.

Arwan hurried to open it. "Thank you, Balam. Your hunts are keeping us all strong enough to fight."

The cat's tail flicked as he sauntered out, vanishing around the corner.

"I think he's warming up to you."

Arwan turned to Zanya, who stood in the hall

with her back against the wall and her arms wound around her body, as if she were cold. A sheer robe hung open, layered over a tank top and pair of shorts.

"At least he's not growling at me anymore."

Zanya tucked strands of wild hair behind her ear—a gesture that drove him crazy. Her hair was tousled and her robe wrinkled, but she was the single most beautiful thing he'd ever laid eyes on.

"What are our plans for today?" she asked.

They both sensed the sudden tension in the air, though neither of them acknowledged it. The anticipation of an attack was worse than an attack itself. But maybe in this case that wasn't completely true, considering *this* war might end the middleworld as they knew it.

"The king will only wait so long for me to return."

"Why do you think he's waiting?"

He frowned. "I've been dreaming...having visions, maybe. I see his eyes." His stomach tightened. "Just his eyes."

She walked toward him, her bare feet pressing silently over the stone floor. Bright rays from the rising sun beamed through the windows, casting a warm light over her skin.

She looked like an angel.

She settled her hands on his chest and pressed a kiss onto his lips.

In that moment he let himself forget about everything but her. He wrapped his arms around her pulled her closer, this time taking care to be gentle. She was different now—fragile, and it was his job to protect not just her, but their child she carried.

Zanya parted her lips and glided her tongue over his. His skin flushed when she pushed her fingers under his shirt and ran her hands over his stomach.

Heat flared inside him, spiking his blood with adrenaline. He pulled away enough to look into her eyes. "What are you doing to me?"

She pinched her bottom lip between her teeth and shrugged. "Enjoying the morning." She leaned back, creating space between them while displaying a shy smile. "I thought I had lost you. Seeing you this morning is like..." She stared up at him from behind a curtain of dark lashes. "It's like getting the best present in the world."

He gripped her by the waist and lifted her up onto the countertop.

There was something different about her today. He tilted his head while tuning in to her body, her breathing, her every movement. "You're...happy."

"Why wouldn't I be?" She wound her arms around his neck and pressed her forehead against his. "Besides the inevitable war and impending doom, life is good."

He chuckled and skated his hands up her legs. His fingers teased the inside of her thighs before he positioned his hands on her hips. "You're not a normal happy. It's more than that."

"Like you said." She planted her hand on her belly. "It's you and me. There's nothing more worthy of protecting. You and my stone helped me understand."

A sharp knock made Zanya jump.

Arwan tightened his jaw and looked toward the

noise. "Yes?"

"Um…Balam brought something…dead," Tara said from outside, her voice groggy with sleep.

"Thanks," Zanya shouted. "We'll take care of it."

"Good, cuz it's gross. I'm going back to sleep." Tara's mumbles grew fainter until they disappeared completely.

"I guess it's time for you to get to work so we can eat." She hopped off the counter. "While you're doing that, I'll go get dressed. Today we need to train."

"You can't train."

She paused. "What do you mean? I'm the one who needs it the most."

"But it's dangerous. Not just for you, but for the baby too."

Zanya's pressed her hand against cheek. "I know you're worried, but I have to do this." She flickered electricity over her skin, forcing him to step back or get shocked. "Don't forget what you told me when we first met." She rubbed her fingers together and conjured a fire in her hand. "I'm stronger than I think."

CHAPTER THIRTY-FOUR

Zanya

After Arwan left, she changed into the training gear her mother had brought from Renato's home.

She'd never been close with anyone who was pregnant, but she did study human anatomy and reproductive health in the orphanage, so pregnancy wasn't completely foreign.

She hadn't experienced any morning sickness yet—though that probably wouldn't come for a few weeks, at least. Her belly wasn't swollen at all, and wouldn't be for a good while—for a normal human child, at least. In this case, it was anyone's guess. She'd enjoy her figure while it lasted, and use her training gear as long as she could.

She tied her hair into a ponytail and secured her stone into its home on her wrist, then walked outside into the humid jungle air. Everyone was just waking up, and most of the tents were still zipped shut with their sleeping occupants inside.

It was the perfect opportunity to have a quiet,

private discussion with Grima—the other half of the two petrifiers.

The only problem was, besides Tara and Peter's, she didn't know whose tent was whose.

She crept through the quiet campsite, listening for any sounds that would tip her off. Each enclosure was large enough to accommodate two normal sized people, which meant both of the Viking petrifiers would have their own accommodations, seeing they were both larger than the average Riyata.

Snoring tipped her off on Beigarth's location. Grima wouldn't be far. Zanya tiptoed further until she heard loud breaths rising from a nearby tent. She paused beside it, listening to the low, hushed snores. It *had* to be Grima. But Zanya couldn't exactly knock on the tent door, and didn't want to call her name and wake the rest of the camp.

Thankfully, she had a skill that was silent and effective—dreamwalking.

Zanya closed her eyes and used her ability to find Grima and connect with her mind. It was clear she was in a deep slumber, as the bond between her and the lady Viking was clouded. She nudged Grima's mind to wake her, but the haze didn't clear.

Zanya withdrew from the mental intrusion and opened her eyes. The heavy breathing continued. Maybe she didn't snore as loudly, but she was just as heavy of a sleeper as Beigarth. Zanya was left with no choice but to go in and wake her in person.

She pinched the zipper of the tent door and slid it in a clockwise arch. A large bulge of writhing blankets stirred inside. Maybe she was finally waking up. "Grima."

The movement stopped.

"Grima, wake up." Zanya set her hand on what she assumed was a foot.

There was a gasp, and Hawa sat straight up, the blanket secured under her arms, covering her bare chest. Jayden popped up beside her. "What the hell," Hawa said. "A little privacy, please?"

Zanya bolted to her feet and stumbled back, tripping over the tent behind her. She flailed and nearly fell backward, but caught herself on a stone arch instead.

Jayden crawled out of the tent with a blanket wrapped around his waist. "Is everything okay?"

"No, everything is *not* okay," Zanya whispered harshly, now shielding her eyes from Jayden's half-nakedness. "Oh my god, get some clothes on!"

"I'm not the one who barged into a tent! I thought something happened!"

"I told you it was probably nothing," Hawa taunted from the tent. "Now get back here."

"Yes, please." Zanya waved him on. "Go back in there." She covered her face with both hands, heat filling her cheeks.

"I was just making sure," Jayden said.

"Yeah, well, now I'm cold," Hawa snapped back. "You let all the heat out."

"Mmm, I can warm you—"

"No." Zanya covered her ears. "Absolutely not." She turned away from them, determined not to hear another word of their sexy banter.

She wasn't upset Jayden had moved on—even though Hawa was a surprising choice—but at this

279

point, Jay was more like a brother than a boy she once loved, and the thought of him with some girl was just too much.

Her skin crawled, and she did a little cootie dance to shake it off.

"Are ye looking for me, lass?"

Zanya dropped her hands and stared down at Grima, who had poked out of the tent Zanya had tripped over. Zanya nodded, doing anything and everything to forget her horrifying encounter with the lovebirds. "I need to talk to you." She fanned her face with her hand, trying to ease the heat in her cheeks.

"I felt ye knock." Grima tapped her finger on her temple. She stood from her tent, her strawberry hair glistening in the soft morning sun. The others would be up soon, and Arwan would be ready to cook the meat he cleaned. Luckily, the slight disruption didn't wake anyone else, but she had better make this quick and not push her luck.

She waved Grima toward the tree line. "Can we take a walk?"

Grima slipped her feet in a pair of leather shoes and tied a leather belt over what looked like a cross between a vest and robe. "Aye."

Zanya walked toward the fruit trees, where Cualli had been keeping a plentiful stock for the group to eat freely. Not all of the fruits they had were native to Mexico, but it was a perk of having a flower and plant goddess as an ally.

"What can I do ye for?" Grima asked, her soft tone both curious and cautious.

"I wanted to ask you something." Zanya reached

up and plucked a ripe, red pomegranate from a branch. She pressed it to her nose, inhaling the sweet aroma. "Why is Beigarth so determined not to show me how to petrify? I may be the guardian, but if nobody teaches me how to use my abilities, I'll have to try on my own."

"That's not a keen idea, lass. Not in the least bit."

"But why?" she asked, though she knew exactly why. The ability was deadly. Not only that, but it was non-reversible, and it could turn on her if she lost even the smallest bit of control. But if she didn't push the subject, she'd never get answers. Sorry to say, a scare tactic was her last resort.

"Beigarth's heart is in the right place, dear. Ye have to trust that."

"I can't just pretend I'm not capable of petrifying. It's a valuable tool. I saw how Beigarth dealt with that hellhound in the underworld."

"Aye. And did ye see what happened to the beast? It turned to dust."

"Yeah, so?"

"Dear, when ye petrify a thing, yer taking away its soul. Ye turn it to stone. A dead, lifeless thing that's cold when it's cold outside, and hot when it's hot. There's not a grain of life left in it. Not ever again."

Zanya held up the fruit. "Can you show me? Just once, and I won't ask you again." She extended the ripe fruit. "Please."

Grima examined it a moment, then took it from Zanya's hand. "Lass..." Grima's eyes narrowed. "This is no ability to use without thought put into it first. Once ye learn how to use it, ye must control yer emotions and never let anger tear it out of ye. It can…" The corners of Grima's mouth turned down. "It will take something from ye if ye let it. It will take someone dear if ye can't control it." Grima lowered her gaze. "And it will tear yer heart out."

***

Arwan

He washed his hands clean of blood and bits of flesh from the white-tail deer Balam had caught for the camp. The edible organs were harvested and sat in a pail of water, while the deer hung upside down from a tree, its back legs spread to show a gaping, empty torso exposing its ribs.

He crinkled his nose from the smell of blood that overwhelmed his senses. But the deer would feed the group for a few days before Balam would have to hunt again.

The only task left was to section the animal and haul the meat back to the house. That was another task entirely. First he'd skin it. The fur would make for a good lining to a crib once the baby arrived. Meanwhile, it would keep Zanya warm at night.

He removed a knife crafted from bone—ideal for skinning animals. It kept from punching holes in the hide, unlike a steel knife that cut through anything it touched.

He had Renato to thank for teaching him how to process an animal. It was a survival skill he would use for the rest of his life, and hopefully pass down to his daughter when the time was right.

"I was sent to check on you."

Arwan ground his teeth and stood, the blade secure in his hand. Eleuia never found him alone unless she wanted to antagonize him. Whatever she had to say, it couldn't be good.

Without acknowledging she was there, he approached the deer and pulled aside a flap of skin, then nicked small, precise cuts in the white layer of tissue bonding the skin with muscle.

"Actually, I volunteered to come check on you and your project here."

He sensed her behind him, and kept a sharp ear out for any quick movements. Though she'd tolerated him up to this point, there was no telling what she had up her sleeve. If she did come here with ill intent, it wouldn't be the first time.

Arwan worked to skin it as quickly as possible. Hair stuck to his fingers as traces of blood began to dry.

He paused and pushed down a wave of nausea.

He'd never been disgusted by blood in the past. But after his last experience in the underworld, it made him think of only one thing.

"Listen…" Eleuia walked to his side, where he watched her in his peripheral vision. "I'm just trying to do what's best for my daughter."

He made circular incisions around the hooves of the animal, and then straight cuts up its legs toward the belly. "What's best for her is not making her stressed every time you're around her."

She said nothing in response.

"What do you want?" He made one last cut, and

then lifted the whole pelt off of the deer and laid it fur side down on the ground.

"We're going to be in each other's lives," Eleuia said. "That's impossible to avoid now that you got Zanya pregnant."

He paused and clenched his jaw. "You should try not to talk about your grandchild like she's some kind of infectious disease."

"She?" Eleuia shifted her weight. "Do you know it's a girl?"

He rolled the pelt and shoved it into a pack to clean when he got back to the house. "Zanya says it has to be a girl. You should know better than anyone." He stood and cut the animal down from where it hung, then began slicing into the meat. "You haven't told me why you're really here."

She crouched and balanced her forearms on her knees, her fingers laced in front of her. "Renato saw something in you. Cualli sees it too. But most importantly, Zanya sees it."

Arwan looked up at her.

"You're the father of that baby. As long as you take responsibility for that, and treat Zanya as she deserves…"

"She means more to me than my own life, and I would gladly lay it down to protect her. I have, and I will always put her and our family first. No matter what."

Eleuia held his gaze, and then nodded. "All right, then." She stood. "I guess that's all there is to talk about." She grabbed the sack of deer pelt and hauled it off the ground. "We're waiting for you back at camp. It's time to train."

"She shouldn't be training. I tried to tell her that, but she won't listen. Maybe you can talk some sense into her."

Eleuia snorted. "No one can talk sense into her. You should know that by now. Besides." She paused and looked back at him. "She's not training. You are."

CHAPTER THIRTY-FIVE

Zanya

"Please," Zanya said. "I know it's a risk, but…" Arwan would be done processing the deer soon. They were running out of time. "Everyone else is going to fight with their lives, and if I can't protect them, everyone will die. Including me—and my baby."

Grima's lip twitched.

"Please. I can't learn this ability without you. All of our lives depend on it."

Grima turned the pomegranate in her hand, staring at its red, smooth surface. A deep exhale followed the tightening of her jaw. "If ye swear not to use it unless ye have no other choice. No practicing. Not even a wee bit. Do ye understand me clearly, lass?"

Zanya nodded. "I swear it."

"Ye need to stand away from me if I'm to show ye how it's done."

Zanya shifted back. "How far?"

Grima's features hardened. "Far, lass. Very far."

Zanya did as she was told, and moved under the shade of the trees while Grima cupped the fruit in both hands.

"Is a terrible thing ye do when ye petrify a thing," Grima went on. "Ye must clear your mind and concentrate on not a single thing. Find a void inside—a quiet place where nothing lives. Close your eyes not to be distracted by anything around ye."

"In the underworld, Beigarth didn't seem to do any of that."

"Aye. My cousin is a master of the curse."

"Curse? Our abilities aren't a curse. They're a gift."

"No, lass." Grima spread her fingers over the pomegranate. Bits of red showed through the gaps in her fingers. She brought it up to eye level. "Not this." Grima closed her eyes, and the jungle suddenly stilled. It was as if the wind stopped blowing, the birds quieted, and everything around them muted in anticipation—or maybe fear.

There was no light to signal Grima was using her ability. No obvious sign to tell it was over. Just the silence, and Grima's saddened expression.

A tiny ripple punched through the air, so small it was almost unnoticeable. But Zanya sensed it. It carried the same cold, desperate panic as when something was terribly wrong, and there was no way to fix it. That hollow, carved-out hole in the gut—that was what the ability felt like.

When Grima opened her eyes, she unveiled the once vibrant fruit to show a gray, lifeless stone resting in her palm. "Ye see, lass. There's not a hint of life left in it."

Zanya stepped forward to inspect it closer. "Is it safe to touch?"

"Aye."

Zanya picked up the heavy ball. It was cold, though it had the same smooth surface as it did before it was changed. "Does everything come out like this? I mean, it looks exactly the way it did."

"Aye. But when ye change a living thing that's more than a wee fruit, you feel it deep in yer bones." She gestured to her face with two fingers. "Anything with eyes. They become hollow, and ye know yer to blame."

Zanya nodded. "So there's a price to pay."

"Aye." Grima turned halfway, making it clear she was done with the demonstration. "A terrible price."

***

Arwan

Back at the training house, Arwan handed the meat off to Beigarth, who had more experience handling a fresh kill than the others. While the Viking washed and stored the meat, Arwan rinsed the brown, dried blood from his hands.

It had been a long time since he'd scrubbed blood from between his fingers. It reminded him of the possibility…the possibility of having the blood of his fallen comrades stain his skin.

When he was done, he walked out to the

campground in search of the others. Eleuia waited for him with her hands shoved into the pockets of her fleece sweater, her hair pulled back in a tight ponytail.

It was amazing how much Zanya looked like her, though he'd never been willing to see it until now.

"Ready?"

He narrowed his eyes, still apprehensive of her sudden change of heart. "For what?"

"Like I said." She extended her hand toward the protected circle, where the others were loosely gathered. "Training."

"We have bigger things to worry about than *my* training."

Eleuia tilted her head, her features suddenly sobered. "What does that mean?"

He walked past her to the center of the training circle. The group quieted and gathered around. He spotted Zanya, on the far right beside Grima, while Eleuia stood on the opposite side of the group beside Marzena.

"Listen up." There was no polite wording for what he was about to tell them, so it was better to be as straight and concise as possible. They were almost out of time. "The situation is worse than we thought."

The group stole silent glances at one another.

"Contessa was dangerous, but she was the only one standing between us and something worse."

"Worse?" Hawa said.

Flashes from the underworld tore through his mind—the warmth of his own blood as it flowed from his veins, the sounds of tearing flesh and bone while the hellhound tore Contessa apart, and the pile of half-eaten guts mounded beside him on the scorching ground.

"I know you all want me to tell you what happened down there." Only Zanya had seen him suffer every night since his return. If he expected the others to fight, they needed to know. "Contessa was not alone in the underworld. The king...my father, was there too."

"I've told them that much," Zanya said. "But nothing more, and you don't have to either."

"To hell with that," Jayden said. "I want to know. Was he the one who killed Renato?"

Arwan could only manage a simple nod.

"Then I say we fuck him up."

The others nodded in agreement.

"We won't have to go looking for him," Arwan continued. "He's going to come to us. He, and an army of damned souls."

"When you say army..." Tara coiled her arm around Peter's.

"It will be like a sea." Marzena's voice filled them in where Arwan could not. "They will rise from the dark realm and there will be no end to the soldiers at his command."

"How the hell are we supposed to fight that?" Hawa said.

"We will not," Marzena said. "We will flee."

"No." Zanya stepped forward. "We can't."

Marzena tilted her head ever so slightly. "Then we will die."

"We're going to die anyway if we run like cowards. They'll take over the middleworld, and millions of innocent people will become victims before they get to us." Zanya lifted her chin. "But it *will* get to us, sooner or later."

"Then we fight," Eadith said, her eyes gleaming with fire.

"Aye." Grima nodded. "We fight."

The Arab windthrowers pushed out their chests. "We fight, and if we die, we die with honor."

"We must send Tara to safety," Marzena said. "Back to Renato's home in Belize."

"What? No way." Tara pushed out her chin. "I can't leave you guys. Not when—"

"This isn't up for debate," Peter said. "You're going."

"There *is* another option." Eleuia looked at Zanya—at the stone. "We could use another fighter, and the stone *was* created with the power to turn humans to Riyata."

Tara's already pale complexion drained of color. She pursed her lips. "What, like…change me…into one of you?"

Marzena's features hardened. "That is not a decision to be taken lightly."

"And it would take a whole hell of a lot of energy from Zanya," Eleuia said.

"Which we can't ask her to spend." Arwan shifted his weight. "Even if she were changed, she would need time to adjust and train in both combat and her new capabilities."

"We don't have that kind of time," Peter said. "Maybe…" He looked at Tara. "Maybe when we go home we can talk about it more. We are going home." He wound his arm around Tara. "All of us.

Together."

Tara swallowed and nodded. "Yeah." The word came out in a breathless whisper. "When we go home, maybe."

"Then it's settled. But make no mistake. Everyone understands your lives are at risk," Marzena said. "You are all willing to die for this cause?"

Eleuia stepped forward. "Before everyone goes full-on martyr, I have an idea." She inspected Arwan closely. "You." She walked in a circle around him, her stare boring into his skin. "You're pretty impressive when you're..." she whirled her hand in the air, "...the other you."

Arwan tightened his jaw. "No."

"You even somehow escaped the underworld on your own, without any help from your father. In fact, you left that realm against his will, didn't you?"

"I will not fight as a beast."

"Why not?" She stopped walking. "You have to admit, you'd be a more valuable fighter if you did." She counted the points out on her fingers. "You're stronger, faster, and more deadly. You can take more hits, fight harder and longer, and you can protect them." She gestured to Zanya—*them*, including the baby. "Isn't that what you want?"

Arwan narrowed his eyes. He should have known Eleuia's act of accepting him—even for a moment—was a tactic to get something out of it. He would do anything to protect Zanya, but he would not change simply to amuse Eleuia. No matter what she used as bait.

Besides, he had one more piece of news to share.

"That's not going to be a problem, because Zanya is going with Tara, back to Belize." He looked at Zanya. "And she is going to stay there."

Zanya snorted. "The hell I am."

"I won't allow you to put yourself at risk."

"Excuse me?" Her lips parted and she took on a defensive stance. "I'm sorry, did I just hear you right? You won't '*allow me*?'"

"This is not only your decision to make," Arwan said, heat rushing through him. "Not anymore. You are carrying my unborn child, and I will do what it takes to keep you both safe."

"Well, until you grow a uterus and take on the job of being pregnant, you have exactly zero right to make that decision."

He balled his fists. "That's not fair."

"You're right. It's not." Zanya glared. "But that's how it is."

Arwan drew in a deep, shaky breath, working hard to stay calm. The beast rattled inside him, protesting to be set free. Even though Arwan now controlled it, that didn't mean he did not struggle with the urge to be let it out—especially when provoked.

"You'd still be a better fighter," Eleuia said. "Whether Zanya stays or not. Come on. Beast it up." She waved him on, as if prompting him to hurry. "Let's see it."

Arwan scanned the faces in the group, all of them watching intently.

Drina had been silently standing in the back. She out of all people knew what he was, yet she made no effort to interrupt Eleuia's effort at making him into a side-show exhibit.

"You have nothing to say?" Arwan asked, staring at Drina.

Drina smiled—a reaction he didn't expect. "You are who you are, boy. You must be who you are."

CHAPTER THIRTY-SIX

Zanya

After the conflict between Arwan and her mother, the training session stopped and Arwan went back to the house.

Now it was night, which brought its own set of problems.

Arwan's nightmares—or visions—had gotten worse, and he struggled to sleep more than a few hours at a time. She related, but it was hard to reach out to him when he felt so unequivocally alone. So confused. So much like she did back in the orphanage, when nobody truly understood what she was going through.

Even though it was late, Arwan wasn't in bed with her, where he belonged. Instead he took to helping Balam as sentry, probably to avoid sleeping.

She couldn't blame him.

She lay in their bed, wearing a sheer tank top and a pair of shorts. The room was dark except for the light radiating from her stone. She turned it in her fingers, then placed it on her belly button, watching as the tiny light flickered inside.

Arwan swore it was the baby's heartbeat.

Deep down, she knew he was right.

Her stone was warmer than before—now linked to the baby as well as her. All of them shared the same bond. It wasn't until she connected with the child through her stone that she felt any love for her unborn daughter.

The child was more part of her now than it ever had been, in both body and heart.

A knock on the door prompted her to tuck her stone back in its leather carrier on her wrist. She didn't want to share the phenomena with anyone but Arwan. Somehow it seemed too personal to talk about—even to Tara.

She grabbed the sheets and covered herself more, in case it was Peter coming to check on her. "Who is it?"

"Your mom."

"Oh." She sat up. "Come in."

Her mother creaked open the door and walked inside, shutting it behind her. "How are you feeling?"

Zanya shrugged. "Okay. No morning sickness or anything."

"Lucky for you, you won't have any. I didn't. I think it's all a part of our healing ability. Keeps that at bay."

"Nice. So…is there another reason you're here?"

"Actually, yes." She walked across the room and sat at the foot of the bed. "I'm worried about him."

"Him, who?"

"Arwan."

Zanya paused. It was the first time she'd heard her mother show any real concern over Arwan's wellbeing. Maybe she was pretending to put Zanya at ease because of her *condition*. But she'd take what she could get. "I am too."

"He looks exhausted...disjointed. I think I pushed him too far this afternoon."

"You could have been a little more gentle."

"We don't have time for gentle." Her mother sighed. "But you're right." She noticed Zanya's hand pressed to her belly. "Thinking of any names?"

"No. I just came to grips with the idea of..." Zanya's cheeks flushed with heat. She still didn't love this topic, but now that her mother had warmed up to Arwan a little, that made it somehow easier to talk about. "You know, the whole baby thing."

"Yeah. It's pretty overwhelming, isn't it? When your father and I found out we were having you, Renato was the first person we told." She blinked a few times, then lowered her head. "He, uh..." She swallowed. "He was really happy too. He'd always wanted kids of his own."

Tears stung Zanya's eyes. She'd miss Renato every day of her life.

"Anyway." Eleuia sniffled and wiped a tear from her cheek. "I'm sure he was just as happy to learn you're expecting."

"I'm glad he was still here to find out."

Her mother nodded. "Well, if you need help with baby names, let me know. I'm sure we can brainstorm a few." She patted Zanya's leg. "Get some sleep." Just as her mother stood, Arwan opened the door to their bedroom, pausing in the entrance. She pointed to the hall. "I was just leaving. Sorry."

Arwan stepped aside.

Her mother walked past him, paused, gave an awkward smile, and then continued without a word.

"Everything okay?" He closed the door.

"Yeah. She was just asking about me. Wondering how I feel."

"And?"

"Good." Zanya moved the covers off of her, revealing her bare legs and low-cut top. She used to be shy to show off her body, but now that they were bonded, she was free of inhibition. And since they'd experienced each other's bodies, the need to be close to him sometimes overtook her. "I'm feeling great, actually."

Arwan arched a single brow. "I see."

Zanya knew that look. He understood exactly what she wanted, and wasted no time in stripping off his shirt and joining her in bed. Her chest jumped when his skin brushed against hers. He'd been so out of it. Maybe some time alone, with her, would bring him back.

***

Arwan

Hours after Zanya had fallen asleep, Arwan lay awake in bed, staring at the ceiling. Exhaustion sank deep into his bones, but his mind wouldn't allow him to sleep. Every time he drifted, he'd wake himself up, afraid of the visions that waited for him.

But a man, even half-underworlder and half-light, can only stay awake for so long.

His eyes slipped closed and his mind washed blank, leaving his subconscious in a state of limbo.

The blissful rest lasted for mere moments before a vision intruded—showing him his native realm, and the king, who he'd left behind.

The first layer of the underworld was crawling with damned souls. They spewed from the lower levels—tens of thousands of them—climbing up by using each other as ladders. Their flesh tore from their bones, their groans growing more desperate with each passing moment.

The king stood in the center of the madness, peering into Arwan's soul.

Arwan focused on his eyes.

His red, angry, flaming eyes.

"I will not wait any longer for your return, son." The king tilted his head toward the tree above. "You love the mortals too much, and have grown weak in their presence."

Arwan kicked at the sheets, aware he was in a vision, but caught—unable to escape.

"This realm has grown too small for me and my slaves." His father raised his hands toward the tree above. "I am coming. And there is no power great enough to stop me."

Arwan opened his eyes and threw himself out of

bed, clawing at the stone floor.

The ground shook, making the house tremble.

Zanya sat up, disoriented and still half-asleep. "What's happening?" She clung onto the bed. "What's going on?"

Arwan fisted his hands. "He's here." Still wearing his cotton night shorts, he bolted out of the room and down the hall. "Balam, he's here!" The jaguar sprang to all fours and followed him outside to the camp. "Get up! He's coming!"

Half of the group was already awake and gathering their battle gear and weapons.

Marzena was the first to meet him. "We must get Tara to safety."

"It's too late for that." He looked back at the house. "Zanya. We have to protect her."

"Tell her to stay inside." Marzena turned to the others. They all paused, fear clearly streaked in their eyes. Marzena took Eleuia's hand. "Now is the time to come together as warriors, like our ancestors did before us, and their ancestors before them. We must fight for the safety of the middleworld and mankind. That is our cause. That is our calling."

Arwan nodded at the others.

This was it.

The time was now.

An explosion erupted from the earth—thick roots from Yaxche, merging the underworld with their realm.

Underworld stench filled the air.

Then came the souls.

Hundreds of them, crawling up the tree, onto the earth. Their contorted figures were hunched and battered from thousands of years trapped in hell. Tara screamed and stumbled back. Peter grabbed her arm and pointed at the house. "You go inside and lock the door. Do not let anyone in under any circumstances, do you understand me?"

"You have to come with me." Tara pulled on his arm. "You have to!"

"Stop it!" Peter grabbed her arms. "I can't. You know I can't."

She hesitated with tears streaming down her face, and then nodded. She kissed him, long and hard, before running upstairs and vanishing into the house.

"Go with her," Arwan said, looking at Marzena. As powerful as your mind is, you won't stand a chance in the battlefield." He looked at Drina. "You too, old woman."

Drina scowled.

He stepped close—very close—and looked her in the eyes, his features like stone. "I'm not asking."

They watched each other for a brief moment before Drina mumbled and turned back to the home, following Marzena inside.

"Good. Now that they're inside," Peter pushed up his sleeves, "let's hope all that training sank in."

Arwan patted him on the back. "You've got this."

Jayden grabbed a weapon from camp—his bow and a quiver of arrows. "Let's see what you got!" He pulled an arrow and shot his first round, landing it in the center of an underworlder's abdomen. It walked on, as if it weren't fazed in the least. Jayden pulled back another arrow and launched it into the enemy's eye, but even that did not stop the damned soul. He shot one more, straight into its heart. The enemy collapsed on impact. "The heart!"

Arwan grabbed his glaive—a stick with a long, curved blade at the end—and ran at a smaller group sectioned off from the others. One swiped at him with a jagged blade. Arwan ducked and speared it in the chest, then turned and severed the other's head. More came, and he dispatched them the same—twisting and ducking from every attack.

Driving a blade through bone was difficult. It took a force of impact some of his comrades might not have, and just as much to yank the blade back out of the chest.

A scream stole his attention, and he looked to Ahmed—one of the windthrowers who was under attack. He held his arm while blood seeped from the gash as he stumbled back, his eyes wide with fear.

His twin, Yousef, used a gust of wind to throw the underworlder into the trees. The damned soul smacked into several branches on the way down until it collapsed onto the soil, motionless. A sharp stick stuck out of its body, no doubt piercing its heart.

A shadow darted behind Yousef—so fast Arwan almost didn't see it.

Hellhounds.

"Yousef, watch—"

A hound tackled the windthrower from behind, clawing into his back and tearing skin off bone.

"No!" Ahmed ran toward the beast, but was met with a horde of underworlders blocking his path. The second windthrower did as well as he could to kill the group of savages before they killed him first. But it wasn't fast enough.

When the hellhound moved on, Yousef lay in a pool of blood, face down in the soil.

Something else darted in front of him. When he turned, Hawa had an underworlder by its throat. She raised a blade and shoved it in its chest before the tattered body fell limp. She glanced back at Arwan. "You're welcome." She grinned, then vanished in a streak of color.

The air suddenly became warm. Arwan looked to his right, where Eadith conjured a fireball in her hand. She threw it at the hole where more underworlders flooded out, and set dozens of them on fire.

But it didn't stop them.

Flaming corpses ran toward the group.

"In the heart," Jayden shouted, shooting off several arrows.

Eadith extinguished the flame in her hand and pulled a sword out of its sheath on her back. With a gleam in her eye, she conjured fire over her sword. The flaming blade cut through the air, both slicing and cauterizing at the same time.

The stink of cooked flesh rose into the air.

"There are so many," Eleuia shouted. She pulled a pistol from her holster and shot seven underworlders in a row before she reloaded. "We need a plan!" She fired several more rounds, then one into a hellhound darting between the trees.

Peter fought from the stone training circle while the battle raged on. An underworlder swiped at him, but when its hand reached over the blood-barrier, it screeched and recoiled.

"They can't cross over the barrier," Peter shouted. "Attack from the protection of the stone training circle!"

The group fell back, killing anything and everything in their way.

Ahmed fought with one arm, swinging a long, curved sword with Arabic script down the blade. He lunged forward and stabbed an underworlder in the sternum, lodging his sword in bone. Another came down with a hatchet into Ahmed's already injured arm, carving out a chunk of muscle.

Hawa rushed to his aid and drove her blade into its back, then stomped on its head, spewing brain matter over the ground. The underworlder continued to move until she stabbed it a second time through the back, into its heart.

Ahmed screamed and threw himself onto the ground, convulsing with white froth leaking from his mouth.

"Something..." Hawa shifted her weight. "Something's up with their weapons. They're poison! Don't let them cut you!"

"You have to leave him," Eleuia shouted at Hawa from the training ring. "They're closing in!" Eleuia pointed her pistol and shot several rounds, fending off a small group.

Arwan sliced through another cluster while more poured into the middleworld.

Hawa crouched and wrapped her arm around Ahmed. "Let's get him back to the protected ring."

Arwan reached them and grabbed Ahmed and then hauled him off the ground. Hawa carried him under one arm while Arwan carried him under the other until they were able to drag him to safety.

When he let go, Arwan turned to Eleuia and yanked her in close, peering into her eyes. "We don't leave people behind. *Ever*."

Eleuia nodded. "Just a little test." She held up her pistol and pulled back the hammer, the barrel aimed over his shoulder. "Good thing you passed."

CHAPTER THIRTY-SEVEN

Zanya

Zanya finished strapping on her training gear and rushed into the living room, where she plowed right into Tara. Zanya examined her sobbing friend from head to toe. "Are you okay?" She scanned Tara's body. "Answer me! Are you all right?"

"Yes. Yes, I'm okay." Tara wiped streams of tears off her cheeks. "Peter's out there with the others. There are so many of them."

"You have to stay here. Don't leave this house, no matter what."

Tara shook her head while biting her lip.

"I have to know you're safe. So does Peter. If you go running out there for whatever reason, you'll just be a distraction, and right now, a distraction will get someone killed."

Tara froze, and then nodded. "Okay." She sniffled and wiped her face clean. "Okay, I'll stay."

"Good." She hugged her friend tightly. "I love you so much. I'm sorry I got you into this." She pressed a kiss on Tara's forehead, and then ran outside to join the others.

The second she burst through the front door, the foul stink of the underworld smacked her in the face. She stumbled onto the bare soil, shock coursing through her as she took in the scene.

The ground had split open, and Yaxche had invaded the middleworld. But this time the tree was like a highway for underworld souls—a direct portal to their realm.

Small fires burned in the distance along the tree line, making the underworld figures into eerie silhouettes. The entire group fought from the training circle, which was now encompassed with more damned souls.

Peter nudged Arwan and then pointed at her.

Arwan turned, and paled when he saw her. His eyes widened and he ran toward her.

Zanya looked to the right, where an underworld hound was in full sprint in her direction.

Panic streaked through her and she froze.

The beast leapt. In mid-air, Balam plowed into the hellhound and tumbled to the ground, tearing at it with a voraciousness she'd never seen the jaguar deity display.

Arwan yanked her into a crouching position. "What are you doing out here?"

"I..." She couldn't stop looking—taking in the scene. Her gaze stopped on Yousef's lifeless body. Her breath caught and she cupped her hand over her mouth. *"Oh no."*

"You need to snap out of it," Arwan shouted, pulling her back to reality. "You have to stay on the petrified ground. Drina's magic is keeping them at bay for now. We're too outnumbered to fight on the soil."

"I don't think the lad's breathing," Beigarth shouted from behind them.

Zanya sidestepped to see the group crowded around Ahmed, the second windthrower.

Peter loomed over him a moment before beginning CPR.

"Oh my god." Zanya rubbed her hands over her eyes. "This can't be happening."

"If you can't be here, you need to go back inside. Go hide with Tara. I'd rather you do that anyway." He cupped her face in his hands. "Please."

Hide with Tara.

He wasn't trying to insult her, but she couldn't shake his words. She had trained for this moment— to stand against the uprising and rescue the innocent lives that hung in the balance. She was the Stone Guardian, and it was her job to lead them.

The light in her chest flickered to life and her stone buzzed against her wrist. "I'm okay. I can do this." She walked toward the group, Arwan following right behind her. Balam fell in line after he'd finished with the hellhound. Putrid blood stained his muzzle.

When Zanya reached the others, Peter was gliding his hand over Yousef's eyes. "He's gone."

"It's something in their weapons," Hawa said.

Eleuia loaded her gun. "We can't afford any more casualties."

"Afford?" Zanya looked at her mother. "Yousef wasn't *collateral damage*. And neither was his twin brother. They were our friends, and now they're *dead*."

Eleuia's features softened. "I didn't mean…" She swallowed.

"We should bring the lads to a protected space until we can give them a right proper burial," Beigarth said.

"Aye." Grima's bottom lip quivered. "He'll only be tread on here."

Arwan knelt and scooped Yousef into his arms. He glanced at the growing group of underworlders—now thousands, all gathered around their home. "We don't have much time. This spell may not hold forever."

"Come on." Zanya set her hand on Arwan's back. "I'll help you find somewhere to rest him for now."

She accompanied him down the petrified path until they reached camp. Zanya searched the area, spotting a clear space beside the steps. "Here." She kicked away a few rocks and leaves. "You can put him here."

Arwan did, and then placed Yousef's white hat over his face.

"We have to find a way to get Ahmed's body too."

Arwan hung his head. "There's no use."

"They should be buried together. It's what they'd—"

"There's no use, Zanya." He turned and watched the thousands of underworlders gather in tighter around the group, reaching and slicing at them with their weapons. They had begun to pile on top of each other—two, even three at a time—creating a wall of the undead. "We're not going to make it through this. I had no idea what we were up against. I'm so sorry…"

"We will make it. We have to." She took his hand held it to her belly. "Not for our sake, but for hers."

Heat slithered through Arwan, giving him the fuel he needed to push forward. His child would greet the world one day. He would be sure of it—even if he weren't there to hold her for the first time.

***

Zanya

Arwan ran to the others, leaving her alone with Yousef.

She knelt beside him and took his hand. His skin was still warm.

"I'm so sorry this happened to you. I promise I'll do everything I can to get your brother. I'm so…" She choked on her words. She knew they'd lose warriors, but she thought she'd be prepared.

Zanya stood and turned back to the group, who fought just out of reach of the underworlders.

This was her fight.

She tapped the surface of her stone. "You ready for this?"

Her stone buzzed and lit up, pushing light through the clasps of the leather wristband.

"Good. Because we're going to need every

ounce of energy to make it out alive." She sprinted to the group and gathered them close. "I know we all thought our abilities would be more useful. We thought we'd do more damage, but that doesn't mean we can give up. We're protected here, so we have to use everything at our disposal until we're tapped out. We owe it to Yousef, Ahmed, and Renato. We owe it to them to fight as hard as we can, until we have nothing left!"

She walked through the group as they parted a way for her, and then stopped at the edge of the blood-barrier. Underworlders slashed at her with their hatchets. She leaned back, too close for comfort. It was an apocalyptic scene with an unlimited supply of the damned. But the Maya had been fighting this good fight since the early years, and she wouldn't give up now.

Her light burst to life and she conjured a storm overhead. Flashes of lightning pierced the sky and struck the ground, hitting a cluster of underworlders nearby. She squinted and shielded her eyes from the burst of electricity, ignoring the stench of burning flesh.

Beigarth and Grima walked to the barrier's edge and removed their weapons. The cousins glanced at each other before swiping at the underworlders, taking down a few at a time.

It was clear the Riyata could cross over the barrier, while the underworlders could not. Magic didn't have an exact science, but Zanya chalked it up to a spell to block evil. Those who weren't could cross.

Her mother and Hawa approached next, her

mother letting out several shots from her pistol while Hawa threw a row of shining blades at the mob, hitting them in the hearts.

"We'll cut them down from here," Peter shouted. "Then push them out." He took a knife and stuck the blade into one, then yanked it out before it dropped to the ground at his feet.

Zanya looked into the distance, catching sight of another group heading into the trees. She conjured a flame and pitched a firebomb into the jungle. A burst of light followed by a wave of heat kept the stragglers from seeking out unknowing victims in distant villages. There was no telling how far they could reach—or if they had risen from other areas already.

"Make sure they don't go far," Zanya instructed.

Eadith stepped up and formed two balls of fire in her hands. "I'll cover it."

Jayden let several arrows fly, striking three of the underworlders. He stepped closer to the barrier and shouted, then leapt back. Burns dragged over his arms and hands, bubbling into angry, red boils. "What the fuck—"

"Drina's magic." Arwan shook his head. "It must keep underworlders from going in—or out."

"What the hell," Jay shouted. "It hasn't burned you and you're more underworlder than all of us combined!"

Arwan glanced at Zanya, who shrugged. Maybe it had to do with Arwan's split-genes. Jay was pretty much all underworlder at this point—a dead man walking.

Jayden mumbled a line of curse words under his

breath before Peter stepped off the front lines. "I can heal you."

"Don't waste your energy." Jayden glared at the massive, growing army. "It's about to get a lot worse." With a warrior's scream, he charged the barrier, breaking through to the other side. He covered his face as his skin flushed an angry red.

"No!" Zanya stepped to the edge of the circle, but dared not step over it. She couldn't risk being attacked. She wasn't the only one at risk anymore.

Eleuia fired her weapon, putting down a few of the damned near Jayden to give him enough time to get to his feet. He stumbled to the nearest corpses and pulled his arrows out of their heads.

That's when Zanya realized—he was out of ammo.

"Jay!" Zanya swiped her hands, leading a gust of wind to knock an assailant off its feet. "That's enough. Get back here!"

Jayden gathered salvaged arrows and grinned. "Worried about—"

An underworlder came from behind and sank its weapon into Jayden's back. He shouted and scrambled, taking the arrow in his hand and plunging it through the underworlder's chest, dropping it in seconds.

Zanya lunged forward, but Arwan snagged her around the waist, holding her back. "You can't go out there."

She held her breath and watched Jayden, who ran toward the group and plowed through the barrier a second time, doing even more damage than the first. He lay on the ground, screaming and clawing at his

313

eyes.

Balam darted through the underworlders, taking down hellhounds the best he could.

A shrill shriek stole Zanya's attention. Grima stumbled back, holding a gash on her arm.

Zanya searched the barrier. "How did that happen?"

"It reached right through," Grima shouted. "It reached through and cut right into me arm!"

Zanya shook her head. That couldn't be. Drina's spell kept them out. Unless...

"The spell is failing," she said, first to herself, and then to the others. "The protective spell is failing!"

A sense of desperation charged through her, echoed by her stone.

She had to push harder.

Zanya took the stone out of its holster and cupped it in her hand. "You have to help me. We have to save them."

Her stone buzzed and lit up with an affirmative response.

She coiled her fingers around it and drew in a deep breath.

Everything around her went silent. The light in her chest grew colder and brighter by the second. Her head started spinning, slicing into her focus. She wavered on her feet.

"*No.*"

She had to push on.

She had to work harder.

She had to protect them—until she no longer could...

CHAPTER THIRTY-EIGHT

Arwan

When Zanya dropped to her knees, Arwan ran to her side and scooped her into his arms while the others continued to battle the underworld army. "Peter, get over here!"

"I can't help her," Peter shouted as he slashed and jabbed at the enemy. "Get her back inside where she's safe. We can't do anything for her if the baby is taking up her energy."

"But we won't last a second if these things break through completely." Eleuia fired several more rounds. "Not without her." When she reached for another clip on her belt, there was none, and she resorted to reloading the empty clip with a handful of bullets she'd pulled from her pocket.

"What do we do?" Hawa shouted. "I'm out of throwing knives, and my dagger got stuck in one of these things." She swung a battle hammer and cracked it against the jaw of an underworlder. She swung again, hitting its skull and throwing it back, but not killing it. "And—" She stumbled back, covered in murky blood. "This is exhausting. I can't pierce hearts with a battle hammer. It's just slowing them down." Panting, she wiped a streak of blood from her cheek. "Arwan...we're running out of time."

He held Zanya tighter against his chest. He should have told her to run—forced her, if need be. He should have ensured her safety and the survival of his child. Of the others' lives. He should have, but now it was too late to look back. And even if he had—even if he bent time and did it all over again—he wouldn't be able to fight off the army alone. They were all doomed, no matter the course of history.

Grima clenched her jaw, holding the wound on her arm. Her muscles tightened and she seized on the ground, a second victim of the underworld toxin.

Peter knelt beside her. "I'll do what I can to help her, but we have to get Zanya out of here!"

Eleuia looked at him. "Please...save her."

An underworlder broke through and slammed right into Eleuia, taking her down. It was the same underworlder Hawa had gotten her blade lodged in. She yanked the knife from its back and spun, lopping off the underworlder's head. Though severed, its eyes darted side to side while its body continued to move. Eleuia kicked it off and jumped to her feet.

Hawa mounted the flailing corpse and stabbed it in the chest, then rolled the corpse away from her.

Another intruder broke through.

Then another.

The group gathered into a tighter formation as they fought with everything they had.

Eleuia ran out of bullets and held the gun by its barrel, using it as a bludgeon. "Fall back!" Eleuia cried. "Fall back to the house! We're out of time!"

Beigarth scooped Grima into his arms and chased after the group as they fled to the sanctuary of the house.

Tara flung open the door and let Arwan inside. He set Zanya on the nearest step and backed out, shaking his head. "We can't hide in here." He turned to the group. "Keep fighting! They'll break into the house in minutes. We have to fend them off!"

"We're out of options!" Jayden shouted. "There are too many!"

An arrow whizzed through the air, hitting an underworlder in the chest and pinning it to nearby tree.

Arwan looked at Jayden, but there was no bow in his hand.

Another arrow struck. And then another.

Within seconds the sky was blanketed with arrows, all raining down on the dead army.

The group turned, watching in silence as a sea of damned souls covered the ground.

"What's going on?" Eadith said. "Who's doing this?"

A faint smile softened Arwan's lips. "The villagers."

Flashes of snarled teeth and crazed eyes shone from behind masks of colored body paint.

"How…?" Eleuia looked up at the window of the home. Arwan followed, spotting Marzena with her eyes closed and her fingers pressed against her temples. "She called them," Eleuia shrieked. "She called them!"

Beigarth looked into Grima's face. "I have to get her inside. She's ill."

Arwan nodded. "Keep her with the others. She's done all she can."

"Aye." Beigarth stroked Grima's hair. "Ye have done all ye can, lass." He placed a kiss on her forehead. "Ye rest now." Beigarth let her down from his arms. Thankfully, she was now able to walk, thanks to Peter's healing touch.

"Ye be careful," Grima said, her hand clenched onto Beigarth's bicep. "Yer all I've got in the world."

Beigarth fisted his hand and pressed it over his heart, holding Grima's gaze.

Rows of villagers flooded out of the jungle, each marked in body paint. They charged downhill, ululating, with their weapons poised to strike. Villagers leapt over dead bodies and sliced at the enemy, taking down hundreds in a matter of minutes.

Beigarth turned to the battlefield and pushed out his chest. "Well, what are ye waiting for?" He ran his hand over his face and down his beard, glaring ahead. "We have a battle to win." He charged forward, followed by the rest of the group.

Arwan handed Zanya off to Drina, who waited in the doorway. "Take care of her." He held Drina's gaze. "If anything happens to her…" His throat tightened.

Drina waved him off. "Go, boy. I will care for t'e guardian."

Before he could leave, Zanya reached out and touched his face.

The warmth of her skin and familiar pull of his soul mate completely encompassed him.

Pale and weak, beads of sweat collected on Zanya's forehead. "You can't go…"

He took her hand in his. "I have to. I can't leave them out there—"

"They aren't going to make it. None of us will." A tear slipped down her cheek. "Stay with me until it's over. Please."

***

Zanya

"That's not true. Don't think like that." Arwan looked at Drina, who lingered behind her. "Take her inside and lock the door."

Drina braced her hands on Zanya's shoulders. "Come—"

"No." Zanya shook the priestess off of her. "He can't go." She looked back at Arwan. "Don't you see?" She looked at the war raging around them. "Even with the villagers, it isn't enough."

Arwan turned to the scene.

Blood coated the ground from fallen Mayan warriors as more underworld troops ascended the tree to join in the fight. Whatever triumph they'd had was short lived.

There were still too many.

"I can't stand here and watch you die. I…" He worked his jaw. "I'm sorry. I can't."

He slipped out of her grasp and ran into battle. He snatched his glaive from the ground before dispatching several more underworlders.

"Sweet girl." Zanya looked at Drina, who stood behind her. "You must come back inside. T'ere's no other choice."

"Than to hide until we die?" Zanya wiped a bead of sweat drizzling down her nose. "No. I can't go down like that—cowering in a corner."

"He is more capable—"

Zanya turned and hugged the Mayan priestess. "Take care of them—especially Tara. She's terrified. And make sure Grima is comfortable as long as she can be." Zanya slipped out the door and shut it behind her. She closed her eyes and heated it with a charge of electricity until the handle began to melt—as did the mechanisms—locking everyone inside.

Screams and cries saturated the air, morphing into a soundtrack from her most gruesome nightmares. She slouched against the stone walls of the home and gathered her strength. She'd need every ounce of it for what she was about to do.

Zanya took a knife from her boot—a spare Arwan made her carry at all times—then stumbled into battle.

The world seemed to move in slow motion.

Arwan swung his glaive. Strands of blood-soaked hair stuck to his cheeks and neck.

The clouds seemed to stop moving.

The wind seemed to still, leaving the air stagnant.

Zanya fought the fatigue struggling to take her over. More underworlders poured from the hole in the earth. More hellhounds. More roots from the tree.

The enemy closed in around them yet again.

It was clear in that moment—they would all die.

Zanya let go of her knife and let it clatter the ground.

Bodies of the fallen villagers were being consumed by Yaxche. Vines and roots coiled around their bodies, dragging them under until they were nothing more than a bloodstain.

Hawa screamed and stumbled back when a hound leapt on top of her.

Jayden kicked it off, then shoved a blade in its back, piercing its heart from behind.

Another hound tackled Jayden, snapping at his face while he held it just inches away.

Hawa pressed her hand over her stomach as blood pumped between her fingers. She kicked at another underworlder, unable to defend herself from the onslaught of attacks.

Zanya wanted to move—wanted nothing more than to help Hawa escape. But it took all of her effort to stay standing, and she had nothing left to fight.

Nothing.

A shrill cry pierced the air while several underworlders piled on top of Hawa, hacking at her with hatchets and primitive weapons.

Zanya dropped to her knees, reaching out in

despair and helplessness.

Jayden screamed, stealing glances at Hawa while he struggled to keep the hound from tearing his head off. Eleuia ran to his aid and dispatched the hound.

Hawa's legs went stiff, and then fell lifeless.

Blood rolled over the petrified stone.

"Get off her!" Eleuia bludgeoned an underworlder over the head before diving on the back of another of the enemy.

Jayden grabbed a rock and smashed in the head of his last attacker, stunning it long enough for him to see Hawa's body splayed out on the ground.

He stilled and dropped the rock.

The savage rage in his eyes stole Zanya's breath.

The pain was unbearable.

Jayden dropped on his knees beside her lifeless body. Gaping wounds covered her arms, legs, and face. He pulled on handfuls of his own hair while his mouth contorted.

Eleuia checked Hawa's pulse, then looked up at Jay and shook her head.

Zanya covered her eyes and wailed. "No!" A surge of desperation took her over completely. She fisted her hands and slammed them onto the ground, her entire body shaking. "No!" She clenched her jaw and opened her eyes. Hot, scalding wrath coursed through her veins. Her breath quickened and her stone seared her skin, pulsing with untainted force. "No!" She picked up her fists and slammed them on the soil another time.

A cold sickness flushed through her body and the world was tainted in a dusky gray. The air stilled.

The atmosphere grew silent. The ground beneath her hands turned to stone, and the sickness began to spread.

The underworlders fought in slow motion, as did her group. The petrified ground crackled and split as the ability rolled over the battlefield, turning everything it touched to stone.

She screamed and pushed harder, tearing every fiber of ability out of her to bring this to an end. Every underworld soul froze in time as they turned to stone.

Every fallen Mayan villager.

Every leaf or grain of soil.

Even the tree itself—turned to stone.

She would turn the entire jungle into a petrified wasteland if she had to.

Nothing would survive.

The trees her ability touched hardened and split. Branches cracked under their own weight and tumbled to the ground, exploding into piles of rubble on impact.

When the fog cleared from her mind and she finally came back to the moment, the jungle was a massive graveyard.

She opened her eyes and scanned the battleground. The rest of the group had leapt to the safety of the already petrified training ring, and were busy dispatching the few surviving underworlders.

Everyone had fled to safety.

Everyone but Beigarth.

She spotted his stone figure on the battlefield, an ax raised overhead with his eyes focused on the victim in front of him.

Zanya forced herself to her feet. The adrenaline had already begun to wear off. Her hands shook and her legs trembled beneath her weight. She found her mother, who met her gaze. Her mother's lips were parted while she stared at Zanya in horror.

Zanya examined the death and destruction—the consequences of her actions...

What had she done?

Her mother stepped toward her, only to stop after a single stride.

"Zanya." Peter stood, watching Zanya from a distance.

Her entire body was numb—except for a snaking pain winding up her belly. A sharp cramp nearly took her to her knees. With her legs pinched together, she cupped her belly. Warm liquid trickled from between her thighs.

Arwan slaughtered the final underworld survivor before looking at her.

Zanya ground her teeth. "Something's wrong." Those were the only words she managed to say before an excruciating pain tore through her stomach, and everything went black.

CHAPTER THIRTY-NINE

Arwan

"Zanya!" Arwan sprinted toward her and caught her before she hit the ground. Her eyes fluttered shut.

Peter was there within seconds, running his hands over her body in search of the cause of her illness. "She's hemorrhaging." Peter's face went white. "The baby."

Arwan ran her to the door, but it wouldn't open. He saw the handle had been melted, and clenched his jaw. With a swift kick, he broke the door open and ran up the stairs, past the others, and into their bedroom. Tara was the first to arrive in the room, followed by Marzena, and then Drina.

The old priestess hobbled to the bed and pressed her hand to Zanya's forehead. "She is not well. Not well at all." Drina removed some herbs from a pouch tied around her waist and slapped them in Tara's hand. "Go make tea—quickly, child."

Tara nodded and ran into the hall.

"She used too much of herself," Marzena said. "She dug too deep." The seemingly young dreamwalker closed her eyes, only to squint and shake her head. "She is too far gone. I cannot communicate with her."

Arwan knelt beside the bed and took Zanya's hand. "Come on, Zanya." He draped his hand over Zanya's belly. "Please." The word came out in a watery plea.

Eleuia darted into the room, covered in underworld blood. She froze in the doorway, staring at her daughter from a distance.

"She needs you," Marzena said, waving Eleuia in. "Come by her side. Remind her of how much she is loved."

Eleuia clutched her chest. *"So much."*

Arwan pressed a kiss on the back of Zanya's hand. She mumbled and kicked at the sheets. Her words were indiscernible at first, but as the seconds passed, they became clear. "It hurts." She arched her back and clawed at her belly. "Make it stop. It hurts!"

Eleuia sat on the other side of her bed and took her hand. "Come on, sweetie. You have to be strong. Not for yourself, but for your baby. Be strong for your little girl."

Zanya opened her eyes and looked at her mother. Her bottom lip quivered. "Mom…I'm scared."

"It's okay, baby." Eleuia stroked Zanya's hair, tears building in her eyes. "It's going to be okay."

Zanya closed her eyes and curled into a ball, then let out a scream. "Mom!"

Peter skimmed his hands over Zanya's body.

"I'll do everything I can to stop the bleeding."

"T'e herbs will help. T'ey will ease her pain and allow her to rest."

Arwan stood back, fighting to hold down the streak of panic.

Tara returned with a steaming cup of herbal tea. "Where do I put it?"

"Here, child." Drina pointed to the nightstand.

Tara did as she was told, then stood beside the priestess. She scanned the faces in the room. "Where are the others?"

"Eadith is outside with…" Eleuia paused. "With whoever's left."

Tara pressed her fingers over her lips, shaking her head.

"It's my fault," Arwan said. "Their blood is on my hands."

"Stop it," Eleuia snapped. "You can't do that to yourself. You did your best. We all did."

"No." He combed his fingers through his hair. "I could have done more. I should have…" He turned his face away, too ashamed to look into Eleuia's eyes.

Tara scrubbed away tears with her sleeve. "Who's still outside…alive?"

Arwan walked to the bedroom window and stared out at the petrified jungle. There was very little movement. Eadith stood beside Jayden, who cradled Hawa's body in his lap.

Arwan's chest tightened.

"Only Jayden," Arwan said. "And Eadith. That's all that's left."

Tara slowly sat, her features wiped blank from

327

shock.

"I should get out there. Help collect the dead."

"Who's going to tell Grima?" Tara asked.

"She's asleep for now," Peter said. "She went into what I can only describe as toxic shock from her wounds. We should let her rest, and tell her when she's regained strength. Otherwise it may strip her of her will to live, and we'll lose her too."

Drina hobbled toward the hall. "Come, boy. I will help you gat'er t'e dead and rest t'eir bodies wit' honor until we can give t'em a rightful ceremony."

Arwan leaned down and kissed Zanya on the forehead, then whispered in her ear. "Don't give up."

When he followed Drina outside, the air was still and the familiar noises of the jungle had vanished. No birds or humming of insects. No rattling of leaves. Just silence, and the all too familiar stink of death.

Drina approached Beigarth's petrified form and touched his stone face. "You did well, warrior." She sliced her finger and smudged two streaks of blood over his eyes. "May you find your way to t'e heavens wit' ease."

Arwan approached Jayden, who sat silent with Hawa lying limp in his lap.

The seeker, who he'd grown to admire over the months, was not sobbing or rocking his fallen love. Instead, he silently sat, staring out at the lifeless jungle.

Arwan crouched beside him, but couldn't bring himself to look at Hawa's body. He'd seen it once since the underworlders attacked.

"I'm sorry," Arwan said.

Jayden didn't take his focus off the distance. "There's nothing left for me now. I have no one…"

"You still have us." He braced his hand on the seeker's shoulder. "And you are welcome to stay as long as you would like. Forever, even. You're family."

Jayden hugged Hawa tighter against his chest and buried his face in her hair.

Arwan stood, deciding that was enough. The choice was the seeker's now. Whether he stayed or left, the decision was out of his hands.

"Anot'er was petrified," Drina said, standing several yards away. She stared down at one of the twin windthrowers, face down on the ground.

He was just a kid. He deserved better.

"His brother's body is resting beside the house," Arwan said. "We'll bury him as soon as we dig a grave. But…" He rubbed the back of his neck. "It seems inhuman to leave them like this, like statues on display. What can we do?"

"T'ere is not'ing we can do but destroy t'em." Drina smeared blood over the windthrower's stone skull and murmured a silent prayer. "T'at, or leave t'em as t'ey are."

He scanned the surroundings. "How did she do this? Everything—she changed everything."

"Pain, boy." Drina looked at Jayden. "Pain will tear t'ings out of you t'at you never knew were t'ere. And it will make you do t'ings you know are fatal…"

A blip of movement caught Arwan's eye, and he

turned to see Jayden snatch Hawa's battle hammer from the ground, then stomp toward the portal to the underworld. "Come on!" Jayden raised the hammer and brought it down on the tree, cracking the roots and sending shards of stone flying in every direction. "I've got nothing to lose, you son of a bitch! Come on!" He brought the hammer down a second time, breaking one of the roots off completely. His frantic attack tore at Yaxche, creating a crater in the ground.

"Jayden." Arwan walked toward him, but then stopped. Maybe this was what he needed to work through the pain. Who was he to tell him it was wrong?

"I'm coming for you!" Jayden brought the full weight of the weapon upon the tree again and again. A wild gleam in his eyes told Arwan there was no reeling him in. Like Drina had said. It was the pain.

"Boy…" Arwan looked back at Drina, who stared at the ground. Tiny pebbles bounced over the petrified soil.

Arwan looked back at Jayden, who continued to hack at the tree like a crazed lunatic.

"Jayden!" Arwan ran toward him as fast as he could. Before the seeker could strike again, Arwan stole the weapon and dragged him back. "Get away!"

"Let me go!" Jayden threw his head back and cracked Arwan in the nose. Blood dribbled from his nostrils, down his chin. He wiped it from his face and grabbed Jayden a second time. "You have to get back! He's coming!"

Jayden froze and stared at the tree as live roots

burst through the petrified ground and whipped into the air.

Arwan's stomach sank. "The king is here."

CHAPTER FORTY

Arwan

Arwan gestured to Jayden. "Get inside."

"Fuck that!" Jayden snatched the battle hammer from the ground. "I'm seeing this to the end."

Arwan looked the seeker in his eyes. "Zanya needs you. She loves you. Go with her, and keep her and the others safe…please."

Jayden carefully lowered his weapon and looked back at the house.

"She's losing the baby," Arwan continued. "I can't imagine what she's going through right now, and I'm not with her." Arwan's throat ached as he spoke. "But having you beside her would help her through."

The tree purged hundreds of roots from the underworld, tearing an even wider crater in the earth.

Jayden tightened his jaw, clearly wrestling with his choice. After a moment, he exhaled and tossed Arwan the battle hammer. "Be careful." He ran toward the house.

Arwan readied the blood-stained weapon.

The petrified ground trembled and cracked beneath his feet until the putrid stink of the underworld once again flooded his nostrils.

The air shook with dark magic, and the shadow of the king rose from the realm below.

Arwan shifted his weight, terror gripping his heart.

He'd never been truly scared of battle. Never doubted his capabilities, or considered the possibility he wouldn't live to see another day.

Not until he stood his ground, against all odds, and against the one deity who overpowered him in almost every way.

His father, the king.

The broken earth sent a thick cloud of stone dust into the air. As the haze slowly settled, his foe was revealed.

Arwan narrowed his eyes and blinked through the fog.

Something wasn't right.

The king's back faced him, but he seemed...unclothed, exposing mocha skin— wrinkled and deformed.

Arwan stepped forward, straining to get a better look.

Could it be Houn, keeper of underworld souls? No. Houn was not as stout as the figure in front of him.

When the dust fully settled, the figure came into focus.

Arwan leapt back, his hands shaking and his skin

prickled with revelation.

The king turned to face him, showing dark hair splayed over his forehead.

Hair that did not belong.

Hair that was not his.

Arwan dropped his weapon and fell to his knees, staring at the king…wearing Renato's skin.

It was a tradition Arwan had only read about—a common practice in the ancient Mayan civilization among clashing tribes.

Once a rival was captured, his death was guaranteed. If he were a formable adversary, his skin would likely be worn by the victor as a means of drawing strength from the fallen warrior's remains.

But to see his mentor's flesh splayed out like a processed deer was too much to handle.

Arwan vomited on the ground, his stomach clenching in twisted knots.

The king stretched out his arms, displaying the full shape of hanging, wet flesh draped over his body. "The sacrificed Riyata was a brilliant choice. His strength ran deep."

The king's baritone voice was muffled in Arwan's ears. He heaved again, but there was nothing left to purge.

"Stand, son." The king stepped forward. "Stand and fight." As the king walked toward him, his boot crushed petrified Mayan villagers and underworlders alike. "Fight, or die on your knees like a coward."

Arwan wiped his mouth and clenched his eyes shut, working to gather his wits. The horrific display was just that—a display, designed to intimidate and confuse him. He couldn't allow the tactic to work. Not if he wanted to come out of this battle alive.

He gathered his strength and reached for Hawa's weapon. "A fight is what you want." Arwan stood, his focus trained on the king. "A fight is what you'll get."

The king peeled the fleshy remains off and cast them to the ground. Blood matted the king's hair. Renato's blood. Arwan could smell it now, and it made the hairs on his arms stand on end.

The king unwound a flaming whip from his belt and cracked it in the air. "Very well, son. So it begins."

Arwan nodded. "So it begins."

He charged forward, his weapon poised to strike. Before he could get close, he was met with paralyzing pain of a molten whip across his chest. Arwan skidded and clutched his searing flesh. There was no agony more intense than to have one's skin split open with a blazing weapon.

"You could have taken the throne if you were not so weak and attached to the middleworld mortals." When the king lashed out again, Arwan dodged the attack and leapt forward, striking the king with the battle hammer.

The king's arm popped out of place and he shouted, then wheeled his whip in his other hand, slashing at Arwan's back.

Arwan ground his teeth and scrambled away, moving out of the weapon's range.

The king forced his joint back into its socket

with another audible pop. "You cannot defeat me." He rolled his shoulder, as if it had already healed. Perhaps the king had more abilities than Arwan was aware of. He could heal, in or out of his native realm. "We are both made of the same darkness, as you are made from *me*." The king's mouth contorted. "Yet you dare betray me—your own flesh and blood. Your family. Your sire!" The king worked his whip, but Arwan had observed the weapon in action enough to learn its capabilities— and weaknesses. If he were to get close enough to the king to kill him, he'd have to first disable his hellish tool.

When the whip struck, Arwan extended the battle hammer, and the lash coiled around his weapon. Arwan yanked as hard as he could, tearing it from the king's grasp.

Once out of its wielder's possession, the flames fizzled and died. Arwan kicked it away and broadened his stance.

"You believe you stand a chance to leave here alive?" The king glared. "You forsake your realm— your bloodlines." He fisted his massive hands. "You enter into an agreement with me, the King of the Underworld, and think you can transgress the conditions with no repercussions?" The king's gaze moved to the home behind Arwan.

The home where Zanya slept.

The home Arwan would defend with his life.

"I will take everything you love before I take your life. I will smother the admiration you have for these meddling mortals. Then—only then—will I allow you to perish." The king raised his hands, cuing the ground to slither with roots. The layer of petrified remains broke and crumbled as Yaxche reached from the underworld. "You will watch them die!" The king clenched his fist, guiding the roots to coil around the home and begin to pull it apart.

Screams sounded from inside the home.

The king would drag the home down in its entirety if he weren't stopped.

Arwan leapt forward, striking the king in his head with the hammer and knocking him to the ground.

The king's face contorted while he held the side of his head. Dark, murky blood leaked from the gash in his skull, coating his hair and hand.

Arwan raised the weapon to bludgeon him a second time.

The king showed a hideous grin, blood coating his teeth. "You are as I have always pictured you, my son. So dark. So beautiful."

Arwan snarled.

"It is a shame you will not live to take my throne." The king pulled a weapon from his belt and drove it into Arwan's gut. The blade scraped against his ribs as the king pushed it inside, stealing the air from Arwan's lungs.

Arwan leapt back and gripped the handle.

The king pushed to his feet, the wound in his head healed. "I will tear your heart out!"

Arwan stumbled back and collapsed onto the ground. His cheek settled on the jungle floor as he struggled to pull in a breath. The king had surely sliced one of his lungs, causing it to collapse. His vision blurred.

The king walked toward him, his boots now the only thing in Arwan's blurred line of sight.

Warmth and life seeped from Arwan's body, pooling below him on the ground.

"It seems, son, your Riyata friend was sacrificed in vain. You will die, regardless. What a waste." The king knelt beside him and wound his fingers around the weapon, then tilted the blade inside him.

Arwan screamed and grasped onto the king's forearm, desperate to make the pain stop.

"I warned you…" He dragged the knife down an inch, tearing deeper into Arwan's abdomen. "Just like our ancestors, I will slice you open and reach inside of you, then tear out your still-beating heart."

Arwan screamed, which turned into gurgles as blood poured down his throat. Arwan coughed and struggled to stay conscious, barely clinging to life. His eyes rolled back in his head.

While his consciousness slipped away, a familiar voice echoed in the distance.

It was not Zanya, nor his mentor, Renato.

It was Drina, the old priestess who had loved and protected him, and given him refuge since he was a young boy. It was *her* voice that called him back to life, repeating the same message she'd delivered before. *"You are who you are, boy. You must be who you are."*

The king dragged the knife across his belly, splitting him open while he was still alive.

Arwan's muscles tensed and his eyes shot open.

Cool air caressed areas of his body never meant to see the light of day.

Deep, raw parts of himself—flesh and bone,

buried beneath muscle.

The king leaned down and hovered his lips beside Arwan's ear. "Travel well into the underworld, my son. I will meet you there, but not as royalty. As my prisoner."

Drina's face wavered, her eyes coming into focus. *"You are who you are, boy. You must be who you are."*

Arwan lifted his shaking hands, nearly void of strength.

The king had forgotten one key element to Arwan's existence.

He was not only darkness, but also half-light.

He clutched both sides of the king's head and grabbed handfuls of his matted hair. "You may be my father," he muttered, choking on blood, "but I am my mother's son."

Arwan pushed his father back and called on his ability to form a bubble of rippling waves.

He would not be able to hold the timebend for long—if even for a few moments. And once inside, he would hardly be able to move.

There would be no oxygen.

No way to escape.

He would have to do his bidding quickly if he were to change history.

The timebend formed and pressed against his skin, freezing him in place.

A fraction of a second had passed before Arwan closed the bend, and in the blink of an eye, he was back.

A flash of light took over his vision, and before Arwan could ground himself, he found himself in the heat of battle with underworlders surrounding them.

CHAPTER FORTY-ONE

Arwan

Arwan clung to his glaive with strands of blood-soaked hair sticking to his cheeks and neck.

He turned to see Zanya, obviously struggling to fight through her fatigue.

More underworlders and hellhounds poured from the hole in the earth.

He'd gone back. Not far. Just an hour or so—just long enough to make things right.

The enemy closed in around them.

Bodies of the fallen villagers were being consumed by Yaxche. Vines and roots coiled around their bodies, dragging them under until they were nothing more than a bloodstain.

Hawa screamed and stumbled back when a hound leapt on top of her.

Arwan parted his lips. Hawa. She was still alive.

He sprinted toward her and killed the beast before it could tear into her gut.

He spun and pointed to the second one charging

Jayden. "To your right!"

His warning caught Eadith's attention, and she threw a fireball at the hound before it plowed into the seeker.

He turned to Zanya, who was now on her knees, too weak to fight.

Hawa sprinted in front of Arwan and kicked an underworlder back. "Hey, snap out of it!"

Arwan blinked and looked at Hawa.

"We have to retreat," she said. "Get the others out of the house and let's get out of here, or we'll all die!"

He waited, shifting his weight. Zanya would petrify everything in just a few seconds...she had to...

"Come on!" Hawa yanked his arm. "Now!"

What had he done?

By going back and saving Hawa, Zanya no longer had the motivation she needed to petrify the army. She would simply succumb to her fatigue and they would all fall victim to the underworld attack.

Unless he gave her a reason...

First, he turned to the battlefield and waved Beigarth back. The Viking nodded and sliced through several enemies to carve his path back to the safety of the already petrified ground.

Arwan ran to Zanya's side. Her face was drained of color and her eyes were glossed with exhaustion. He grabbed her and shook her, jolting her back to awareness. "You have to listen to me." He cupped her cheek. "Zanya, I need you to be strong right now. We all need you."

She mumbled and grabbed his hand, swaying

from side to side. "I can't…"

"You have to." He looked behind him at the others, who were still fighting their way back. "We are all going to die without your help."

She swallowed, shaking her head. "I'm too weak."

"If you don't help us…" His stomach went queasy. What he was about to do was wrong on more than one level, but he had no other choice. "If you don't, you'll lose the baby. You'll lose me. Everyone will die. I've seen it." He pulled her closer. "I came back."

Her eyes widened. "*Back?*"

He nodded. "I've seen it, and you'll lose everything. Everyone."

Zanya pulled away, horror streaking her features.

But it wasn't enough.

"You'll bleed out, right here on the stone floor."

Zanya cupped her hand over her mouth.

"And the king will cut my heart out in front of you."

Her hands shook.

"Then the tree will consume the house with everyone inside."

Zanya clenched her stomach and scooted back, the fear too raw and harsh for her to react.

He searched for a way to push her over the edge. He would have to be savage. Cruel, even. It tore into him, but it was the only way.

He glared down at her. "I should have known you'd fail." He fisted his hands. "I should have known you'd ruin your chance at being the guardian. At being…" The foul taste of his words coated his tongue. "At being a mother."

Zanya froze, and her eyes narrowed. "I am *not* a failure."

"You've given up. But not just on us. On her!" He pointed at her stomach. "Just like your mother gave up on—" A bolt of energy crashed into his chest, knocking him back into the defending group of Riyata.

He stood upright and looked at Zanya, whose skin pulsed with electricity.

"I will never give up on her!" Zanya screamed and punched the ground, sending a wave of petrification over the land. It crawled over the jungle and froze every underworlder in sight—this time missing Beigarth.

When it was over, Arwan scanned the silent battlefield.

Zanya clenched her belly and contorted in pain. "Something's wrong!"

Peter ran to her side. His face drained of color. "The baby."

Zanya stared up at Arwan, her lips shaky and parted. "You said I would lose the baby if I didn't stop them. What have you done?"

He had lied to her, and forced her to do the impossible. To make the decision between one life, or the life of all humanity. There was no other way.

Peter and Hawa hauled Zanya to her feet. Zanya clenched her legs and buckled over, groaning under the ultimate loss. "My daughter. Something's wrong. Something—" She choked on a sob.

"Is she...?" Jayden approached from behind. "Is she going to be okay?"

Arwan turned to the seeker. It was a relief to know he wouldn't lose Hawa. He needed her—that much was clear. But now, Arwan would ask them all to go inside the house so he could finish what had been started with the king. "I don't know. But you have to watch over her. Will you do that?"

Eleuia approached and stood behind the seeker, underworld blood streaked across her cheek. "Of course we will." She pushed hair out of her face. "We'll do everything we can."

"Go inside, and don't come out—no matter what."

As Arwan walked past them, Eleuia caught his arm. "What are you going to do?"

"Like you said." Arwan stripped off his shirt and tossed it to the ground. "I'm going to beast it up."

***

Zanya

Pain streaked through her stomach and up her back, making her legs quiver. Hawa and Peter hauled her up the stairs and into her bedroom, where they laid her over the mattress. Tara was already in the room, throwing pillows off the bed to give her space to lie down.

Zanya screamed at a sharp spike of heat that tore her womb. She curled into a ball on the mattress. "I'm so sorry, baby. I'm so sorry. I didn't mean to hurt you."

Peter washed his hands in the bathroom, then ran back and sat beside her. "You should be healing.

The baby must be taking too much of your energy. Let me see what I can do. But you have to lie flat for me so I can see your stomach. Can you do that?"

She nodded and forced herself to roll onto her back. "I swear I didn't know this would happen. I had no idea—"

"Shhh." Tara sat beside her and stroked her hair. "We know. This isn't your fault."

Peter slid his hand under the hem of her shirt. His brows turned down, and he felt around a bit more, pressing lightly in some spots, while simply pausing over others. "You're bleeding...a lot. But..." He looked at Zanya. "I'm sorry, I can't do anything to help you. I'm not an obstetrician and I don't have any tools here. No ultrasound, and no way to check and see if the baby is okay. You're too early for me to listen with a stethoscope." He lifted his hands from her skin. "So...you have a choice to make."

Zanya nodded, indicating she was listening.

"If I try to heal you, I'm pretty sure your body will do what any woman's body would—choose your own health over the life of the baby. But if I don't heal you, you'll keep hemorrhaging, and if you lose too much blood..." He pursed his lips. "We could lose you both."

She turned away, shielding her stomach from his touch. "I can't do that." She looked at Tara. "I thought I didn't want this baby. But now I can't stand the idea of losing her." She pressed her hand over her mouth. "This is all my fault." Tears flooded her eyes. "I told her I hated her. I said it. How could I be such a horrible person?" Sobs rolled out of her chest.

Tara wrapped her arms around her and cradled her close. "You and the baby are going to be fine."

The room fell silent when Jayden walked in. He shoved his hands in his pockets. "Hey." He nodded with a crooked grin. It was his familiar face that took the edge off. "Want some company?"

Zanya nodded and reached out to him.

His features sobered. He walked to the bed and laced his fingers between hers, kneeling beside the bed. He rubbed her hands, staring up at her with wide eyes and an expression of pure helplessness. "We're all here for you."

Zanya nodded. "Where's Arwan? He should be here. He should—" Her breath was stolen with another jab to her gut. Heat crawled down her legs. She squeezed her eyes shut until the worst of it passed. "I can't do this. I can't lose her."

"You're not losing anyone. Drina is in the kitchen brewing you some herbal tea. She looks..." He chuckled and wiped a tear from her cheek. "She looks pretty pissed, and I wouldn't be surprised if she came up with some kind of crazy witchdoctor formula just for you."

Zanya held Jayden's hand. His skin was like ice, but it was still him, and that was all that mattered. "I need Arwan here. I can't get through this without him."

Jayden glanced at the others. "Um..." He swallowed and lowered his gaze to the floor.

Zanya forced herself to sit up as much as she could. "Jay...where's Arwan?"

He finally met her gaze. "He's got some

unfinished business. He…" He exhaled and squeezed her hand. "Zanya, I don't know if he's coming back."

CHAPTER FORTY-TWO

Arwan

Standing outside the house, Arwan stripped off his pants and tossed them aside. A shiver crawled over his skin while he stood in his shorts, cool jungle air drifting over his body. The entrance to the underworld was still sealed, though not for long. The king was on his way, and this time, Arwan was ready for him.

The ground trembled beneath his feet.

Arwan took that as his cue to unleash the beast.

The transformation took seconds, and the pain subsided quickly after.

Yaxche broke through like before, creating a portal for the king to ascend into the mortal realm. And as soon as he did, Arwan was reminded that although he had saved Hawa, Renato was out of his reach. His mentor was slaughtered in the underworld, while Arwan was drifting in and out of consciousness. In that realm, time was its own entity, and Arwan could do nothing to change the past.

This time he would make his mentor's death count.

The king rose, wearing the same horrifying pelt. Arwan did his best to ignore it, and braced for the scene.

The king stretched out his arms, displaying the full shape of hanging, wet flesh draped over his body. "The sacrificed Riyata was a brilliant choice. His strength ran deep."

This time, Arwan would not fall to his knees like he did before.

This time, he met the king as a beast.

The king chuckled and peeled off the fleshy remains, casting them to the ground.

As soon as he did, Arwan lurched forward.

The king reached for his whip but Arwan anticipated the move and beat him to it. Arwan was on top of him in an instant, and tore the weapon out of the king's grasp.

The king glared. "It is a shame you will not live to take my throne."

Before he could reach for his second weapon— the blade that had nearly killed him—Arwan plowed into him and pressed his massive paw on the king's chest *and pressed*.

This time, the king's heart would belong to *him*.

Arwan dug his claws into the king's flesh, snapping ribs and tearing through his sternum.

The king flailed and lurched, but to no avail.

His heart was within sight, beating with black, putrid blood.

The blood of a damned soul.

Without hesitation Arwan reached inside with his claws and tore the still-beating heart from the king's chest and cast it aside.

The king's body fell limp and his eyes fogged over with a layer of white.

Yaxche's roots reached from the soil and coiled around the heart.

The muscle beat once.

Twice.

It stalled, and beat one last time before Yaxche yanked it underground.

Arwan stepped back, circling the king's lifeless remains.

After so many years and so much heartache, it was finally over.

"You did well, boy."

Arwan froze and looked up at Drina, who was hobbling toward him.

Still in his beastly form, he was unsure how to react. Drina had only seen him like this a handful of times. She didn't appear scared. Her features were soft as her gaze cast lightly over him.

It shouldn't have surprised him. Drina loved and accepted him for who he was. She always had, and would, no matter what.

"You have done well, boy." Drina walked forward, her stride now smoother than usual. His keen hearing caught the sound of a bird in flight. But not just a bird—an owl. He peered up at the sky as Ishel—the middle world goddess of plants and flowers—soared overhead.

"Do not be bitter, my boy. I asked her to stay away from the fight."

351

My boy?

Arwan tilted his head, listening, watching, and waiting. There was something different about Drina. Her tone was more even, and she had less of an accent.

"This was *your* fight," she continued, "and *your* destiny to fulfill." Drina stood up straighter, no longer hunched like an old Mayan priestess. "And I am very, very proud of the man you have become, my son."

Her appearance morphed and wavered. Glimpses of his mother's features came in and out of focus like a mirage.

Ishel swooped down from the sky, changing into her human form just as her feet landed softly on the ground. The middleworld goddess stood back, her head bowed.

Drina's form continued to alter until a glowing being stood before him.

His mother, the Star.

Her big brown eyes mirrored his own, and her illuminated skin made the moon seem dim in comparison. Arwan whined and lay on the ground. She should not have seen him in this form—his true self.

"Do not be ashamed." Her silken gown draped over her shoulders in the most elegant way. She reached out and rested her hand on his head, burying her fingers into his fur. "You are perfect." She glided her hand down his cheek. "I only wish you had known it was me all along." He picked up his head so he met her gaze. Rolling galaxies existed in irises of her eyes. "I could not part with you, even after my mortal body was dead and gone. My soul is bound tightly to yours, and I gave you my love the only way you could accept it—through the illusion of Drina." Her laugh was like music. "Such a crass, angry woman you needed to love you. But a mother knows her son, and I knew you would not allow anyone else close while your heart was still hurting. Yet you needed guidance."

It all made sense now.

Drina's agelessness was not due to her Mayan magic.

She had been a mere presentation—a mask worn by his mother, so she could raise him in a world he believed had betrayed him long ago.

His memory whipped back to the campfire in previous months, when Drina allowed a glimpse of his mother to show through her. The priestess had claimed she was in communication with his mother's spirit, but in reality, his mother had merely lifted the mask for a fleeting moment to give him hope.

All this time...

"Do not be angry with me. I only did what would save the mortals from the underworld king and his wicked realm. Without you, the middleworld would have surely fallen. You were the only hope of mankind. You, who was born as the prince of both heaven and hell."

Arwan forced himself to morph back to his human form. Ishel waited with her feathered robe to cloak him, while her long, flowing hair shielded the most intimate curves of her body.

He could not stay a beast while his mother stood

353

before him for the first time.

She raked her fingers through his hair and knelt in front of him.

He tried to lift his gaze to meet hers, but now in his human form, he was somehow more vulnerable, and dwarfed beside her majesty

She hooked her finger under his chin and lifted his gaze. "Worry not." Her lips curved into a soft smile. "I will keep your mentor close. Through his sacrifice, he has earned his seat at my table." She placed a kiss on Arwan's forehead. "And in my heart."

"Mother…" The word came out in a croaked whisper. He wove his fingers between hers. "Don't leave. I can't be alone again."

"Do you not see?" She leaned forward and held him close. He breathed in the essence of her being—the bright, clean scent of her hair and the comfort only a mother's touch could provide. "You have never been alone. The guardian is your future. However…" She pulled back and looked into his eyes. A streak of sadness lingered in her gaze. "I fear you will not have the daughter you so desperately tried to protect."

He choked on tears, but managed to hold them back. He had failed at being the man Zanya needed, and the father his unborn child would never know.

"Great things are destined for you, my son. Your bloodline is precious, and once inherited, will bind the heavens, middleworld, and underworld in an unbreakable chain to unite the realms. This is what I had intended with your conception, and why you are not only precious to me, but to all of mankind.

The mortals do not know, my love. And as is their nature, they fear what they do not understand."

Arwan nodded, hanging on every word. But it wasn't enough. "I don't know who I am…"

"You are, and always have been, my son." She stood and gazed down at him. "You must embrace your new role as king and soul mate. It is not an easy task, but with the strength you have inherited from both myself and your father, you are able."

"King?" He pushed to his feet, clinging to Ishel's garment wrapped around him. "But…" He looked at the portal to the underworld. "I can't. Zanya needs me. I need her…"

"Then you must order the tree to retreat into the underworld, and *never* return."

He furrowed his brow as a realization hit him like a charging wave.

Now that his father was gone, he had inherited the role as ruler of the dark realm. Now that the king had perished, Arwan was the rightful heir.

He turned to the portal and tilted his head, staring at the tree's roots lying still, as if awaiting instruction.

Arwan reached out and swiped his hand through the air, willing them to retract back into the soil. The tree obeyed, and recoiled into the pits of hell where it belonged.

He stood a moment, silent and still, and somewhat numb. What did this mean for his future? Now that he was king of the dark realm, how would be fulfill his obligation to his crown while staying true to his heart?

He turned back to see Ishel standing with Balam

355

at her side.

Arwan scanned the area, but his mother was not there.

In his gut, he knew what it meant.

She was gone, forever.

CHAPTER FORTY-THREE

Zanya

The following night, Zanya lay in bed with Arwan beside her, where he belonged.

After the conflict the day before, he explained what happened.

He had killed his father, and Drina had been his mother all along. As a result of his father's death, he inherited the throne to the underworld, and was now ruling king.

It was all too much to process in one day, so for now, Zanya focused on getting well. With the help of Peter's healing, and her own abilities seemingly coming back, her body was on the mend. The bleeding had stopped and the pain had mostly subsided. But the lump in her throat hadn't gone away, and she was too terrified to investigate whether the baby had survived.

Silky moonlight shone through the windows in their bedroom. Zanya turned on her side and gazed up at the sky, admiring the endless amounts of stars, like faraway diamonds hanging overhead.

Arwan turned and wound his arm around her, his body contoured to hers from behind. He propped his chin on her shoulder. "How are you feeling?"

"Okay...I guess." She set her hand on her stomach, still hopeful. "Everything's just..." She couldn't find any word to describe it. Unsure, maybe?

"I know." He pressed a kiss on the curve of her neck. "But Grima is better."

"And Yousef and Ahmed are still dead." She dared not mention Renato, who she missed more than she could ever express. "And Drina..." She turned on her back and looked into his face. "I know she was never real, but she was real to me." She grinned. "I miss that angry, snoring old woman."

Arwan chuckled, the curve of his mouth begging to be kissed.

So she did.

He cradled her cheek and drifted his hand down her body, over the curve of her waist, resting on her hip. His fingers spread over her skin.

She went rigid and pulled away. Her cheeks flushed with heat. "It's too soon." Her throat ached. "I don't even know..."

"You don't have to explain." He glanced at the leather pouch clasped around her wrist where the stone was kept. She knew what he was thinking, though he didn't say it aloud. But she'd been too terrified to look at her stone and see if the little blue light still flickered inside. "You should get some rest." He raked his fingers through strands of her hair and kissed her forehead. "We have a lot to talk about tomorrow."

Zanya nodded and then lay back down, anxiety bubbling in her chest. The room fell silent, and Arwan's breathing steadied as he drifted off to sleep.

Eventually she'd have to face her fears and know the truth. If tomorrow they were going to discuss the future, she had to plan around whether the baby made it through.

She unclasped the pouch on her wrist and drew in a shaky breath as she closed her eyes, and then slid out her stone. She flinched when it was cool to the touch, and not warm as it had been before. After rolling it in her hand for a moment, she built the courage to open her eyes.

Bright white and blue lights wavered inside as they always did, reaching out to her with the invisible connection they shared. She peered at it closely, searching, hoping, desperately wanting to find the tiny flashing light…but there was none.

She pursed her lips and coiled her fingers around the stone as a tear slid down her cheek. The deepest sense of sorrow settled in her chest and coiled around her heart. She pulled her legs to her chest and wept silently into her pillow, the pain too raw for her to speak.

The mattress bounced with movement, and Arwan's strong arms slid around her and lifted her into his lap. She buried her face into his chest and wept freely and openly, with no effort at holding back.

He stroked her hair with a long, soft touch. "*Shh,*

mi amor. No llores. Sé que duele pero no llores. Estoy aquí para ti y siempre lo estaré. Siempre."

"I want to go home," she sobbed. "This place isn't home. We've lost so much. I can't bear to live here and be reminded every day—"

"Shh." He hugged her tighter. "Whatever you want, *mi corazon*. We'll tell them in the morning, and tomorrow we'll make plans to go back home—to Belize."

CHAPTER FORTY-FOUR

It had been nearly a week since they had returned to Belize—to Renato's estate, where it had all begun.

It was strange without Renato there. Each time Zanya walked into the large study in the back of the house, she could almost see him sitting behind his desk, smoking his bone pipe with stacks of books piled around him. The room still smelled of the earthy tobacco, and his energy seemed to live in the walls. It would never be the same as it was before, but this was truly home.

Tara and Peter had taken the west wing, along with Jayden and Hawa. It had gone from a bachelor pad to the couples' retreat. They were a strange combination of people, but it worked, and they all seemed happy. Besides, with Marzena in the north wing, there was no way the dreamwalker would tolerate Jayden living in her space with Hawa. It was either relocate or die—according to Jayden, at least—and Hawa took pity on his phobia of being around the 'creepy child of the corn' as Jayden

361

called her. Only when she wasn't around, of course.

The main wing had become hers and Arwan's, almost solely. Her mother took Renato's old wing, and seemed at peace there, among the treasured belongings of her late brother. Eleuia had started to play the cello again. Zanya listened from the main wing as the low, smooth tones echoed through the house, filling the air with music once again.

Zanya had missed the comfort of a melody. She knew when she was ready, her violin waited in the music room for her to claim. Maybe she would find it one day and begin to play. But for now, she had to focus on finding direction and meaning in their now-quiet lives.

Eadith, Beigarth, and Grima all parted ways when the rest returned to Belize. The fire conjurer was eager to return to her life in Paris, and the two Vikings had adventures to seek on the high seas. Zanya was pretty sure there were no Viking ships still sailing the oceans, but she wouldn't tell them that. They had dreams of living quietly on farms and raising livestock to feed the nomads of Europe. It didn't sound so bad if Zanya thought about it, and she wished them both the best.

Before they parted, Grima demanded Zanya keep in touch with her dreamwalking ability. Zanya offered a phone number, but Beigarth gave a hearty laugh and smacked her on the back.

She could only guess that meant they didn't believe in phones.

Eleuia walked onto the veranda, where Zanya sat, watching Arwan and Peter practice martial arts on the beach. They'd fallen back into a familiar routine of training. Maybe they were eager to resume their normal lives—whatever normal meant these days.

Zanya cradled a cup of tea in her hands, inhaling the scent of herbs and mint. Lately, coffee made her feel queasy. The last few weeks' events had taken their toll, both emotionally and physically, and she was determined to give her body anything it needed to mend. Even if that meant sipping herbal tea over coffee in the morning.

Her mother strode to the alabaster railing and leaned against it, inhaling the crisp morning air. "It's a beautiful day. Want to go for a swim?"

Zanya crinkled her nose. "No, thanks. I've had my fill of water for a while." Ever since she and Arwan drowned to go to the underworld to rescue Jayden's soul, the idea of swimming had never been quite as appealing.

Her mother shrugged. "Maybe I'll paint, or play the cello a little…" She rubbed her face and exhaled, then looked at Zanya. "Is it just me, or are you bored out of your mind too?"

Zanya laughed. "If I've learned one thing, it's that boring isn't always bad." Zanya sipped her tea. The seagulls soared overhead, screaming their usual tune. Other than that, there was only the sound of distant jungle trees being tousled by the coastal winds. "It is pretty quiet, though."

And quiet gave her time to think, which usually brought back memories of all she'd lost…

"Yeah." Her mother inspected Zanya a silent moment. The corners of her mouth turned down. "How are you feeling? Any more pain?"

363

Zanya shook her head. "Just some nausea, and I'm still pretty wiped out, but Peter says that's to be expected."

"And I'd expect he's right." She walked to a nearby chair and sat.

Zanya watched Arwan while he instructed Peter on certain martial arts moves she knew nothing about. But it was nice to see him in his element again—training and sharing his knowledge with others. It gave him purpose.

"How have things been with him?"

"Okay. Quiet."

Arwan kicked Peter to the ground. Both of them laughed as Arwan extended his hand and helped Peter off the sand. Arwan's smile was genuine, but Zanya knew deep down he was still in pain over the loss of Renato and their daughter.

He stayed awake some nights staring into the distance. Even when she would rest her arm over his chest and curl her body against his, he would remain silent.

"What about…" Her mother swirled her finger over the crown of her head. "You know. The whole king thing. What do you think he's going to do with that?"

"I honestly don't know. He hasn't been back there, if that's what you're asking. He doesn't talk about it. But one day…" She exhaled. "One day his realm will call for him. And when it does…" A heavy weight settled in her gut. "We'll face it together."

There was a bang at the front door. "Zanya!" Tara screamed. "Come quick!"

Zanya dropped her mug of tea before darting into the main foyer, where a lanky teenage boy swayed on his feet, his eyes rolling back in his head. A second later, his knees buckled.

Zanya caught him before he could hit the floor.

Arwan, Peter, and the others joined them in the foyer. "I heard a scream."

They stared at the stranger, half-conscious in Zanya's arms.

"Who are you?" Zanya pushed silvery hair out of the stranger's face and looked into his ghostly eyes. They were white or, more like void of pigment completely. Now that she noticed, his skin was as light as powder.

"Help…" He reached up to touch her face.

Hawa grabbed his wrist. "Don't let him touch you."

The boy's appearance changed into a teenage girl—Hawa.

Hawa gasped. "He's a shifter." She pulled back, and as soon as she did, the boy's appearance changed back.

"What do we do?" Zanya looked up at her mother.

"We need to get him out. He's a stranger, and we don't know what he wants."

"Help…me," the boy whispered before passing out completely.

"We need to get him inside and let him rest." Jayden crouched beside him. "He's obviously one of us."

"That doesn't mean he's peaceful," Eleuia responded.

"I'll take care of him," Jayden said. "I'll be responsible for whatever happens."

The entire group stopped and stared in silence.

"What? Like I can't be responsible?"

Hawa set her hand on Jay's shoulder. "I'll help…just in case."

Zanya's mother looked at Arwan. "What do you think? This is your house now. Should he stay?"

Arwan was silent for a long stretch of time.

"Please." Jayden shifted his weight. "I was this kid…we all were. We were all lost until Renato found us. The least we can do is pay it forward and carry on his legacy."

Arwan's rigid muscles relaxed, and he nodded. "Okay. But he stays in the west wing, with you. Put in him a bedroom with a door that locks, and keep it locked until we know who he is and what he wants."

Jayden acted without hesitation and scooped the boy up off the floor. "It's gonna be okay, kid. Hang in there." Hawa followed him to the west wing.

Tara clung to Peter. "How do you think he found us, or knew who we are?"

"I don't know, but we can't take any chances." Arwan scanned the faces in the group. "This means there are others out there. Others we don't know about, but who know about us."

"And that means we're vulnerable," Eleuia said.

"But I thought it was over. Now that Sarian, Contessa, and the old King of the Underworld are dead…" Tara bit her bottom lip. "It is over with, right?"

Arwan's eyes narrowed as he seemingly

searched his mind for an answer. "The truth is, there is no way to tell for certain. New threats could rise any day. We have to always be prepared, just in case."

Jayden and Hawa walked back into the main foyer. "Well…" Jay ran his fingers through his hair. "The kid's asleep."

"He can't be older than thirteen," Hawa said. "What's he doing out there alone like that?"

"I don't know," Peter said. "But it's kind of cool—his ability, I mean."

Zanya recalled shifting once before, and it hurt like hell. If she could avoid it, she would, and couldn't imagine that being the only ability she had.

"Maybe…" Jayden shoved his hands in his pockets and shrugged. "Maybe we can keep him?"

Eleuia snorted. "Like he's a stray dog who wandered in?"

"No. Like he's an abandoned kid who needs someone to protect him."

Tara furrowed her brow. "Who *are* you?"

"He has a point." Hawa leaned in close to him and lowered her voice. "Like at Thirteenth Street." She glanced at him shyly—the first time *ever* Zanya had seen her look even *remotely* close to being shy.

Jayden grinned and winked at her, then looked back to the group. "I'm just saying. Everyone needs a place to call home."

CHAPTER FORTY-FIVE

Arwan

Hours passed and night had fallen over the quiet estate. Tomorrow they would break ground on the graveyard project, where Eleuia had already mapped out the tombs for Yousef, Ahmed, and Renato. To think they needed their very own graveyard was a chilling reminder.

Arwan walked barefoot through the silent house to do his nightly rounds. The familiar wooden floors in the main wing gave him comfort. As he passed by the entrance to the west wing, he could hear Jayden and the newcomer talking from the living room on the other side of the door. He paused and listened to Jayden's calm, steady tone as he investigated the kid's background. Arwan couldn't help but be surprised at the seeker's softer side. He would be good at welcoming any others in the future—if they were to come. Perhaps that had been his calling all along.

Tara's quirky voice raised above Jayden's—

loud, as was her nature, though he'd grown to care about Tara more than he ever imagined. He recalled the first time he met her in the kitchen, while she picked at a stack of Peter's burned pancakes. Everything was new and confusing. He had no idea what to expect of the spunky redhead, and now saw her like a younger sister.

They still hadn't figured out what to do about her mortality. The idea of changing her to Riyata was not out of the question, though it was something they hadn't revisited since they returned home. Perhaps one day soon they would speak to Zanya about it. But for now, they would have to leave it in the hands of fate.

Arwan continued past Renato's old wing where Eleuia now stayed. It was quiet, except the sound of gentle sobs from somewhere inside. Arwan's throat tightened. Eleuia had lost so much. It was only natural that she would need time to mourn the loss of her stone, her brother, and her granddaughter.

Arwan lowered his head as a sharp pain pierced his heart.

He also needed time. Thankfully, Zanya had tuned into that, and was giving him the space he needed to heal and move forward.

He continued his rounds, past the north wing where Marzena lived. Classical music flowed from inside. She and Renato shared the same passion for classical music, and now the dreamwalker—who had been Renato's friend and confidante for many centuries—was alone.

He moved on, making a full circle back to the main wing.

Smooth, gentle notes carried through the air, catching his attention. He followed the sound up the grand staircase and down the hall to the bedroom he shared with his soul mate, and opened the door.

She played another note, then paused and lowered her violin to her lap. "Oh, hey." Her cheeks flushed with color. "I hope I didn't bother you."

"Not at all." He stepped inside and closed the door behind him. "I'm glad to see you playing again."

"Yeah. It's been a long, long time."

He walked to the far end of the room and sat on the chaise, watching her. She fiddled with the strings, plucking them one at a time with her fingertip, and stealing a glance at him every few seconds.

He crossed his arms and slouched down, fatigue coiling his muscles. He hadn't slept well for the last week, and it was taking its toll. Maybe a little music would help. "Don't let me stop you." He nodded at the instrument. "Please, keep playing."

She tucked the violin under her chin and held the bow with a soft, delicate hand. As she dragged the bow over the strings, the room filled with a relaxing melody, easing his mind.

Arwan closed his eyes as he fell deeper into the song. With each note, his spirit swelled with admiration for the woman who owned his heart.

Moments later, a stretched note ended the tune. He opened his eyes to see her stand from the bed and walk toward him with her hand extended. "Come on. You're tired, and you need some sleep."

"That noticeable?" He took her hand and forced

himself to stand.

She didn't walk back to the bed, but instead stood in front of him and slid her arms around his body. Zanya breathed, her chest rising and falling with the action, her heart rate rising. She slid her fingers under his shirt and slipped her hands around to his stomach and down his abs. "I miss you."

He may have been exhausted to the bone, but no amount of fatigue would keep him from being close to the woman whose soul was bound to his. He kissed her, softly at first. But the way she pressed her body against his made his skin rush with heat.

He wrapped his hands around the back of her thighs and hauled her onto his waist so she straddled him while he stood. Zanya coiled her arms around his neck and parted her lips, kissing him deeper.

He walked to the bed and eased her down, hovering his body over hers. She stripped off her shirt and threw it aside, then buried her fingers in his hair and pulled him closer.

Hot breath rushed from her nose as she slid her tongue over his.

His skin prickled and his stomach flipped. He would be forever obsessed with the way her mouth tasted, and the warmth of her body against his.

He broke their kiss and ran his mouth down her neck, chest, and down her stomach, where he worked to unhook her leather belt. She arched her back and breathed in, her heart racing under his touch. He could hear it, just like he sensed the wave of heat over her skin and the rise in her endorphins. Sometimes having inhuman senses was overwhelming, but in this rare case, they enriched the experience.

When he unclasped her belt and worked open the button to her jeans, he trailed more kisses over her stomach.

Her heart skipped faster.

Abnormally faster.

He paused and looked up at her face. She didn't seem to be in distress.

He positioned his hands on either side of her waist and looked at her belly…

It was impossible.

He pressed his ear to the gentle curve of her stomach below her belly button, and closed his eyes.

Quick ticks echoed from inside.

He pulled back and gazed at her stomach, then at her face.

Zanya pushed up on her forearms. "What's wrong?"

Arwan smiled—a full, uninhibited smile.

Zanya tilted her head. "What?"

The grief in his heart lifted, pulling a laugh out of his chest. He had never been so happy in his life. Not ever.

EPILOGUE

Zanya

Two years later…

"Ren, you can't put that in your mouth." Eleuia picked Zanya's son up off the beach and wiggled the shell out of his chubby hand. "It'll cut your gums."

"His name isn't Ren, Mom." Zanya crinkled her nose and wiped grains of sand from her son's olive skin. "It's Renato. I don't want him getting used to nicknames."

"Fine, fine." Her mother handed her son over and brushed her hands together. "I'm going to get lunch ready. Where's Arwan?"

Zanya sensed his approach and turned to see him walking toward them on the beach.

"Speak of the underworld king."

Zanya rolled her eyes. "Very funny."

"Oh, come on. You've lost your sense of humor since this little boy came into the world." Her mother pinched Renato's cheeks and kissed his neck, making him giggle. Renato threw his arms around Zanya and hugged her neck so tightly he nearly cut off her air. She widened her eyes and took his arm, uncoiling it so she could breathe. "Careful, son. You're stronger than you know."

"He's stronger, faster, and more skilled than all of us," Arwan said with a broad smile.

Renato flailed his arms and screeched, reaching out for his father.

Arwan stole him from Zanya and threw him in the air, making her son's eyes light up with joy— and maybe a little magic.

"Okay, I'm off," Eleuia said. "Salad with fresh bass and gnocchi. Sound good?" Without waiting for a response, her mother spoke in the high-pitched baby tone she often used when talking to Renato. "Because my big boy loves his gnocchi, doesn't he?" She tickled his tummy. Renato belly laughed while kicking the air with his bare feet.

While her mother walked away, Arwan set Renato onto the warm sand and crossed his arms, staring down at their son. "Enough play. Now it's time to train."

Zanya arched an eyebrow. "Train? He's barely walking, and you expect him to do any of the fancy capoeira moves you try to teach Peter?"

"It's never too early to start."

She bit her tongue. If teaching their son made Arwan happy, it made her happy too.

She'd learned to pick her battles.

Just two years ago, having a child had been wiped out of the equation when they thought they'd lost their chance.

Then to discover, despite all odds, their miracle had pulled through after nearly vanishing forever—undetectable in its weakened state, even to the stone itself.

And on their child's birthday, to find out the daughter they had been so elated to welcome into the world was, in fact, a son.

Her son.

Nobody knew what it meant for the long line of stone guardians. Was she the very last? Or would Renato one day inherit the stone? Nothing was certain anymore.

"Hey, hey, hey!" Zanya pointed at the wobbling toddler. "Stop that right now."

Renato hovered his hand over the ground, with a tiny tree sprouting from the earth. It grew leaps and bounds in front of their eyes.

Arwan snatched him up and tickled him, breaking his concentration. "You know how your mother feels about you growing trees when you're bored."

"It's only a problem when he decides to do it in the house. How many times do we have to fix the floors? I'm trying to break him of the habit now, before our home is turned into a rainforest."

Arwan chuckled. "That doesn't sound so bad."

"Lunch is almost ready." They turned to her mother, who shouted from the kitchen door. "You guys coming inside?"

"Be right there," Arwan shouted. When her mother went back inside, Arwan looked into Renato's face. "How about you show Grandma how

375

to grow trees later? She'd get a kick out of it."

Renato nodded.

Arwan put Renato back onto the sand and waved them forward. "Come on, let's get inside before your mom comes out here. You know how she gets when she has to repeat herself."

Zanya snorted. "Yeah, I know." She extended her hand to Renato. "Come on. Time to go inside for lunch, and then a nap."

Her son's light gray eyes darkened, and he pushed out his bottom lip.

"Nope. That's not going to work this time." She wiggled her fingers with her hand still outstretched. "Let's go."

Renato looked at the tree he'd grown. Still upset, he touched one of its leaves, making it shrivel. The rest of the tree quickly wilted, turning to a dry, brittle stick in the ground.

Zanya watched her son stomp back to the house with his arms crossed over his chest.

Zanya signed.

The burden placed on such a new soul was cruel, really. Her son was not just a boy. He was a unity of bloodlines, tying together all three realms.

He was a Stone Guardian, the underworld prince, and the grandson of Star.

More power and magic coursed through his veins than Zanya would see in her entire lifetime, and even a thousand lifetimes after she was gone.

He would have to learn how to harness his powers and use them for good, just as Arwan struggled to do through his youth. But this time, he had his family.

This time, the future was bright.

THE END

ACKNOWLEDGMENTS

Wow. I can't believe this is the end. Birthright is the fifth and final book of the Stone Legacy series, and i'm both excited and heartbroken to see Zanya and Arwan's story come to a close. I've spent years with these characters and in this story world. It is almost like a small piece of me is going with it.

I'd like to thank my amazing editor, Lori Whitwam, who has stood by me book after book, challenge after challenge, and fought for my series just as valiantly as I have.

To my critique partner, Susan Walsh, who held my hand during the early days of Mayan Blood, when I was still developing my craft. Your mentorship has been invaluable, and your friendship has enriched my life in so many ways. I'm so thankful to know you.

And to all of my other critique partners, you're amazing. You know who you are.

A special thanks to Limitless Publishing and Deranged Doctor Designs who gave this series beautiful covers.

ABOUT THE AUTHOR

A long time enthusiast of things that go bump in the night, Theresa began her writing career as a journalism intern—possibly the least creative writing field out there. After her first semester at a local newspaper, she washed her hands of press releases and features articles to delve into the whimsical world of young adult paranormal romance.

Since then, Theresa has gotten married, had three terrific kids, moved to central Ohio, and was repeatedly guilt tripped into adopting a menagerie of animals that are now members of the family. But don't be fooled by her domesticated appearance. Her greatest love is travel. Having stepped foot on the soil of over a dozen countries, traveled to sixteen U.S. states—including an extended seven-year stay in Kodiak, Alaska—she is anything but settled down.

Wherever life brings her, she will continue to weave tales of adventure and love with the hope her stories will bring joy and inspiration to her readers.

Facebook:
https://www.Facebook.com/theresa.dalayne

Twitter:
https://www.twitter.com/theresadalayne

Goodreads:
https://www.goodreads.com/author/show/7847410.
Theresa_DaLayne

Website:
http://TheresaDaLayne.com/

Instagram:
http://www.instagram.com/authortheresadalayne

Newsletter:
http://bit.ly/22DZ0BY

Google+:
https://plus.google.com/+TheresaDaLayne/posts